DREAM
PHAZE

Also by Matt Watters

Dream Phaze
Dream Phaze - Imagination

Standalone
Dream Phaze - Germination

Watch for more at www.dreamphaze.com.

Table of Contents

DREAM PHAZE
Imagination
Book 2
Matt Watters

Red Giant Publishing
Australia

Copyright © 2021 Matthew S. Watters
Edited by Anne Foxx
Cover art by Andrew Ostrovsky
Book Two: Paperback ISBN 978-0-9578199-7-9
Book Two: Paperback first published 2022 by
Red Giant Publishing
Sydney, Australia
Dream Phaze Trademark owned by Matthew S. Watters

DREAM PHAZE

Imagination - Book 2
in the continuing series

Read
DREAM PHAZE
Germination – Book 1
first.
Consult the
Expanding Glossary
at the back of this novel
for clarification.

Introduction by Dr Keith M.T. Hearne

British psychologist Dr Keith M. T. Hearne conducted the world's first sleep-lab research into 'lucid' dreams for his PhD research in 1975. Several years later, his research was replicated in the United States. Dr Hearne also invented the first 'dream machine'. His book 'The Dream Machine', and his PhD thesis, can be downloaded free from: www.keithhearne.com[1]

******

Shared dreaming usually involves dreamers trying to meet up in the same location and have common experiences. However, I feel that a device is in the offing to link a network of dreamers and achieve that goal in a meaningful way.

The result will be key thoughts that will send the imagery-flow in the same direction in users. By training, dream manifestations will become more similar between users.

Motivated dream disruptors might indeed induce unpleasant experiences in others, and in the real world the Dream Police could well knock on the door of some uncooperative users.

With great prescience, author Matt Watters has anticipated that sort of scenario in the not-too-distant future. He has figured out the issues that will occur with mass public involvement in dreaming (of all things!).

Hardly anyone has realised the changes that will inevitably happen in society. I salute Matt Watters' insightful revelations of times to come.

---

1. http://www.keithhearne.com

Chapter One

Merlin approached the dim city alley with trepidation. Pausing, he peered down the narrow lane at the single light towards the end. Just one more Kilpepper and he would advance to the next level, the exalted Foxtrot. Only 58 players had achieved Foxtrot to date. Proceeding cautiously, his gaze attentively followed his crossbow pistol spotlight as he swept from left to right and back again. He checked behind garbage bins, and rubbish piles large enough for a Kilpepper to hide under. A shadow ahead near the dumpster caught his attention. Focusing his weapon in that direction, he took out his scanner and searched for an ultra-aura...nothing.

An instant later, a Kilpepper dropped onto Merlin's back, latching on. Merlin immediately felt the proboscis from the hirsute slug-shaped creature drill through flesh at the nape of his neck. He dropped his scanner, reached back and began pulling at the sucker. Its four needle-like mouthparts inflicted rapid pain. Grabbing around the girth of the 30-centimetre-long critter, he squeezed as hard as he could muster, forcing the Kilpepper to excrete warm waste down his back. The unconscious creature withdrew its feeding prong and Merlin smashed it to the ground and stomped on it with extreme disgust.

Everything around Merlin swam with movement. He emerged from the game level transition standing by a fast-flowing magenta coloured river. Three blue moons of differing sizes hung in the pale mint sky. Merlin immediately recognised the environment from the game tutorials. This was Hoyok, the Kilpepper's home planet. The weapons in his hip holster had been replaced with a laser pistol and garrotting cable. The cable provoked instant anxiety; he had to get up close and personal with these blood sucking creatures.

Merlin reconnoitred his immediate area. The caked, dark grey soil crumbled under the weight of his steps; he realised he could easily be tracked. He looked to the river. *'Should I travel by river? What's in the river? What type of liquid is it?'* Merlin heard a distant engine noise as a plume of dust rose a kilometre away. He searched for somewhere to hide. The lack of vegetation forced him down to the riverbank. A small ledge gave him cover as he watched the vehicle's dust cloud. It was heading directly towards him. Merlin drew his laser pistol.

A single eye on an extended black tentacle slowly ascended from the river, then another, and another. By the time Merlin turned around, 100 eyeballs were watching him. Alarmed by the forest of gawking eyes, he shifted nervously, not wanting to draw attention from the land travellers or the river creatures. Cautiously, he glanced down at his arm, five seconds remained in this episode cycle, he exhaled. A nanosecond later, a marbled-sized projectile burst from the water and pierced Merlin's left eye, wedging in his brain, before exploding.

The following day, Merlin sat working on a project brief in his office on level three of the ZynnComm facility in Port Augusta.

Arrow approached, putting her hand on his shoulder. 'Got time for lunch?'

'Always got time for lunch,' he replied, wrapping his arm around her waist. 'Do you like to die when you dream phaze?'

'Depends, on the experience I mean. Why?'

'You know I've been playing Kilpeppers. I reached Foxtrot level last night. The experience is totally unpredictable, totally exhilarating, but I die a lot. These experiences I'm dying in...are the best I've ever had,' he admitted.

'Is there something wrong with that?' Merlin didn't answer. 'Merlin? Have I lost you? Merlin?'

'I suppose not,' he responded vaguely. 'Will that become the norm for dream immersion experiences? It won't be rated high unless you die?'

'For a certain user demographic like you, yes. I played Kilpeppers once. I didn't like how the small Kilpeppers could quickly merge to form a large alien. Scared the shit out of me.'

Merlin's stomach growled loudly.

'Boris is awake,' Arrow said as she reached down and rubbed Merlin's tummy.

'Come on, I'd better feed him.' They walked towards the elevator. 'How's the Porterman project going?'

'Rendering. I finished it about an hour ago.'

As the elevator door opened, Bhang pulled them both in. 'Have you heard?' he asked with urgency.

'Heard what?' Merlin puzzled.

'Walt's in a bad way, he's in hospital.'

'What's wrong with him?' Arrow asked.

'Not sure. I just saw the news feed,' the codester muttered, fiddling with his blonde man-bun. 'Just said he was rushed to hospital last night.'

'Is Margo here at the facility?' Merlin questioned.

'Someone said she's in New York,' Bhang replied. 'This could turn sour for ZynnComm.'

'Why?' Arrow enquired.

'Rumour has it Walt and the Tremaine Board have an agreement with Margo and Saxon not to sell their share of ZynnComm for 12 months, which ends next month,' Bhang explained. 'If Walt dies, then the agreement would more than likely expire, so we might be sold to HBU Electronics.'

Merlin glanced at Arrow then back to Bhang. 'Aren't you jumping the gun a little? Walt has plenty of printed organs in storage.'

'What if it's not an organ? Something that can't be replaced?' Bhang argued. They all considered the possibility for a moment. 'I'm not saying he won't recover, but we have to be prepared. I won't work for HBU.'

'Why won't you work for them?' Arrow probed.

'I'm Korean. My father was working for those bastards when he died in an industrial accident and they refused to compensate our family. They said it was his fault.'

Merlin considered Bhang before he spoke. 'I'm sure Walt will be fine,' he rested a hand on his shoulder. 'We're going to get some lunch. Want to join us?'

'Sure.'

Margo stood in the waiting room at the Hackensack University Medical Center in New Brunswick, New Jersey. Her diamond flecked nail lacquer was intact, despite her nervous picking for the past three hours. One of her minders hovered in the room while two waited in the corridor.

Walt's surgeon entered the room. 'Margo, walk with me. Walt's out of surgery and in recovery.'

'How is he?' she demanded as they took their time along the corridor.

'Coping, just,' came the honest response. 'He'll need plenty of time to recover, no more work.'

'Easy enough to say, but Dad has adult ODD,' Margo advised tongue in cheek.

The doctor considered Margo with a sly smile. 'I know. He'll be here for the next week, then he needs bed rest for a few months with a cardiac rehab team supporting him. Surviving myocardial infarction at his age is rare, less than two percent make it.'

'He's a strong old bastard.' They entered the recovery ward. Margo couldn't help but weep when she saw Walt lying unconscious with drips, catheter, a bank of machines and nurses monitoring his vitals. The father that made her giggle so hard, sometimes to the point of peeing herself, appeared lifeless. Her PD vibrated in her hand. The number was unknown, she declined it. *'Probably media,'* she thought.

Walt's cardiac specialist approached Margo. 'His new heart is an improved version of the last, but he must stop drinking, and Walt needs to retire.'

'You and I both know that should happen...now we just have to convince him.' Margo's PD vibrated again, same number. 'Excuse me, I have to take this.' She left the room for the corridor. 'How did you get this number?' Her manner was terse.

'Hiya, Mum,' came the reply.

'Hugo? Is that you, Hugo?' she melted. 'Oh, Hugo, where are you?'

'Just checking on Pop. How is he?'

'Erm...he's alive, just. He has a new heart. Where are you?'

'Darwin. But you already knew that,' he teased.

'What? What are you talking about?' Her tone was unconvincing.

'I know you've had your hounds on me for the past year.'

The dead air stretched into seconds before Margo conceded defeat. 'You wouldn't have expected anything less, would you?'

'Nope. I'll be in Sydney for Christmas.'

Margo smiled. 'Will we see you?'

'Do I still have a bedroom at the house?' he fished.

'Forever. You know that.'

'I'll be down there for a block of prac for my Uni course.'

'Where at?'

'ZynnComm...if you'll have me,' he responded with trepidation.

Margo was thrown for a moment. 'ZynnComm? In what capacity?'

'I was studying astrophysics online through ANU, but then I turned 21 a couple of months ago–'

'Yes, I know,' Margo interrupted, rolling her eyes.

'I've since swapped to neuroinformatics. I'm so fucking impressed with what Dad has created; this whole dream immersion thing is going through the roof. I want to be part of it.'

Margo was apprehensive. 'Are you kidding me? Is this another one of your projects you'll drop in a few months' time?'

'No! Honestly, I want to work in this field and where better than the business that started it all, the family business. So, I thought I should come back to Sydney.'

Margo grinned to herself again but was reluctant to cave into the arrangement automatically. 'I'll talk to your father.'

'On this 11th anniversary of the Gambaldi incident, we pay tribute to the 923,093 people who lost their lives in the largest ever mass murder by a single individual,' the TV news anchor began. 'In this devastating event, on November 12th, 2037, just under one million people from around the world lost their lives.'

Saxon watched as he waited in one of the Green rooms within the Toronto Convention Centre. He was the keynote speaker at the inaugural 2048 International Dream Immersion Symposium. Two of his three-man protection team lounged in the comfy chairs around him, the other stood by the door.

The Gambaldi incident was a decade old but due to the unprecedented death toll it was never far from the public's mind. There was always new information to be gleaned. Archival footage of Qantas aircraft wreckage being pulled from building rubble in downtown Hong Kong played as the commentator continued.

'Most would remember where they were on November 12th, 2037, when they heard the news that 919,291 individuals had died simultaneously. Alexander Augustus Gambaldi hacked the Forsythe Corporation's Medical Gateway network at 8:15 am local time on the outskirts of Turin, Italy, November 12th, 2037, initiating the incident. The Gateway neurochip, which had been voluntarily implanted close to the base of a patient's brain stem just below the skull, had allowed the network to control all patient information. The chip had been marketed as biological hardware or bioware, a psychopharmacological neuroaugmentation medical device monitoring and enhancing psychostimulants, 24-7. A decade of clinical trials had proven the device to be an effective and safe mood stabiliser. On that day in November, Alex Gambaldi the Italian SFT neurological developer, manipulated the neurochips initiating an electrical surge within patients' brain stems, causing massive seizures resulting in immediate death. An additional 3,802 deaths were attributed to accidents caused by those immediate deaths.'

A montage of photographs and video footage populated the screen as the voiceover continued. 'Alex Gambaldi had been repeatedly taunted by provocative New York Times journalist, Bud Rosen. The journalist had claimed in numerous interviews that Alex Gambaldi was wrong in his belief that the Gateway neurochip could be hacked and sabotaged. As one of the head developers at Forsythe Corporation, Gambaldi had been forced to resign because of his publicly expressed warnings. On October 12th, 2037, Bud Rosen publicly dared Gambaldi to bypass Gateway security and directly control the neurochip. One month later, Rosen's recklessness delivered staggering consequences. Bud Rosen, himself a Forsythe neurochip patient, fell victim to his own foolish actions. On November 13th, a clearly maniacal Gambaldi posted a video across multiple platforms arrogantly defending his actions—'

'What happened to Gambaldi?' one of Saxon's security men asked.

'He's locked up on Blackreef Island,' Saxon told him. 'Highly intelligent man, with all the characteristics of a psychopath.'

The Green room door swung open and a young male attendant walked over to Saxon.

'We are ready for you, Dr Zynn.'

Saxon stood and straightened his sports jacket. He pulled out his PD, checking his speech prompt app was running before placing it back in his jacket. One of Saxon's security detail followed the young man, Saxon followed him. His other minder fell in behind as they manoeuvred their way through backstage passages to the wings where they were told to wait. His remaining bodyguard scanned front of house before entering the auditorium and stood at the rear. Saxon nervously tugged at his earfonic.

The MC was alerted by the stage manager through her earpiece before spying Saxon. 'Now the formalities are over, let's hear from the unassuming man who created extraordinary tech that changed the world. The man who has single-handedly revolutionised not only the entertainment and training sectors but has spawned an industry of which we have barely scratched the surface. His dream immersion is not just about dreaming, it has invigorated many real-world industries inspired by in-dream environments, from themed restaurants to games in VRXLR8 complexes to theatrical stage shows and a plethora of merchandise. Please welcome to the stage, friends, our keynote speaker, the dream master and CEO of Zynn Communications, Dr Saxon Zynn.'

The 5000 strong audience erupted with enthusiastic applause as Saxon strode confidently to the apron stage in front of dancing holoprojections and the simple rear wall projection of the symposium name and logo.

'Good morning, good morning and welcome to the inaugural International Dream Immersion Symposium here in frosty Toronto. Over the past seven months, we have witnessed what can only be described as a Cambrian explosion of business start-ups developing and pushing the dream immersion envelope using our Gatekeeper of Dreams authoring unit. We can't make them fast enough to keep up with demand,' he grinned. 'Young DI content producers are quickly becoming the next wave of nouveau riche as they take advantage of over 240 million personal DI units sold worldwide, and the half billion unique, regular users accessing Dreamplexes, and dream pods at airports, shopping centres, in workplaces and on aircraft and trains. In total, an impressive 740 million plus users. We are fast approaching the tipping point to significantly impact and change the entertainment industry landscape forever.' Applause rose and fell quickly as Saxon continued.

'This morning, I'm going to give you a brief overview of where we are and where we're heading before we breakout for specific discussion groups,' Saxon explained. 'Our DI platform or dream phaze as the media and public refer to it, has been described as the "ultimate social media platform", or "dream collective platform", eclipsing anything before it and likely anything for several years to come. Early adopters have taken full advantage of the new medium with gusto. Like many new technologies before it, DI has developed or invented its own jargon to describe different aspects of itself. Users, for example, have become known as "dippers" for occasional users and "big dippers" for daily users. This of course has evolved from the acronym DIP, for Dream Immersion Platform. Subcultures reflecting specific dream networks and clusters are materialising in the real world, as fans and clubs flaunt unifying dreamspeak, tattoos, clothing and haircuts. This type of social propagation will continue to develop and flourish as the platform matures.'

'Based on our staged implementation strategy, we initiated the DI Classification Tool for all experiences across the platform four months ago. This has resulted in a backlog of new releases because all general public experiences through to gratuitous ultraviolence and explicit sex have to be rated by our classification unit before publication. We don't trust AI to do all this, we have a team of real humans in an office, occupying an entire floor in fact, classifying every experience released on the platform. They don't censor any experiences. Let me repeat that, we do not censor any experience content. Our classification tool is a perceptive algorithm using specific criteria to carefully analyse then classify experiences into a simple five colour rating system so users immediately know what to expect. Now you can search by colour rating, genre or experience name.'

'Production companies and advertisers are feeding users' insatiable appetites by creating new formats from old concepts like the Dream Shopping Network and Try B4U Buy.' The popular BMW Dragonfly G3400 hoverbike materialised in the void above Saxon, complete with female model flaunting ultra-white teeth. 'Dating experiences like Dream Lover, D Harmony and Luster have exploded with memberships doubling month on month. We've also been working with the producers of two of the most popular real-world streaming dramas, Melton Place and Timeless Warrior. We've transitioned these shows to the platform by producing what we call dreamcasts and they are becoming highly addictive in-dream destinations. MMDG's or mass multiplayer dream games of roleplaying and adventures like GalNexus, Spawn, WarCry, Star Quest, My Secret Life, Alien Dogfight, Visigoths and Vandals, Starpendium, DreamSeeker and Timorpheus have proven to be the fastest growing sector as people crave alternate realities. Growing almost as quickly are people gambling on DI sports such as World Obelisk League and Exoskeletal Combat. DI sports betting has appeared virtually overnight, creating a multi-billion Nukoin industry. Not to be left out, faith-based users can speculate with their spiritual capital through the established religions as well as emerging doctrines. Larger faiths have created dedicated networks for their worshipers while enthusiastic devotees of developing dogmas are producing dream clusters for followers.'

'Next month, ZynnComm will release our much-anticipated DI short format experience of only seven minutes. This format will be used for dreaminars for craft and DIY courses, real estate renovation walk throughs or as tasters for potential buyers of new cars, boats, real estate, travel products and luxury goods. Five short format experiences will be allowed per user in a 24-hour period.' Saxon paused to refocus.

'Unfortunately, there will always be individuals, organisations and countries opposed to ground-breaking technology. Case in point, Sir Tim Berners-Lee developed the World Wide Web protocols to exploit the internet almost 60 years ago. Countries and organisations blocked or suppressed access to the platform because they were afraid. They were afraid of what it was, how it could influence, and the fact that they couldn't control it in a way they wanted.' Saxon gazed out over the audience. 'Some countries have banned our DI platform outright. Countries have singled out and blocked networks, clusters and experiences such as Sinnerverse, Frightmare, DreamScream and Hellfire Haus from being accessed. In those locations underground DI enablers, black marketeers, have sprung up, circumventing country network firewalls and thriving. Prohibition has never worked. As I said before, we have the DI classification rating system to help individuals decide their experience, but the individual, not organisations or governments, must be allowed to make their own choices. Our organic dreams are not censored nor should dream immersion be. One authority should not dictate or censor what a person dreams.'

'There have been recent media reports accusing ZynnComm of secretly mining user data for our own benefit, even selling it. Let me reassure you all, we are not. The bad old days of multinational corporations collecting individuals' information and selling it have long gone ladies and gentlemen. Privacy legislation worldwide has seen that type of unsavoury practice completely prohibited. Anonymity for all users is the cornerstone principal ZynnComm safeguarded for individual users. The platform was designed from the ground up with civil liberties and privacy at the forefront, so every user could feel secure in the fact that they could visit any experience without judgement, without criticism. Your dreams are your business. None of us see each other's organic, natural dreams, and we made sure that same right, that same expectation, existed for dream immersion from the start. If you choose to share an experience with friends or family, or to rate an experience on social media, that is up to the end user. That's one reason some countries have banned our technology; they can't monitor or control the choices of the user.'

'These false reports quote that our quantum ID code is the culprit tracking you. This is 100 percent false. Our QuID code works on several levels, but its primary role starts when you switch the DI wrist device on for the first time when you purchase a unit. That's when your anonymity begins. Sure, we know when you purchased the DI device, but that's it. This unique QuID code conveys how often a device is used, the number of people using that device, their location, their age, and their level of intoxication. This information is based on GPS and cell analysis from the wrist sensor when you attach the device. Now here's the important part, we can't access, analyse or cross reference an individual's personal experience, choice or history based on a quantum ID code, GPS or cell analysis. That specific information sits behind complex encryption and simply can't be accessed. We know there are users in an experience but not the identity of those users. We can see which experiences are popular or trending by sheer volume, but not the identity of individuals in those experiences. This muckraking against ZynnComm is fodder for fake news sites, calculated attempts to tarnish our good reputation by those who oppose our technology.' He stood silent. 'Okay, I've said enough on that, I don't want to dwell on negatives this morning.'

'On an extremely positive note, all three of our Dream Immersion Academies have waiting lists of two years as the largest corporations and institutions on the planet incorporate DI into their training, education and prototyping requirements. Medical professionals, police, emergency services, astronauts, engineers, pilots, the military, trades people, are all taking advantage of employing real-world scenarios in the safety of DI. Studying, practising the scenario in the real world followed by actually participating in that scenario in-dream is invaluable. I can announce today, due to increased demand on the subcontinent, we will be opening our fourth Dream Immersion Academy in Chennai, India within six months.' The passion in his voice intensified. 'Universities have created research experiences conducting ongoing DI experiments allowing the best and brightest to network and problem solve vexing scientific issues in physics, bioengineering, space tech, AI and sociology. But,' he paused for emphasise, 'that is just the tip of the iceberg.'

'Let's cut to the chase, I am here because I have very important news to share with you. We are not prepared to publicly demonstrate what I'm about to tell you just yet, it's still early days with years of research in front of us, but believe me, we have functioning prototypes and preliminary evidence and data to back it up.' Saxon paused for dramatic effect. 'ZynnComm has made a massive breakthrough in the evolution of dream immersion technology, with help from Professor Hamasaki and his team at Kyoto University.

We've dubbed this new process, Neurocoalescence, or NCL.' The word grew larger on the rear wall screen before exploding from the screen into a hologram hovering above him. 'To put it simply, the harnessing of collective wisdom. Neurocoalescence is the confluence of minds, the unification and synchronisation of multiple brains working in concert as a single, superintelligence capable of problem solving at unprecedented speed and capacity. Superintelligence that will benefit everyone.' He waited, to let the concept permeate the now muttering audience.

'Centuries ago, when universities were founded, great minds came together to research and debate the big questions for the advancement of mankind. Just over 75 years ago the internet extended that collaboration between institutions and individuals across the entire planet. Now we have Neurocoalescence, where individuals can work together in real-time at the source of thought, in the mind itself. Over the past nine months, ZynnComm has been collaborating with Professor Hamasaki and a diverse group of experts. We've conducted research combining the neural capacity of 136 leading scientists to exploit Neurocoalescence, to accelerate and expand thought processes to solve abstract problems in minutes, instead of weeks and months. We are embarking on an evolutionary surge in human consciousness, shifting up a gear in the Great Acceleration from a technological perspective. By combining human brain power at the source, in a symbiotic relationship with our Norus quantum network, the sum becomes far, far greater and more powerful than the parts. We can use Neurocoalescence to answer complex, intuitive questions that computers alone will never answer. We honestly believe we have reached a neurological inflection point, launching into a new era in human evolution.' The audience burst into spontaneous applause as Saxon soaked up the rapture.

'He who owns the knowledge makes the rules,' Sterling Lindquist muttered to Iminka in the back row of the auditorium.

'No, they own a shitload of code,' Iminka responded.

Someone towards the front of the auditorium stood and yelled. 'What about the victims of dream immersion, those with DITS? What are you doing to help them?'

Saxon stood his ground as the audience admiration fizzled out. 'It's still too early to determine if so-called dream immersion trauma syndrome actually exists. Is it the result of dream immersion or the result of a pre-existing undiagnosed psychosis? There is not enough data–'

'Tell that to the 20,000 people living with it,' the same speaker, who wore an Organic Dream Alliance t-shirt heckled. 'Trauma in dream phaze from extreme violence, horror and abuse is very real, Dr Zynn. Rather than wasting your fucking time on Homo superior dream tanks, you should be addressing problems with your existing technology. You have to be accountable!'

'The evidence is anecdotal and sketchy at best, sir. That number you quoted is a relatively small sample compared to overall usage,' Saxon challenged. 'But whatever the number, believe me, we are investigating.'

A group of young women joked as they strolled along the bustling shopping strip, stopping occasionally to ogle the exquisitely dressed store windows. Dance music filtered along the strip, providing a festival-like atmosphere.

'I love the idea of having all these stores in one place,' Charmaine remarked.

'Much more fun doing this with my besties than with Ricardo,' Brigit boasted.

'C'mon,' Emma encouraged. 'We need to keep moving, I want to see Louis Vuitton and Versace. And I can't tell you how excited I am about seeing Korozu Umami!'

'I want to see Bergdorf Goodman!' Dana exploded.

'Nugent's is my all-time favourite experience,' Charmaine declared.

Brigit lingered, taking in the eye candy of Oscar de la Renta as the others ventured ahead. Brigit was oblivious to the partially concealed walkway between buildings as she passed by and was grabbed by her arm and dragged into the darkness. A sizable, gloved hand covered her mouth from behind to stop her vocalisation as her body was pinned against the cold brick wall. She assumed the acute pain in her lower back was the point of a knife blade.

'Stop squirming or I'll gut you,' he whispered in her ear.

Brigit ceased her struggle.

'Put this around your right wrist.' The knife pain momentarily disappeared as he handed her a set of old handcuffs.

She felt nauseated as she fumbled with the handcuffs and heard the rachet mechanism close around her wrist. Brigit tried to pull away, but the other cuff was quickly fastened to the metal pipe running up the wall. She seized the opportunity to strike back with her free elbow, hitting him in his ribs, forcing him to drop the knife to the ground.

Her attacker grabbed her left arm and twisted it back behind her. 'Stupid girl.' He rested against her for a long moment, inhaling her. 'To work.' He quickly swapped hands over her mouth.

Brigit felt her left-hand slide through a plastic loop, tightening. She struggled in the darkness but now her other hand was tethered to the wall somehow. His hand over her mouth was ever so briefly removed, as his other hand slapped a length of gaffer tape over her mouth. She felt his hand under her skirt pulling her underwear down, before spreading her feet with his leg. The man was small, inside her within seconds. Brigit deliberately tried to force her mouth open, attempting to pry the tape loose. Gradually pushing her tongue against the edge of the skewed tape, the tape under her bottom lip peeled from her skin. 'Gobbledygook,' she uttered. Cloaked in red, she vanished.

Saxon and Kris sat outdoors at Barron's Bar along the esplanade leading to the Sydney Opera House as the western city skyline masked the setting sun. Saxon's personal protection detail were scattered in a loose triangular formation around him.

'No...Walt's taken leave, he hasn't retired,' Saxon said.

'Why doesn't he just call it a day?' Kris questioned.

'You know what he's like; the old bugger thrives on being in control,' Saxon responded before sipping his beer. 'Hopefully, Margo will talk some sense into him when he gets back to Sydney in a few days.'

Kris grabbed a handful of macadamia nuts from the bowl on the table and started munching one at a time. 'So, a few ideas from the symposium have made headlines, Sterling pushing for extended DI experiences and this idea for a DI Advisory Council.'

'That's not an idea, that's Lindquist driving brand promotion. Every time they mention him, Sinnerverse is always mentioned in the next sentence,' Saxon replied. 'As for the DI Advisory Council, it's a voluntary gig, however, we can nominate and approach potential members. It was agreed one representative at an intergovernmental level from a democratic country should be nominated for transparency. We should have been on the front foot on this I suppose. Certain individuals, Ethan Tan being one of them, were vocal about privacy concerns relating to user DNA information stored on the network; they want it protected beyond any doubt.'

'This is fuelled by those fucking fake news reports last month. Ethan should know better. Did you explain that was the primary prerequisite for voluntary interconnection agreements with governments? We can't access DNA profiles!'

'I knew you would be all over this,' Saxon smiled. 'Did I mention I put you forward as our representative on the panel?'

Kris laughed. 'I'm already a global nomad, as if I can spare the time. You know we start night classes next year and we have another Academy opening.'

'They'll only be meeting four times a year and it's all expenses paid as usual. You're the perfect fit as the DI Academy CEO. Besides, it gets you on the inside to drive our agenda. Ethan will be on the Council.'

'Okay. Lookout Sinnerverse and other DI nasties.'

'The DI Advisory Council will be an advisory body only, not a regulator. I can't see Sterling or Santoro allowing Acid Spear Studios to be dictated to by a toothless advisory body. Sterling will do his own thing and that's why we have classifications, so we don't have to censor content on an adults only platform.'

'Maybe I'll push for the DI Council to grow teeth and pressure countries like Denmark and Sweden to stop harbouring debauched developers like Acid Spear.'

'Acid Spear is evolving into a steady cashflow for us, generating profits; I don't want you disrupting that. I don't give a fuck where Acid Spear and the like have set up shop and I don't want you going in gung-ho and jeopardising that.'

'As with all fledgling industries, players evolve, the cowboys are weeded out by the more powerful members,' Kris argued. 'I'd imagine this DI Advisory Council will develop into a global governance body over time.'

'All the more reason for you to be in there from the get-go. If customers are willing to pay a premium for Acid Spear products, that's up to the users, not governments or the DI Advisory Council to police. We can't interfere with people's taste in entertainment,' Saxon reinforced.

'That's where we disagree. We're in the wild west stage of DI, lawlessness until the law steps in and restores some sort of decency. I wouldn't call hunting and murdering people of specific ethnicities entertainment,' Kris countered.

'Nor do I, Kris. Look, even if those experiences do exist we wouldn't access them and neither would 99 percent of DI users.'

Kris drank his beer before changing the subject. 'What do you make of this dream immersion trauma syndrome?'

Saxon didn't hesitate. 'Our research always indicated there would be a very small number of individuals who wouldn't cope with the tech for one reason or another. Now someone's attached a name to it.' He shrugged and sipped his beer.

Kris nodded. 'We did.'

'So they won't use the platform and we risk-manage the fallout.'

'Margo said Hugo's coming home.'

'That boy confuses me. He disappears for a year then pops up and announces he wants to work for us.'

'Sounds like he needed time to find himself, to sort himself out.'

Saxon thought about Kris' insight. 'I suppose he did.'

'Will he be working with us?' Kris probed.

'Margo definitely wants him to...and so do I,' Saxon finally confessed, before selecting a macadamia nut. 'Did you hear about Andrew McTavish?'

'Just that there was an accident. He was hit in the head with a paddle board?'

'He's holidaying in Hawaii. Some guy was learning to paddle board, fell off and the board shot out from under him and hit Andrew in the side of the head. He's been in a coma for two days.'

'Poor bastard. Wasn't he camping?'

'Yep, by himself around the islands. Ingrid and their two boys were supposed to go, but the boys got sick so he went by himself. He wanted to walk to the rim of an active volcano.'

'Did he do it?' Kris questioned.

'Ingrid said he was booked to go yesterday, so no.'

'Shit.'

'We've organised a medical flight back to Brisbane for him tomorrow.'

The first man's skin colour was overtly white, too white, so Kris knew he was in the right place.

Kris had researched forums and blogs about this experience, full of opinion, cryptic clues, rumour and urban myth, there were no reviews for Hunters and Collectors. To gain membership to the secretive real-world darknet website he had registered under an assumed identity, which he thought all users would do anyway. Kris had bought a burner PD to verify his contact number and to provide a specific MC1R genetic profile. This profile, along with a 3D wrist scan revealing veins through translucent skin, had confirmed his skin colour. An extensive psychometric test had completed the entry exam. Kris' real-world membership had one purpose, to gain access to the Sinnerverse virtual proxy dream network to enter Hunters and Collectors. Without the correct VPDN code, users were denied entry to the Black rated experience. Members of Hunters and Collectors promoted white supremacist and separatist principles, harbouring deep-seated hatred for dark skinned and Asian people while championing Christian ideologies.

Half a dozen of the men in the pack of 40, behind the first man, were also blatantly white in colour, signifying players of rank. The rest, all fair Caucasians, wore necklaces of dark, tan and white skinned human ears, signalling subordinate players. The entire group, including several women, were dressed in military fatigues. They stood in a forest clearing, facing Kris. He wore civvies.

'Welcome, newbie, I'm Hunter One,' the first white man with silver grey hair said to Kris. 'We have two rules before we begin. We do not discuss what we do here in the real world, ever, and we don't use names in here. We have a strict hierarchal structure you must obey if you get through today. Before we start, you'll have a chat with Hunter Two,' he gestured to the chubby, bleached man standing to one side and behind him. 'He'll explain the finer points of the experience. Today we will forgo our usual prey to begin your initiation. Today we hunt you. If you survive, you can return to participate. If you are killed, you can never return.' He pulled a knife from his belt. 'This is your weapon.' Hunter One handed Kris an impressive stainless steel 30-centimetre hunting knife.

'Thank you,' Kris responded, checking out the size and balance of the intimidating weapon in his hand.

Hunter One turned around to address the group. 'Today we hunt the newbie.'

Kris took the initiative; he plunged his weapon deep into the soft throat of Hunter One and twisted. Withdrawing the knife quickly, Kris took a few steps back in a defensive stance waiting for an attack. None of them helped Hunter One as he unceremoniously thumped the forest floor. A heavy-set white man in the pack instantly drew his knife and moved towards Kris.

A tall, golden-haired, blue-eyed man wearing a single ear on his necklace, held out his arm and stopped the hefty man's approach. 'Wait. We all want a chance at this prick.'

Hunter Two took a step forward. 'You have one minute before we start the hunt,' he growled. 'Take his ear before he vanishes, then fucking run, mister.'

Ten minutes later, hiding in a tree fork several metres above mossy ground cover, Kris watched and waited. The tall, blonde man inched his way along the rough path below, searching undergrowth. Kris dropped from above and felt his generous blade sink into the soft flesh between the hunter's right collarbone and shoulder. Both men collapsed to the ground. Kris extracted his knife and rolled the man over, preparing to cut his throat.

'Wait!' he pleaded. 'Please,' he panted. 'I'm with you.'

Kris held his blade hard against the Caucasian man's neck. 'What the fuck are you talking about?'

'That was a ballsy move, to kill Hunter One,' the man praised, wincing from pain. 'My shoulder's fucking killing me. I'm not going to bleed out and die here. I have to exit.'

'Wait.'

'Dreadnaught,' he muttered before glowing a soft red and fading away.

Liam sat in the office trying to write. He was easily distracted by the show projected on the wall from his PD.

'Explosive revelations today from the wife of convicted murderer Locky Slade,' the news anchor began, 'the man responsible for the assassination of Fundamental Purists founder Jeremy Abernathy. June Slade stated her husband was reportedly recruited by the man himself for the job. Abernathy was apparently in remission for colon cancer, but the week after his return from Australia it was confirmed the disease had returned and he was given only months to live. June Slade decided to go public after she was not paid promised money from the Fundamental Purists. Slade admitted her husband was paid 100,000 Nukoin up front with a further 100,000 promised after the shooting. She named Amanda Voss, Abernathy's wife and now CEO of the Fundamental Purists organisation, as being in the meeting with Abernathy when he and her husband planned his very public execution. June Slade said Amanda Voss had reneged on a promise to pay the money to the Slade family as agreed. Slade believed the plan to martyr Abernathy and immortalise him in their dream immersion network was made clear from the sta–.'

Liam's PD unexpectedly shutdown, out of power. Picking it up, he passed the device over the Swipe Charge point in the wall above his desk. It immediately popped back on, but he decided to switch it off to concentrate.

The DI Experiences website owned by ZynnComm was the source of all truth when it came to available experiences on the DI platform. Liam had carved out a niche by donning the nom de plume, Jonny Fab, and compiling a weekly review blog called Hit or Miss. New releases from mainstream, indie, garage start-ups as well as trending experiences were reviewed by ZynnComm employees, rated accordingly and presented in Jonny Fab's blog. Hit or Miss had influence. It could drive an experience to the backwaters of the platform to languish or propel it into the stratosphere and turn developers into overnight millionaires. He began tapping keys again.

'*Mutsumo Fairy Tails has been trending for the past 24 hours. This weird little indie redemption experience comes from Saskwa Studio where users catch fairies, pull off their wings and tails and feed them to trogs, a walking fish-type critter that lives in a stinking swamp. Fairies of all shapes and sizes attract varying points, the Glaxon being the fiercest and hardest to catch. Scores accumulate and are converted into real-world credit for the plethora of Mutsumo products. Seems to be a hit.*'

'I need you in the lab, Liam,' Wendy said as she entered their office.

'Can it wait? I'm just finishing Hit or Miss.'

Wendy slumped in her desk chair. 'Sydney are reporting qware probes spiking across the network from two state actors in particular. Cybersecurity want us to run a few diagnostics our end.'

'The usual perps?'

'Yep. There's also chatter about a couple of new subversive US domestic terrorism experiences they want us to check. The usual thing.'

'Okay.' Liam saved his blog, 'Let's do it.' He stood and stretched.

Wendy's PD buzzed on her desk. 'It's Saxon, I have to take this first. Hi, Saxon.' She listened. 'Are you serious? Now?'

Five minutes later, Wendy was sitting in Saxon's office with two Australian Federal Police agents.

Agent Kosteska watched Saxon and Wendy as she listened to her partner, Agent Makkouk, outline the reason for their visit.

'Sorry for the short notice, Dr Zynn, Dr Setri. Just between us, this is a new role for Agent Kosteska and me. We are charting new territory, territory we don't fully understand yet. Our jurisdiction is cybercrime, and there seems to be a grey area regarding which federal department has jurisdiction or responsibility when it comes to your DI platform. Victorian State Police referred a matter to the AFP regarding a Melbourne woman who has made a complaint that she was assaulted and raped in a DI experience, and we've been asked to investigate the matter.'

'I'm very sorry to hear that. Have we had a complaint of that nature, Wendy?'

'Not that I'm aware of. Which experience, Agent Makkouk?' Wendy quizzed.

'Nugent's Luxury Plaza.'

'That's White rated, a general public experience isn't it?' Saxon again deflected to Wendy.

'Yes it is. A shopping experience,' Wendy answered with a concerned face. 'Were there witnesses?'

'Unfortunately, no,' Agent Makkouk replied.

'You do realise this incident is impossible to verify,' Saxon insisted. 'I'm not saying this woman is lying, but you only have her version of events. There is no evidence.'

'Possibly,' Agent Kosteska chimed into the conversation.

'We've been investigating a private online group known as Konqwest, that's spelt K-o-n-q-w-e-s-t,' Agent Makkouk continued. 'Members are predominately male university students, but by no means exclusively male or students. A private DI experience called Pleasure Planet has popped up several times during our ongoing investigation of the website. This experience is misogynistic, based on men behaving...let's say, very fucking badly. In the real world, the aim of this Konqwest group is to convince as many women as they can to disrobe on camera and have sex. They post the video to the Konqwest website. Nukoin is the prize for the most posts per month and we've traced the funds through several bank accounts and the Transcredit app to Mumbai. A week ago, we logged chatter on the Konqwest forum about a rape inside dream immersion. By itself, that information was meaningless until this complaint dropped on our desks. We need to know if this chatter is linked to the woman in Melbourne and if members of the Konqwest website and Pleasure Planet experience are involved,' Agent Makkouk concluded, sniffing and wiping his nose with his hand.

'Which network is Pleasure Planet part of?' Saxon asked Wendy.

'If it's the one I'm thinking of, Sinnerverse.'

'Surprise, surprise,' Saxon mocked in a cynical tone.

'Sinnerverse network experiences generally have a Black rating, mostly gratuitous explicit sex and ultraviolence. Pleasure Planet has a Red rating, more geared towards explicit sex.' Agent Makkouk stated. 'We know all DI users are anonymous, and Sinnerverse has an added VPDN layer. We need access to user information for the Pleasure Planet experience and Nugent's Luxury Plaza to cross reference users,' Agent Makkouk finished, pulling his handkerchief from his suit pants pocket and wiping his nose.

'That's not possible, Agent Makkouk. We don't collect or have access to that type data from the platform,' Saxon responded honestly.

'We need your cooperation on this matter,' Agent Kosteska interjected with a gentle smile.

'It's not a matter of cooperating,' Wendy snapped. 'Saxon has already told you, we simply don't have the need to collect that type of data, so we don't. End of story.'

'We need to know who accesses these experiences,' Agent Kosteska insisted, disregarding Wendy's response.

Saxon laughed at her request. 'If you had of done your due diligence, Agent, you would know very well we don't collect that information and if we did, that breaches every privacy and confidentiality law governing DI–'

'We're aware of the laws,' Agent Kosteska continued, irritation creeping into her tone. 'We want to know if it's possible, then we'll get the appropriate court order for you to collect that data.'

'Tens of thousands of users access the platform every hour,' Wendy explained. 'We can't possibly track the experiences they access. Our software is specifically designed not to track or monitor individual user choices because of privacy laws. Even if we could, we wouldn't disseminate that information to you.'

Agent Kosteska glared at Wendy. 'There are laws and there is federal law enforcement disclosure–'

'We know, we know, law enforcement have privileges, special dispensation,' Saxon derided. 'Not here, Agent Kosteska. We monitor devices, not people. We simply don't have the technology to access that information, and there is specific legislation that forbids us from disclosing any user information. One of the reasons this was done was because law enforcement has a reputation for abusing systems to benefit the few. Sorry.'

'So, you can't access that information?' Agent Makkouk continued to probe.

'Look,' Wendy began with growing frustration, 'the only user information collected by the DI device is location, which is pointless if a VPDN layer is used, time of use, frequency of use, user age and intoxication levels–'

'Using an epidermal DNA microsensor,' Agent Makkouk finished. 'Which also checks body temperature.'

'Correct, that's where the information collection stops. That data is stored behind an encrypted DNAsafe key, and no one, and I mean no one, has access to that key except the system to check for usage within a 24-hour period.'

'So sweat is checked for intoxication levels and DNA checked for cell age, and that information is stored?' Agent Makkouk pushed.

Wendy didn't respond immediately. 'Yes, but–'

'You just told us you don't know who has jurisdiction over this in-dream incident on our platform, so where is the court order coming from?' Saxon challenged.

Agent Kosteska stood. 'Thank you for seeing us today, Dr Zynn.' She smiled at Wendy.

Saxon stood and shook her hand. 'I'm sorry we can't be more helpful.' Both agents left his office for the elevator. Saxon turned to Wendy. 'Keep an eye on that experience and get a report together on all complaints, no matter how trivial. Something's not right.'

'Will do.'

Chapter Two

Hammerhead One glided through the ocean effortlessly before coming to a complete stop. The substantial submarine had the characteristics of a hammerhead shark, featuring entirely transparent pressure and outer hulls. Hundreds of observers packed the vessel from the forward viewing deck to aft, gawking at Cretaceous Period Mosasaurs. Diffused shafts of light stabbed the sunlit layer of ocean revealing a spectacle of energetic marine reptiles. Dallasaurus and Platecarpus, four metres in length, preyed on fish and nautilus molluscs, enthralling spectators. From the dark depths rose much larger apex predators, Tylosaurus and Hainosaurus, attacking their smaller brethren chomping them in half in outpourings of pure ferocity. Plumes of blood stained the water as prehistoric reptiles gorged on one another.

'Pretty cool, huh?' Hugo asked.

'Very...realistic,' Margo agreed. 'What's that?' Nodding at the tri-hull of a massive vessel approaching on the surface.

'Watch,' Hugo advised.

The vessel came to rest above Hammerhead One, blocking much of the natural light. At that moment, hull lights on the imposing surface ship lit the entire area around the submarine. Fenrel emerged from the light towards the Mosasaurs. The divers were propelled through the water at speed, quickly surrounding the larger Tylosaurus.

'The Fenrel are natives in these parts, they hunt the marine life,' Hugo told Margo.

'To eat?'

'No, they use their blood the catch Hig worms. They eat the worms,' Hugo clarified. 'One worm can feed hundreds of Fenrel for months.' The mass attack on the marine reptile was swift and efficient. The overpowering lights temporarily blinded the beast long enough for the hunters to shoot spears into its eyes, disorientating the animal, enabling the captors to surround it with a fine net and attach it to their vessel. 'The spears are coated in a neurotoxin that quickly stuns their prey, then they drag them back to port and drain them of precious blood.'

'You seem to know a lot about this experience,' Margo commented.

'I love this experience; I spend a lot of time here exploring. There are 56 humanoid species on a planet the size of Jupiter. Remember the novels I used to read by Franklin Fritz–'

'I know that name. He wrote...erm'

'Star Storm. Sam Pendleton was the protagonist.'

'That's right,' Margo remembered. 'You always seemed to have one of his novels going on your device.'

'There were nine in the series, this experience is based on those novels.'

'Is it true to the novels?'

'As much as I've seen. The characters and worldbuilding are accurate. Fritz was known as the train writer.'

'He was a train enthusiast too?'

'Not quite. He wrote the series riding trains throughout the late '20s and '30s. He didn't have an office and didn't like writing at home, so he jumped on a train in the morning and travelled the system writing all day. Getting off one train, changing platforms and jumping on another, never leaving a station. He did this all over the world in different cities for each novel. He travelled four days a week like a regular job and it cost him next to nothing. It inspired him to write, watching passengers and meeting characters on trains that ended up in his novels in some form. He called it an exercise in human observation.'

'Sounds like an interesting way to write. Where's Sam Pendleton, the hero?' Margo asked.

'His starcraft is docked on the other side of the planet. You can travel with him or explore the planet. The developers of this experience have taken Fritz's story lines in a hundred different directions, that's why I keep coming back.'

Margo studied her son. 'Thank you for the invitation to the experience, it's great to see you. When will we see you in the flesh?'

'That's one of the bonuses of Dad's tech, you can feel me right now, in the flesh,' Hugo joked, wrapping his arm around her.

Margo grabbed his hand on her shoulder. 'You know what I mean.' She kept hold of his hand. 'We've missed you.'

'Closer to Christmas. I have a few loose ends to tie up in Darwin. Look!' he pointed.

Wendy sat at the table watching her PD, under the dome above Saxon's residence.

'Chris Reddy, Minister for Correctional Services in South Africa has been arrested and charged over falsifying records, embezzlement and dereliction of duty for the past seven years,' the voiceover reported over file footage of the minister. 'South Africa has an increasing incarceration rate, while maintaining the same number of correctional facilities. And how did they do it? By feeding maximum security prisoners to sharks. The whistleblower from Craydenhurst, the maximum-security facility in Umhlanga, north of Durban, covertly filmed his part in a three-man team who routinely ferried bound and gagged maximum security prisoners offshore at night to the shark feeding grounds off Umhlanga rocks.' Rough footage shot at night showed prisoners being tossed into churning water aft of a fishing trawler. 'The facility, operated by the minister's brother in-law, James Muller under Duke & Duke Enterprises, charged the government $800 per day, per prisoner. The facility inmate numbers have reportedly swollen from 1200 seven years ago to housing 3400 prisoners today. Craydenhurst was virtually impossible to gain entry to without ministerial approval until yesterday. Craydenhurst maximum security facility is home to inmates whose files are marked "never to be released". They are the worst of the worst. These men enter the facility and are never allowed to meet with visitors, instead family and friends are deceived by Cubicapture holoprojected meetings with specialist staff masquerading as inmates, the whistleblower has told authorities. To compound this already extraordinary story, comes the admission that–'

Saxon and Veejay Kandy joined Wendy at the table. Saxon brought drinks for the three of them. Wendy put her PD down and picked up her tablet device.

'This makes the second extreme complaint for the month and we're only four days into December,' Wendy told them. 'Harvey said they're increasing–'

'Refresh my memory,' Saxon jumped in. 'What does Harvey do?' Saxon slumped into his chair with a small carton of coconut water.

'Head of Customer Solutions team in Sydney,' Veejay answered. 'His team monitors and responds to all complaints; the vast majority are disgruntled users, insignificant to minor on our Complaint Severity Matrix. Most have ended up in the wrong experience by their own choosing. He's been tracking extreme complaints in White and Yellow rated experiences for the previous four months.'

'His report has one in August, two in September, three in October, three in November,' Wendy rattled off. 'All in White experiences to date.'

'Extreme complaints, like the Melbourne woman?' Saxon asked.

'Worse. All raped, most killed,' Wendy responded.

'Shit!' Saxon exclaimed. 'Why the fuck do we get a visit from the AFP before it appears on my radar?'

'Harvey mentioned he had some extreme complaints, but only escalated it a few days ago,' Veejay explained.

'You should have escalated this months ago, Veejay!' Saxon stressed in a terse tone. 'This is the type of issue that could stop us in our tracks,' Saxon grew more annoyed. 'They could just pull the fucking plug on the entire platform.'

'You're a busy man, Saxon,' Veejay nervously offered in his defence. 'Given we have hundreds of thousands of visits a day, the ratio is miniscule, and we thought they were just isolated events until recently. I discussed it with Wendy yesterday, she told me about the AFP visit, and here we are.'

'Jesus.' Saxon sat forward and rubbed his forehead. 'How the hell do we track down these arseholes? Is there any evidence assembled echoes are being raped and killed?'

'I wondered the same thing,' Wendy said. 'We don't have any methodology for checking when and how assembled echoes die. There are so many of them across the platform, we didn't really need to know until now. Do you remember Jardene's temporal disphage algorithm from his 2038 paper?'

'Not really,' Saxon honestly admitted.

'Well, since yesterday, I've used that as a starting point to write a search method within the assembled echo database across three of the reported experiences. As we speak, I already have four females in the target demographic attacked and killed.' Wendy concluded.

'Users can't differentiate between live and assembled echoes, so it makes sense victims are mixed,' Saxon reasoned.

'It may not be one person?' Veejay proposed. 'It could be several.'

'Possibly, but I don't think so. The patterns of attack are too similar,' Wendy scrolled back and forth through the complaint summaries. 'Very crowded general public experiences, at night, with lots of mixed echoes. The women are all in their early to mid-20s. Problem is the description of the attacker is vague in all but one incident. They said he was light skinned with black hair. So, no consistent descriptions.'

'That doesn't tell us anything given skin colour can be modified.' Saxon fidgeted, wiping imaginary dust from his sleeve. 'How were they killed?'

'As I said, the pattern is so similar. All eleven were assaulted and raped from behind. Nine had their throats cut from behind. All victims report being dragged into a dark place. If there was more than one perp we'd have variations in the attacks.'

'Any of them have active safe words or kill switches?'

'All of them, only two were activated.'

'Why?' Saxon queried.

'Most had their mouths taped shut and hands bound.'

'Premeditated,' Veejay concluded. 'Definitely has the behaviour of a serial offender.'

'The victim last month, Brigit McKenzie, the woman from Melbourne, managed to use her safe word,' Wendy read. 'As we know, she reported it to authorities and has been one of the most vocal in the media about her ordeal.'

'Do we know if the victims have returned to DI since their attacks?' Veejay asked.

'None have. All said they wouldn't return,' Wendy reported. 'Can you fucking blame them? But it's word of mouth through social media that's keeping women away.'

Saxon thought before asking, 'All attacks in our experiences?'

'Nine in ours across four different dream clusters. Two in Nugent's Luxury Plaza experience.'

'None from the other one...the one the AFP mentioned, the—'

'Pleasure Planet has no complaints. But it has a Red rating, users would anticipate violence. I haven't checked assembled echoes yet.'

The trio sat quietly for some moments. 'I thought we had clear protocols from preliminary risk analysis covering violent crime?' Saxon directed at Veejay.

'We do, to a certain level.'

'What does that mean? I need a better answer then that, Veejay,'
Saxon asserted.

Veejay picked up his container of apple juice. 'All our data is
based on an algorithmic prediction, that's the best we could do. Our
social algorithm, Social Dynamic, which Wendy helped develop, was
an educated assessment of outcomes,' he explained, trying to share
the blame before taking a quick sip of his drink. 'Social Dynamic,
coupled with our behaviour modelling, focused on consequences
not causes. As you know, from the beginning we banned certain
individuals from entering DI based on their known criminal
background. Anyone who had committed violent crimes like
predatory, premeditated murder, or predation leading to sexual
assault, rape or grievous bodily harm, for example. We created an
offenders list across 160 countries, painstakingly obtained their
DNA profiles and consequently banned those profiles from the DI
platform. From that point forward, we calculated the risk of random
violent attacks in general experiences to be almost non-existent
when all behavioural analytics were evaluated. According to all our
modelling, our anticipated user demographic would not be
intoxicated, come from developed, industrialised countries who had
the disposable income to buy or use our product, and where rape and
murder were both low. We never really knew what we were dealing
with until the platform was launched.'

'We had to make a call to largely rely on unconscious bias data
sets within the algorithms from existing socialisation modelling,'
Wendy added in their defence. 'Because we simply didn't have the
data to draw upon.'

'And that historical data possibly skewed the predicted
outcomes,' Veejay said. 'Now we have ten months of evidence-based
data. DI take up was so fast in the first few months we simply
collected data with minimal analysis. But now we're beginning to see
trends and anomalies.' He took another mouthful of juice.

'So, how do we fix this anomaly?' Wendy probed.

'There are upfront warnings every time people use our tech, to limit our liability. Users know they may die in certain experiences; they are warned before they enter, and they accept that risk. The numbers you quoted, Wendy, are comparatively miniscule given usage,' Veejay argued.

'But that's not the point, these are White rated general experiences, Veejay,' Saxon stressed. 'Women don't expect to be raped and killed in these experiences and they shouldn't have to accept that risk when they go in.'

'True,' he uttered sheepishly. 'Here's something else to consider. On average, more than ten percent of homicides worldwide go unsolved each year. This may be an anomaly we are starting to see, a percentage of murderers who have flown under the radar, who have never been caught, are using our platform. The frequency and premediated nature of these attacks seems to be pointing to a serial offender. Our modelling concentrated on trauma outcomes in the real world that could impact our bottom line. Emergent mental health issues such as what we are starting to see now on a small scale with DITS. We never factored in an in-dream serial killer.'

'Perhaps we should be looking for real-world cold cases, serial murders that are not solved?' Saxon proposed.

'Definitely, I'll do that,' Wendy volunteered. 'What was our modelled prevalence of assaults pre-launch in general experiences?' Wendy asked Veejay.

He tapped his device screen. 'Once we removed the known violent criminal element, we calculated the remaining random assaults–'

'By male users,' Wendy interjected. 'Let's be accurate.'

'Predominantly, who could take advantage of participants–'

'Do you mean indiscriminate acts of rape and murder?' Wendy clarified.

'No, not at all. Common assaults such as striking or kicking someone, groping, harassment, and minor aggression. The rate was 10.8 incidences per 345,000 users–'

'I hear a "but" coming,' Wendy told Saxon.

'But as I said, our pre-launch modelling focused on consequences from experiences like Medieval Madness where decapitation, drawing and quartering or disembowelling, high impact violence, could result in psychological trauma for users in the real world. Fallout from experiences we now rate as Red or Black.'

'What's happening to these women is far more traumatic than seeing a fucking head chopped off, Veejay. A grubby, feeble-minded individual is preying on and violating female users then killing them.'

Veejay squirmed in his chair, before taking a gulp from his juice, buying time to think of a response. 'I think the vast majority of men in White experiences are good, decent, law-abiding people. Most men would think they could be identified, caught and banned from the platform if they participated in this level of abuse in a White experience.'

'I think you're right, Veejay,' Wendy agreed. 'But this animal knows his anonymity is protected, which adds power to the mix, making him more brazen.'

'Sinnerverse caters for men who indulge in demeaning, abusive, misogynistic experiences, why isn't he using those experiences?' Veejay questioned.

'No challenge for him,' Saxon suggested. 'I think Wendy's right, it's the power as much as the act that stimulates him.'

'We did discuss abuse against women early in project development, and we did discuss an in-dream policing unit if I'm not mistaken, but it was decided not to go down that path because of jurisdiction complications,' Veejay paused. 'We could recommend disabling memory for the target demographic in the short term until we sort this out?'

Saxon studied Veejay for a moment. 'No. If we draw attention to this issue so will everyone else, especially the media. Your daughters, do they dream phaze, Veejay?'

He glanced from Saxon to Wendy and back again. 'Yes, Saxon, they do.'

'They are in this sick bastard's demographic. Would they dream phaze if they couldn't remember it, or there might be a chance they could be raped and killed and have no memory of it?'

'Probably not,' he quietly agreed.

'In hindsight, even with violent criminals excluded, violence towards women should have been flagged as a higher risk concern,' Saxon said.

'It was flagged, but underestimated I would argue,' Veejay added.

'This is going to have serious ramifications and every one of us are accountable. I need you to extrapolate what this could cost in financial terms, Veejay. I'll have a chat to a few colleagues about the psychological fallout.'

'I'll get the team onto it right away.' Veejay took another drink as Wendy and Saxon stared at him.

'Well...' Saxon prompted.

'Yes, I'll get onto it now.' He left the table with haste.

'We need to mitigate this quickly and quietly,' Saxon confided in Wendy. 'Talk to Harvey in Sydney, I want his team to monitor in-dream violent attacks reported to police worldwide. We need a database of information. This has to be tracked.'

'I've been thinking about how we approach this too,' Wendy alluded, grabbing her orange juice, twisting open the lid and drinking. 'If we can access DNA samples of users in all experiences where the attacks took—'

'Whoa, we are not breaking international privacy laws. We can't access DNA samples,' Saxon emphasized. 'Even if we could technically do it.'

'Hear me out, Saxon,' Wendy's tone was compelling. 'We can't let this fucking maggot ridden festering haemorrhoid prey on female users–'

'Don't hold back, tell me how you really feel,' Saxon said.

Wendy remained focused. 'Miranda was raped when she was 15. She will carry the trauma, that violation, to her grave. It's no different for these women, it's very real to them. I would say most of these women are going to counselling for DITS.'

'DITS...the evidence seems to be mounting,' Saxon thought aloud. 'I think there's no doubt the pendulum has begun to swing from unwavering support for dream immersion to concerns about unintended side effects and abuses.'

'These won't be isolated incidents; we'll absolutely need a strategy to identify certain individuals in the system moving forward. Our psychographic data from users is useless in this situation; this predator won't be completing satisfaction questionnaires. We need one person who can do this covertly...you and I need only know,' Wendy suggested with raised eyebrows.

'That's why you wanted the meeting up here, privacy.'

'I don't think we can track this prick using his DI device, he would be using a VPDN to hide his connection point on the network.'

'I would imagine so, yes,' Saxon concurred.

'So, we need to follow the DNA. I have a background that suits this task and I'm in the position to do it. I can access the DNA records to track this fucker down in the real world.'

Saxon sat silent, contemplating the repercussions of not acting, against acting covertly. 'I don't think it will be that cut and dry. We need to maintain transparency at all levels, for customers, business to business and government. Just attempting this could...how are you going to bypass the DNAsafe protocols?'

'You know as well as I do, there's a crack in everything, that's how the bugs get in. I'm relying on a zero-day vulnerability, human error somewhere in the code. The more moving parts the greater the chance of error. We are the biggest moving part likely to fail, and I'm counting on it.'

Saxon considered her response for a moment. 'Kris must be part of this. Quietly escalate this to him, I want him helping you. I'll talk to Margo, and just the four of us will meet. I don't think we'll have time before the Christmas break, which gives you and Kris time to formulate a plan. Early January definitely.'

Wendy and Miranda walked through the circular Moongate stone, wading knee deep into a sea of gorgeous flowers. Every single plant was in bloom. The riot of vibrantly coloured hills undulated for kilometres before receding to the horizon.

'It's...beautiful,' Miranda remarked. 'So, we are the very first in this experience?'

'Guinea pigs we are.' Two comfy chairs, side by side, awaited on a slight mound. 'Here, take a seat. We've been running simulations, but I wanted to check it myself.'

Almost immediately the chairs activated, slowly moving forward to glide from the ground in a low trajectory, gradually gaining altitude. Their hair gently blew as their speed increased.

'What's this experience called?' Miranda asked.

'We haven't decided yet, maybe Moongate, but Joyville seems to be popular,' Wendy confessed. 'The codesters are pushing for Joyville.'

'Joyville?'

'I'll explain shortly.'

'Did you create any of this?'

'No, not these days. My role is mainly administration, workforce coordination and troubleshooting.'

'How many codesters in your department now?'

'We're up to around 80, maybe 85 in the Lucid division.'

'Eighty-five! Wow, that's a lot of responsibility. I'm so proud of you,' Miranda smiled.

The confectionary-coloured flowers under them transformed into a striking patchwork quilt that stretched on forever.

'It's so beautiful,' Miranda repeated.

'That's where we're going,' Wendy pointed to their right. In the distance, a city of high-rise buildings of unique shapes and sizes stained kilometres of landscape. 'That's Joyville. It's still in development.'

Miranda snorted. 'It doesn't look like it needs more development.'

'Not that type of development. Anyway, Liam wrote a story about a city called Joyville and Arrow came up with a new model for in-dream micro developers. So, we're merging the two ideas to trial a new concept. Micro developers can buy their own building and customise it from an in-dream menu of furnishings, activities, events, assembled echoes, etcetera. They don't need to own or know how to code a Gatekeeper of Dreams unit. It can be for personal use or they can charge users to visit if they wish. Instead of creating standalone, unconnected experiences, we're creating a themed dream park, incorporating multiple distinct destinations, multiple storylines.'

'Fractal storytelling,' Miranda said.

'That's right. How do you know about fractal stories?'

'All stories are fractal, made up of stories within stories that follow rudimentary patterns developed over time. Three acts, four acts, five act stories all have basic rules, repeating patterns that reaffirm themes, ideas and events.'

'Where the fuck did that come from?' Wendy asked in astonishment.

'My Uni days. I took a writing course to help with my essays. I remember that much.' Miranda paused. 'Does everyone dream, even people with aphantasia?'

'I repeat, where the fuck did that come from?'

'I just wondered,' she answered with a smile.

'Everyone dreams, but not everyone remembers their dreams. Saxon did some dream research with people living with aphantasia,' Wendy explained. 'I recall...people with aphantasia do dream but less often, and their dreams are less vivid than more visual dreamers. It's when they're awake they seem to have trouble, they can't visualise, their mind's eye is blind. Saxon wanted to know if those living with the condition experienced sensory interpretation in dream immersion as the rest of us do, and they did.'

Their chairs ascended through cumulonimbus cloud higher into the troposphere as a passenger jet could be heard nearing their location. The rumble intensified, before the aircraft broke through cloud and passed underneath them.

'That was cool,' Miranda said grinning.

Their chairs banked right heading for Joyville. In an instant, the chairs began to dive, plummeting faster and faster.

'What's happening, Wendy?' Miranda questioned, clinging to the armrests. 'Is this part of the ride?'

'Erm...no it's not. There's still an issue with the gravitational modulation code.'

'Do we crash and burn or do we exit early?'

'I'm exiting before we hit,' Wendy told her. 'Excalibur.' She began to shimmer red.

'Mudderfucker,' Miranda uttered to end the cycle, as flower beds quickly loomed.

Stage Two of the Port Augusta facility had been plagued with problems from the outset. It had been fast-tracked a full 12 months ahead of schedule given the uptake of the DI platform worldwide. Issues with power and networking had been just the beginning, meaning elevators shut down between floors and communications dropped out on a regular basis. The second underground structure was larger, three times larger. Dedicated levels for more R&D, developers' labs and overnight accommodation meant Stage One was now rid of clutter and overcrowding. The two facilities shared a common food court and extended gym on level four. At ground level, a climatically controlled single clear dome protected recreational seating sprinkled throughout the meandering, tree-lined running and cycle track.

The manicured grass was soft and inviting under Merlin and Arrow, both lying on their backs, eyes closed, in the warm sun under the dome.

'How did your day pan out?' Arrow asked.

'I had a lot on my plate today, but I managed to lick it clean. You?'

'Started the Hubert Merriman project. It'll take longer than allocated.'

'Okay. Did you see Tristan Grazer has licensed his likeness for a custom experience?'

'Who can afford 1000 Nukoin per experience? He might be a megastar, but that's fucking ridiculous,' Arrow replied.

'I can see well-heeled women, and men, paying that and more for a personal love shack experience with Tristan. We have exclusive rights to develop and distribute the experience. We'll need to test his echo in a few of our experiences before his people sign off on the final release.'

'What are you thinking?'

Merlin was unaware of her cheeky grin but heard it in her tone. 'Well, I think Tristan Grazer will accompanying us to GalNexus. Give users a sneak peek to work the bugs out of his echo.'

'Can you do that?'

'I run uDream custom experiences, of course I can. Do you want to work on his echo development?'

'Fuck yeah!'

'You don't have to be so enthusiastic,' Merlin quipped.

'It's Tristan fucking Grazer, Merlin, I'd be stupid not to be.'

'It's not Tristan Grazer the action hero, it's Tristan Grazer the man, with all his foibles and eccentricities. His well-documented carcinophobia, narcissism and cat grooming will be on display. People need to know the secret life of Tristan Grazer and his love of Morris dancing.'

'Morris dancing? I've never heard that he liked Morris dancing?'

'Oh yes, it's a closely guarded secret very few know about,' Merlin speculated. 'At the utterance of a trigger word he stops everything and breaks into Morris dancing.'

Arrow laughed. 'You are a fucking idiot, Merlin; you can't do that to him.'

'Oh yes we can.' He rolled over onto one elbow looking down at her. 'We are the puppet masters who create distraction for the world.' He gave her a quick kiss.

'Remember what you did to old Elon Musk? If Saxon finds out, he won't be happy.'

Merlin dropped from his elbow onto his back. 'Saxon didn't see the funny or the scientific side of it. Either way, the Bull Terrier and Elon clearly enjoyed it. You know I was inspired by that old movie Bad...erm...'

'Bad Grandpa. Classic.' They both laughed.

'Do you ever think about how much money we could make if we went out on our own, you know, if we started our own production company?' Arrow questioned.

'Occasionally, but then I realise we're at the epicentre of dream immersion tech. We are where most developers would love to be, at the company who created the medium, who keep exploring the fringes with new techniques. The largest corporations and celebrities come to us to create their vision; they don't go to small production companies competing in a sea of wannabes.'

'I suppose so...still, one day maybe.'

'Maybe.'

'Turn that off, will you?' Wendy asked Liam.

'Wait on, I want to see this.'

'The phenomenally successful in-dream World Obelisk League is slowly seeping into the waking world as teams begin building arenas and vehicles to train,' the reporter said as Liam watched the monitor. 'Two of the first professional teams, Zig Zag from China along with The Giants from South Africa, have poured considerable capital into building training venues to mimic in-dream competition. Chen Zhao, the team manager for Zig Zag, reinforced she wants to give her team maximum advantage to win the next WOL cup.' Vision of the Zig Zag dodgers parkouring over obstacles played as Liam stood engrossed. 'However, there are fundamental dangers in this type of sport in real life, as one player from Zig Zag found out the hard way, now permanently disabled–'

'Liam, Liam!' Wendy stressed.

'Coming.' He waved his hand down to put the monitor to sleep before wandering over to her workstation. 'Just checking out the competition. You know DI sports bookies have Zig Zag at four to one odds of taking out the next cup?'

'I don't bet on real-world sport let alone in-dream sport,' Wendy pointed out. 'Besides, they have a team full of gymnastics and parkour champions, they have an automatic advantage.'

'Do you think Saxon would build us an arena?'

Wendy's face distorted into an expression of bewilderment. 'Ah, no. I would never play Obelisk in the real world.'

'I suppose so. What's the problem?'

'What do the DI sports bookies have us at?' Wendy's asked out of curiosity.

'Most are around 200 to one.'

'Makes sense. Okay, our deadline's looming; we need to control the gravitational modulation anomaly in Moongate–'

'Moongate? Don't you mean Joyville?'

Wendy offered a sly smile. 'We'll see. The neuromitter synapse sequencing has to be synchronised to compensate for oscillation dampening between nodes C345 and G419. I want it online by the due date.'

'I'll start adjusting that now. Do you want to run the simulation with Zen again?' Liam sat down at his workstation and opened the Moongate folder.

'Yep.' Wendy was distracted with a text message on her PD.

Liam stopped when he heard Wendy's sharp intake of breath. 'Are you alright?'

In a small voice she responded, 'Andrew McTavish is dead.'

Liam sat back in his chair. 'Shit.'

'They turned his life support off this morning...his third week in a coma.'

'I didn't know him well, just to say hello to in the corridor.'

'Poor bugger. I knew Andrew well,' Wendy confided, settling back in her chair. 'He has two teenage sons. I remember he said to me once, that he struggled to leave a job that gave him financial security; it killed the bohemian in him. That precarious dance between financial responsibility and the freedom to live life spontaneously was beyond him. He said he wasn't a good dancer and always erred on the side of commitment. He said it more succinctly than that from memory.'

'I lived life pretty much on the fly for a few years after I left Uni. I just travelled the world picking up odd jobs here and there. You get tired of that lifestyle after a while. My father told me it was good to get it out of my system, now I can focus on being a grown up with responsibilities,' Liam recounted wistfully. 'Sometimes I wish I was back there, just packing my bag and moving to the next place, next adventure.'

'I only occasionally think like that. I'm more like Andrew, leaning towards obligation to other people. I sometimes wish I could just turn my back on it all and roam freely...but I never have, too scared to let go I suppose to live by the seat of my pants.'

'We all do it vicariously now, through DI. Go anywhere, once a day.'

'True that,' Wendy agreed.

The lack of breeze was obvious. A stifling Brisbane afternoon at the family home of Andrew McTavish made it uncomfortable for family and friends as they gathered after his funeral. There were too many people to fit inside the modest airconditioned house, so many spilled into the backyard, around the generous pool.

'What happens to the Rapid Sun project now?' Kris asked Saxon.

'No shop talk today please,' Margo insisted.

'Sorry,' Kris half whispered.

Saxon, Wendy, Kris and Margo stood in silence sipping their drinks under the shade of a jacaranda tree as a waiter circulated offering sesame king prawn skewers.

'That water looks so fucking good,' Kris commented.

Margo agreed before she took a skewer and dipped into the sauce.

'No thanks, allergy to shellfish,' Kris told the waiter.

'I'll have yours,' Saxon offered, taking two.

Wendy took one of the skewers but no condiment.

'Did Nikola come with you this trip, Kris?' Margo enquired.

'No. This is a day trip for me, back to New York tonight. I'm meeting with Transcode Media day after tomorrow. They want to reserve five places in all eight Cadet Certificate courses for 2051. It seems to be the trend for the larger media concerns and great for the Academy.'

'Did you just slip back into work talk?' Margo badgered.

Kris gestured to zip his mouth as Wendy and Saxon smirked at the pair.

Ingrid McTavish came out onto the deck wearing a one-piece swimsuit with two large plastic bags full of clothing. 'Listen up everyone. Andrew would have wanted us to enjoy the pool today instead of standing around sweating our arses off. We checked the forecast when we were organising today, and we thought everyone would enjoy a swim on a 39-degree day with no breeze. The invitation said to bring your swimwear, if you didn't, I have loads of board shorts and cosies here. They're all brand new, tags still on them. Feel free to grab a pair and jump in the pool. Food and drinks will be circulating all afternoon.' With that she dumped the bags of swimwear on the deck and dove into the pool.

'I've got my budgie smugglers on,' Kris revealed.

'Me too,' Saxon said. 'Bit unorthodox, but so was Andrew.'

They looked at the women.

'Alright,' Margo yielded. 'I'm going to change.' She handed Saxon her drink.

'I'm in,' Wendy decided, following Margo inside.

Kris waited for the women to be out of earshot. 'I've been doing a bit of research into some of Sinnerverse's lovely little experiences.'

'And?'

'That hunting experience I mentioned, Hunters and Collectors, does exist, it's not an urban myth.'

'You visited it?'

'I did. It's as abhorrent as I thought it would be.'

'Was it easy to access?'

'No, it took quite a bit of effort to get the VPDN code and—'

'That's what I was saying, Kris, people have to go to a great deal of trouble to gain access, and 99 percent of users won't go near it. It appeals to a very select clientele. We can't censor an adult platform.'

'I also visited a red room where people are tortured and killed while others watch.'

'Red rooms or snuff rooms aren't new. Those places have reportedly been on the darknet for decades and in the real world before the internet.'

'Torturing and killing animals and people with an audience watching is fucking disturbing, Saxon.'

Saxon stared at Kris. 'Just as disturbing as the human experimentation experiences I've heard about emerging in DI. I'm not saying it's right, what I'm saying is they are classified accordingly, and people can't access those experiences easily. Unless they have a tenacious curiosity or twisted underlying psychosis, they won't. It's a miniscule minority. DI is an alternate representation of the real world, and those individuals exist in the world here and now in exceptionally low numbers. They will also exist in-dream in low numbers.'

Kris accepted his argument for the moment. 'So, what's going to happen with the Rapid Sun project?' Kris asked.

'Phase one trials were extended by four months; they have another month to run. They're going well but I think we'll keep the project on the back burner. I'm still concerned about the tech being misused.'

'Sell the tech outright and wash your hands of it.'

'That was an option, but not what Andrew would have wanted.'

'True,' Kris agreed.

'We'll keep it under wraps for the moment.' Saxon wiped sweat from his hairline. 'I need to get out of this bloody suit. Come on.'

Ingrid came up the pool steps as Saxon and Kris walked by. 'I just wanted to say thank you, Saxon, for the very generous words you delivered at the service.'

'No need to thank me, Ingrid, it was the truth. Andrew was a very dedicated research scientist.'

'Very dedicated,' Kris agreed.

Ingrid smiled at the two men. 'I want to ask a favour, Saxon.'

'Anything at all, Ingrid. Name it.'

'I want to elevate Andrew for dream immersion, so the boys can know their father when they get older.'

'I was going to suggest it, but I wanted to wait until after, you know, after today,' Saxon responded awkwardly.

'Thank you. There's no rush. You're sweating, Saxon. Get your gear off and get in the pool.'

'We were heading in to do just that, Ingrid,' Kris concurred.

Chapter Three

Deep notches and scars on the dorsal fin of the white pointer shark suggested significant previous encounters as it thrashed in the narrow enclosure. The rider, wearing a lemon-yellow wetsuit and helmet, gingerly lowered himself to straddle the seven-metre man-eater in front of that gnarled fin. He tucked his hand firmly under the flank strap and rested his feet on its pectoral fins. Inside the fenced arena, in an open expanse of ocean, shark clowns bobbed in the water wearing jet boots and forearm thrusters, waiting for the chute to open. Floating spectator stands held hundreds of eager onlookers anticipating the event to begin. Shark Deus was not an experience for the faint hearted, be it rider or audience. Multiple screens showed underwater perspectives as the vision mixer switched between them and helmet cams worn by the rider and clowns.

'Remind me again why we're here?' Saxon asked Margo, crammed into the stands like sardines.

'All Hugo said was it's a surprise. He shared an experience link and access code,' she explained anxiously. 'I don't like the look of this.'

'Our first rider today is Vincent DeLorean riding Slasherfin,' came the announcement over the speakers. 'In previous shark riding outings, he scored three, five and six seconds, surviving his last ride on Razortooth, the six-metre monster who killed three of its last ten riders.'

A siren sounded. The release gate on the bobbing chute sprang open, triggering the crowd to cheer. Vincent on Slasherfin immediately disappeared under the water as all spectators turned to the screens. Clowns followed the shark as it dove rapidly to 30 metres, before turning and swimming towards the surface at speed. The shark breached with rider still holding firm, as fans screeched and pounded their palms at the breath-taking display.

'Six seconds!' The announcer screamed.

A barrel roll mid-air by Slasherfin smashed Vincent headfirst into the water, ramming him backwards against the dorsal fin of the plunging 2230-kilogram shark, forcing him to lose his grip. The pair parted company. As Vincent languished in wet space trying to gain his bearings, Slasherfin instinctively turned. The beast powered in the direction of the muddled, vulnerable rider. Shark clowns sprang into action with stun guns that proved totally ineffective. Vincent turned his head, his helmet cam broadcasting his point-of-view as Slasherfin closed in on him. At that moment, the water and everything in centre arena transitioned to slow motion. Slasherfin deliberately launched Vincent out of the water. The audience, still in real time, fell silent in disbelief at the jaw dropping scene unfolding before them as Vincent DeLorean burst from the water agonizingly slowly. Water spray crept metres into the air in all directions as he gracefully somersaulted over and over. Slasherfin followed him out. Its powerful body torpedoed spectacularly from the ocean in slo-mo, catching Vincent headfirst into gaping jaws before ferociously chomping his body in half in a single bite and slamming back into the water.

'Ewww!' The entire crowd spontaneously cried as normal motion returned to centre arena.

Vincent's limp bloodstained yellow remains were cloaked in a faint glistening red aura before vanishing.

'Seven seconds for Vincent DeLorean, if he survived. Better luck next time, Vincent,' the announcer consoled. 'Next up, we have Hugo Z.'

Saxon woke with beads of sweat across his top lip and heart thumping. He remained in bed, thinking about the dream—the experience—no, the dream. Finally, he got up and called Margo.

'I just had a dream about an experience, but it was dream,' he gibbered.

'What? What do you mean?'

'You know, it was a regular, organic dream, about Hugo,' Saxon explained. 'But it was an experience he invited us to, an experience where he was going to ride a shark.'

'A shark? What for?'

'It was a shark riding competition, you know, like they used to ride wild bulls and horses. I've seen promos for the Shark Deus experience,' Saxon told her quickly. 'I thinks that's why I dreamt about it. There's prize money if you can stay on for eight seconds and stay alive.'

Margo's frustration grew. 'I can't talk now, darling, I'm about to go into a meeting. Christine Knox's lawyers have started legal proceedings, she wants to sue me.'

'What? For what?'

'I have to go. I'll call you later.' She disconnected.

Saxon sighed and threw his PD on the hotel bed. 'TV on,' he ordered. The wall monitor sprang to life. 'Channels.' Using his index finger mid-air, he scrolled through the multitude of channels. The alarm on his PD sounded.

'Shit!' He looked at his watch–*8:30am*. He hurried to the bathroom undressing as he went.

Merlin arrived late to start the morning briefing.

'How are you feeling?' Arrow asked quietly.

'Brave enough to fart again,' he whispered out the side of his mouth.

'I told you that dal was too old to eat.'

'I know, I know.' He cleared his throat to address the group sitting with morning beverages around the oval meeting table. 'I want to stand for this morning. Raise table.' The table rose slowly as the dozen meeting participants begrudgingly stood. 'Morning everyone. Let's start. We've got a lot to get through today.' He paused. 'A terrible event can lead to something fantastic; out of tragedy comes positive outcomes,' Merlin said, trying to inspire his young crew of codester supervisors. 'You all know about the death in Mumbai last week being blamed on our DI interface the woman was wearing. News is, it wasn't ours.'

Murmurs of relief swept through the gathering.

'We received a report this morning from our Counterfeit Monitoring Unit confirming it was a bogus unit with a false quantum ID code from Turkey. Subsequently, our team, along with local authorities raided a factory in Tuzla, Istanbul, and over 300,000 fake units were seized and destroyed. The six arsehole owners are now languishing in a Turkish prison.'

'Six!' Arrow scoffed. 'For each one they take down, there's another five to replace them. They'll be back up and running in months I bet.'

'That's probably true, Arrow, but there's no alternative. It's taken 300,000 dangerous devices off the streets and that's a huge positive,' Merlin countered.

'Execution? Lobotomy?' Arrow jokingly proposed for the counterfeiters. The grumble around the table agreed. 'Someone has died, and they should be held accountable.'

'Proving liability can be difficult, but in this case, they have been found and are being prosecuted.' Merlin paused to give the topic some distance. 'So, the next item for this morning's briefing is this issue of corrupt data in the Dunbar project source files–'

'We've isolated the workstation and taken it offline. We've been data cleansing for the last hour,' Bhang explained.

'I've detected corrupt output signals from a single M50 Gelchip,' Mercy Vander, a Worimi woman said. 'I've systematically isolated multiple neuralusion q-circuits, but it continues to occur. It'll take time to go through all the q-circuits.'

'Good. That's positive at least, Mercy, you've isolated the problem,' Merlin praised. 'I'll come and have a look. As a last resort we may have to reformat the Gelchip. But before I look at that, we have one more item this morning. I need someone to help finish the Chesterfield project.' The group stood in silence, not one looking at Merlin. 'Bhang?'

'Sorry, Merlin, my team is backed up with the Aziz project, we're days behind.'

'Arrow?'

'Madison Penelope Chesterfield and entourage,' everyone knew what was coming from her tone. 'I told you we shouldn't have taken this project on. They're all fucking arseholes, her entire entourage. Not my circus, not my monkeys,' Arrow mocked, waving her open hand at Merlin.

Merlin smiled. 'I like that saying. Where did you get it?'

Arrow returned his smile. 'It's Polish...in a novel I'm reading.'

'You're rubbing off on her, Merlin,' Otto teased.

'I wish–' Karl began.

'Don't you fucking say another word,' Arrow warned Karl with a stern face.

Members of the group snickered as Merlin and Arrow exchanged an awkward glance.

'Mercy?' Merlin pushed on.

'Any bonuses involved?'

'I'm afraid not for this project.'

She shook her head. 'My team's calendar is solid for the next six weeks.'

'Thanks for your support people. Otto and Karl, your teams will finish it off. I'll show you what I want.'

The pair looked at each other puzzled. 'What the fu–' Karl started.

'Please, I need your finesse and deft touch to complete this project on time,' Merlin sugar-coated.

'That's why you asked Bhang, Arrow and Mercy first,' Otto pointed out with attitude.

Everyone laughed at their expense.

'That's it. Thanks everyone,' Merlin finished.

Saxon waited in his Budapest hotel suite for a call from Margo. One of his security detail watched a show on the wall screen as he worked on projected keyboard and screen from his PD. Saxon's attention was temporarily seized by the discussion on the wall.

'Imagination is the cornerstone, the driving force behind the DI entertainment juggernaut that has propelled the entertainment experience economy through the roof. Developers have gone above and beyond to create some of the most fantastical worlds that defy description, like Magix or Psykosonic Extinction,' Stark Green commented to his guest, Quinn Cameron.

'Absolutely. We all experience alternate worlds through films and TV, VR, novels and now DI. The entertainment experience economy has matured exponentially in the past 12 months due single-handedly to DI. It has delivered the ultimate user experience and it will do so for many years to come. But we have to remember the experiences themselves are only part of this embryonic industry. Behind the scenes job opportunities for new writers, producers, developers and manufacturers have risen sharply. Roleplaying experiences for example, generate income for copywriters and video creators producing backstory content for users in the real world so they know the intricacies of gameplay. Fan clubs with merchandising for those roleplaying DI experiences have emerged, feeding real-world interest–'

'I saw data yesterday mapping Holoflix and location based VRXLR8 use in the last quarter and it has dropped off a cliff as total immersion in alternative realities begins to gain momentum. This captivating, fast evolving DI revolution has seized the imagination of the entire planet.' Stark enthused. 'Which leads us to your venture into the medium, Quinn. Your inspired films have captured the hearts of millions for over a decade, now you've partnered with cutting-edge DI production houses to create Mind Traveller. Tell us a little about how that came about.'

'Mind Traveller emerged out of a collaboration between Epic Dreams and DreamNet, the Norwegian DI start-up. They approached me with the concept that could be developed into an evolving dream cluster, so I jumped on board as director. We had some teething problems trying to find experienced codesters, developers who could push the envelope with Gatekeeper of Dreams programming. Because this new medium has exploded so rapidly, experienced, qualified codesters on the ground are few and far between.'

'Bedroom or garage developers are doing quite well,' Stark threw in.

'True, but to achieve the look and feel we were after required a more nuanced approach and knowledge of the tech, and we found that in our Lead Developer, Hadrian Judge.'

Saxon bore a satisfied smile when he heard Hadrian's name.

'Explain what Mind Traveller is about,' Stark continued.

'Users are embedded in some of the largest and most cataclysmic and catastrophic events to shape humanity and our Solar System. We take users on a journey of discovery, of awe-inspiring beauty and adventure.'

'Would it be fair to call it a form of disaster voyeurism?' Stark asked.

'That term has been thrown around for some of the experiences in the cluster, but there are over two dozen experiences so far. Most experiences are natural events, but yes, there are events of manmade destruction. We witness first-hand time lapse mass extinctions on our world, and we also explore the creation and evolution of each planet within our system. We are in preproduction for experiences that go beyond our heliosphere into interstellar space, and it's all based on up to the minute science-fact.'

'I must admit I was stunned by the sheer scale and beauty of the experiences I researched for our conversation.'

Saxon's PD buzzed. He grabbed it and went into his bedroom for privacy.

Margo's image beamed from his device. 'Hello, darling, sorry I didn't get back to you earlier.'

'I imagine you were busy.'

'Very. Looks like Amanda Voss is financing Christine's legal team.'

'To what end?'

'Compensation for the wrongful termination of Christine's child,' Margo replied.

'How much does she want?'

'A million Nukoin and a public apology.'

'Where are they getting their evidence?'

'There's a record of the termination from the medical clinic and a statement by a nurse. Michelle and the team are looking at it.'

'That's it? Nip it in the bud and offer her ten thousand.'

'That admits guilt. We have a signed NDA and video of her agreeing to terminate. The entire world has seen that.'

'True, but we don't need the—'

'I know, the media circus that goes with it. We'll nip in the bud,' Margo said. 'It won't get to court.'

'You could dig up a bit more dirt on Abernathy's public martyrdom to pressure Amanda into withdrawing her support. This won't happen without her.'

Margo smiled. 'That's why I love you, we think alike. Michelle's team is exploring a few options. We'll see what they come back with.'

'I was just watching Stark Green's show. Remember Hadrian Judge?'

'That name rings a bell.'

'He was one of our best and brightest when the Academy kicked off.'

'I remember him, his parents were killed.'

'Correct, in the Gambaldi incident. Well, Amanda Voss poached him from us, but now he's a lead developer with Epic Dreams.'

'Epic Dreams! Good on him for getting away from that bitch. Looks like we've landed the Global Disaster Rescue account too. I spoke with Red Anderson today, their CEO, and he wants us to develop a cluster of rescue craft and equipment training experiences.'

'Well done, they have about 40,000 employees.'

'More, 44,000 Red told me. Lots of money in natural disasters these days. What time's your flight tomorrow?'

'Seven. I'll be in London for two days now, Kris managed to get a meeting with InnerVision.'

'It's great to have Disney's DI studio onboard.'

'You should be going to London, not me. You did all the hard work.'

'You know Dad flies home tomorrow and I want to be here for him. He's going straight to the house.'

'Okay. I'll come up to the house when I get home.'

'You had dinner?'

'Not yet. Been eating all day at the conference. I've eaten enough chicken paprika to last a lifetime.'

Margo was called by someone off camera. 'I have to go. Have a safe trip, darling. Love you.' She blew him a kiss.

'Love you.' Her hologram disappeared.

The boat ride to Walt's lavish estate, Wildwood or Fortress Tremaine as Saxon liked to call it, on the northern peninsula of Sydney, was an anxious journey for him. Saxon's first visit to Wildwood as a young man was memorable. The speedboat Walt had sent to collect Saxon and Margo late that afternoon hit a submerged vessel on their way back to the house, throwing him and Margo into the water. The driver was knocked unconscious, and the craft sank within minutes. Saxon managed to pull the driver to shore as Margo, a particularly strong swimmer, followed them to safety. The violent storm the night before had caused widespread havoc across Sydney, knocking out power and communications for hours. Over 50 yachts and small pleasure craft along the river broke their moorings and were either destroyed or had sunk.

The impressive Tremaine estate perched on the banks of majestic Hawkesbury River was encircled by hectares of forest. Today, the Rural Fire Service command had commandeered the Tremaine helipad to orchestrate the air crane water bombers fighting bushfires surrounding Walt's property. Saxon watched as guzzling choppers hovered above the river, mechanical mosquitoes sucking precious water from the veins feeding the surrounding country. The noise was deafening. He spotted Margo waiting for him at the jetty.

As they kissed, a gust of wind from an aircraft's rotor blade passing overhead almost toppled them into the water. They rushed up the stone stairs beside the 20-metre-high sandstone retaining wall to seek solace from the assault on their senses.

'Thanks for coming, Saxon.' Walt appeared frail and gaunt. 'I've been watching these choppers drinking from the river. Bloody noisy dinosaurs. Give me an electric drone any day.'

'Welcome home for Christmas.'

'I thought I'd better come back home, might be my last one.'

'Oh, Dad, stop talking like that,' Margo scolded.

'How are you feeling?' Saxon asked.

'Not bad for an old dog,' he managed with laboured breath. 'Margo tells me Hugo's coming home to work for the business.'

'He flies in tomorrow,' Saxon answered.

Margo and Saxon found a chair either side of Walt's powered wheelchair. Their panoramic river view was interrupted by antiquated noisy helicopters, so Walt remotely closed the massive glass door to the sprawling multi-tier deck, severing the outside world. The Wildwood mansion, designed by distinguished architect Stafford Bruce in 2023 with interiors realised by Kirsten Richards, was characterised by classic art deco curves and geometric forms in timber and stone.

'In what capacity, we're not sure at this stage,' Margo said, relaxing into the comfy leather chair. 'We'll bring him over for Christmas lunch if you like.'

'It'll be good to have him home,' Saxon admitted.

'Of course it will,' Walt agreed. 'Family is all we really have in this world. Which brings me to why I wanted this meeting.' Walt caught an apprehensive glance from Saxon to Margo. 'Don't give her that fucking tragic look, Saxon, it's not about Tremaine's half of ZynnComm if that's what you're thinking.'

Saxon raised his eyebrows. 'Not what I was thinking, but carry on, Walt.'

'I have a request. I want you to recreate Sylvia in dream immersion.'

'Mum?' Margo questioned. 'Why?'

'I don't think I have too much time left, and I want to see her before I die.'

'Stop talking like that, Dad, you're in recovery, you're getting better,' Margo insisted.

Walt shrugged. 'Maybe. But I'd like to see her just the same.'

'We can do that, Walt,' Saxon decided, giving Margo a look of reassurance.

'Now, I don't want to appear to her as an old man. Is there any way to make me younger, about 30 years younger?'

Saxon hesitated before answering. 'I'm sorry, Walt, we haven't cracked that nut yet, you'll appear as you are now. We can construct any world around you, but we can't change your age. However, we can create Sylvia so she doesn't acknowledge any age difference. There are gimmicks such as skin colour changes, but–'

'No, no, no. I thought that might be the case. No matter. How quickly can you do it?'

'Depends on how quickly you can gather the primary assets, you know, the base content to work from. We need digital video, audio, photos, those early holographic clips of Sylvia–'

'Yep, got all that. I'll get James to get all that together. I'll get him to upload it to you.'

'Better still, I'll give James the address to our uDream depository for custom orders. There's a questionnaire you'll have to complete for Sylvia's backstory, like her brand of perfume, clothes and jewellery she wore–'

'You can help me with that,' Walt told Margo.

'Erm...sure,' Margo complied, not completely committed.

'We'll need experience locations, food and music preferences and so on,' Saxon continued, 'but Merlin will contact you and walk you through it. I'll tell him to make it a priority–'

'How long?' Walt's old face beamed with anticipation.

'Depends on the complexities around environment settings, character development and interaction, storylines, compiling, revisions...probably a few weeks at most.'

'Good.'

'Are you sure you want to do this, Dad? After all this time?'

'Definitely. It's been keeping me awake at nights thinking about her. Lately, I really miss her. It's been 22 years since we lost her,' Walt paused and studied his daughter's face. 'You look so much like her. Wouldn't you like to see her again?'

Tears welled in Margo's eyes as she reached out and touched her father's arm. 'Of course I would, Dad, of course.'

Walt patted her hand and smiled. 'Good. Now that's settled, let's talk about succession plans.' Walt reversed his chair leaving Margo and Saxon staring at each other. 'Follow me...James!'

Merlin could see the breeze. It swirled in faint pinks and greens through trees and shrubs. Mesmerised, he watched wind currents flow through his fingers, turning translucent red as he tried to grasp it in his hand. The encounter was breathtakingly beautiful. Merlin immediately took a liking to Magic Dust, the title of this experience. Walking backwards with arms outstretched, he watched the undercurrents streaming around and over his body. He laughed to himself that something so simple, so basic as wind could create such a magical element.

Hearing a noise behind him, he turned to see a glimmering red spiral cone ascend from the sand. Grains were picked up on the coloured zephyr to create a glittering wave wafting past him and carrying on until the weight of the sand fell back to ground. '*Synapse chromaspark coding*,' he thought.

Merlin's environment began to churn, to transition to another experience. Now he was standing on a monochromatic wharf at the edge of a black and white metropolis soaked in drizzling rain. He spied Liam at the stern of a cargo ship docked at the wharf.

Liam suddenly jumped from the ship into the water 40-metres below. Looking back up to the deck rail, Liam could see a man peering down at him. He wasted no time swimming to the wharf and scrambled up a rickety timber ladder.

Merlin wandered over to Liam. 'What's this experience?'

'Wha...what are you doing here?' Liam questioned, a little perplexed and out of breath.

'I'm in a Dream Sampler, ten experiences in 30 minutes.'

'A Dream Sampler?' He panted. 'Is that a thing now?'

'Not yet. It's new code I'm testing, like a showreel for prospective buyers. We selected ten random experiences and edited them together, just to see if the concept works before we offer it to our uDream customers.'

'Like a series of dream vignettes.'

'Sort of.'

'I like that idea. Our Lucid division could use that for our customers, they could bookmark experiences they want to try.'

'True, we could add that feature for you. The random experiences are from Lucid's library. We can't use our customers' experiences due to privacy. What's this experience?'

'Beyond the Secret Door. It's based on film noir from the late 1940s.' He pulled a damp canvas map from his pants pocket and laid it out on the timber planks, patting it flat.

'Arrow deliberately picked this experience,' Merlin thought as he bent down to take a look. 'What's this?'

'A map of six safe houses I could hold up in.'

'How long have you been playing this game?'

Liam thought. 'About three months now, every Tuesday. I love it.' He looked back at the ship. 'I've got to keep moving, he'll be here soon.'

'This looks like an experience I might like,' Merlin commented, looking around him. 'Some distinct subtleties that give it a very authentic feel. What's the aim?

'I work for The Institute. I'm part of a small team who infiltrate Trindon government agencies to covertly investigate employees lining their own pockets by feeding strategic information to private companies bidding on Trindon government contracts. There are networks of people inside and outside Trindon with their own agendas. It's seedy, it's intriguing, it gets complicated. There are no computers, PDs, autonomous cars, it's all old school with telephones and notepads.' Liam saw his pursuer disembarking the vessel. 'I've got to keep moving. This guy–'

'Go, go!' Merlin urged, watching the man. 'I'll slow him down if I can.'

Liam snatched up his map and disappeared behind a row of packing crates as Merlin approached the man in a grey flannel suit.

The meeting room was on the 14th floor of the Crowhurst building in Surat, India. Kris sat in the room of delegates and studied each one. Justine Vanderberg, the CEO of Dutch equity firm GeoSpace, was a very wealthy, stylish woman in her mid-50s. Reportedly, a staunch feminist married to her job and a patron of several women's charities. Ethan Tan, the 40-something tech guru responsible for Swipe Charge technology, was Kris' business associate and the instigator behind the DI Advisory Council. Jorma Despirito had been a board member on half a dozen of the largest EU banks for the past 20 years. At 65, she was the oldest member of the group. Professor Winston Singh, a man in his late 30s, the youngest member, was Department Chair of Psychology and Professor of Social Ethics at Harvard University. Christopher 'Kit' Bombo, the sixth member of the panel, had been Angola's Permanent

Representative to the United Nations since 2039. Kit had a background in international law and Angolan politics, and had sat on the United Nations Social, Humanitarian & Cultural Issues Committee of the UN General Assembly since 2044.

'Let's get started,' Ethan Tan began. 'We need to select a Chair for the Council. Then we should look at our purpose and terms of reference–'

'Let's make it clear from the outset,' Kris interjected, wanting to be on the front foot with the group. 'We do not serve a governance function and we shouldn't promote the interests of stakeholders we represent outside this meeting room. I feel we should create a neutral, objective Council. So, Ethan, what do you see as the Council's purpose?'

All eyes fell upon Ethan Tan. 'You clearly represent the key stakeholder, Kris. When I suggested this group, this panel, at the symposium I was thinking the purpose would be to ensure the privacy of all DI users was kept front and centre and not eroded away around the fringes by governments and corporations for their own purposes.' Ethan unwrapped a Spacestix bar and began eating.

'You all know my role at the DI Academy for ZynnComm, but that shouldn't be construed as a conflict of interest. If that were the case, that could be said for most of us,' Kris accused, casting his gaze around the table. 'Winston, your department is working on a project with Saxon on PTSD DI therapy, which could possibly help those who profess to suffer from in-dream trauma. Justine and Jorma, both of you have brokered finance to bankroll the Tremaine Group for a decade or more. Ethos, your company, Ethan, has partnered with ZynnComm from our beginning to supply key components for our DI device, so we go way back. All but Kit has a finger in the pie so to speak. I'm going to leave my self-interest at the door, and employ an unbiased, balanced viewpoint to discuss whatever it is we're going to discuss. Having said that, I absolutely agree with your purpose for this group, Ethan.'

'I see your presence on the Council as...a sign of cooperation, Kris,' Jorma Despirito flattered. 'Your knowledge of the platform and the privacy protocols are perhaps second to none, so I welcome your insight during our discussions.'

'I see our purpose in a duty of care context,' Professor Singh added. 'DI users need to know if they wish to participate in any type of experience, their identity, their privacy, is paramount. But there must be a balance between protecting privacy and protecting vulnerable participants in experiences from individuals preying on them.'

'I absolutely agree, Winston,' Justine Vanderberg jumped in. 'Kris, you alluded to DITS–'

'Anecdotal at present,' Kris interjected.

'The research on dream immersion trauma syndrome may still be scant, but there are women being attacked and raped, even killed in White rated experiences. This isn't happening in the dark and nasty Sinnerverse crap, but in general experiences. Women now suffer from a form of PTSD and that must stop. The reports I'm seeing are describing vicious attacks that mirror real world abuse; they are equally as traumatic and legitimate as real-world incidents. One of the victims, Brigit McKenzie, is pushing back and calling for dream violence controls in White and Yellow experiences. She wants an investigation.' Justine paused momentarily before continuing. 'What I'm about to say may not sit well with some of you, but I'll say it anyway. I think we need some sort of in-dream policing to track individuals and I think this Council should be used to influence governments to implement those safeguards.'

'It's difficult to police, Justine,' Kit Bombo commented. 'The essential problem is how do you police an in-dream environment? Who gives them their power to act? It comes back to the question, who has jurisdiction over events happening in someone's mind? It would be a political, legal and philosophical minefield.'

'I think that defeats the purpose of this group, Justine,' Ethan Tan uttered, drawing the attention. 'We need to protect the anonymity of users; any sort of investigation would identify individuals.' Ethan was fashioning something out of the Spacestix foil wrapper.

'We are in a brave new world of collective dreaming,' Winston reflected, 'Where identity can't be authenticated, where everyone speaks your language, where rogues target the weak. I think we have to seriously consider weighing up user privacy against their safety. Which takes priority?'

'Finding those individuals responsible would be virtually impossible,' Kris said. 'As you all know, before ZynnComm was given the green light for the platform, we were required to methodically identify all known criminals worldwide who had been charged with murder, rape or vicious assaults and ban those individuals from the platform. We did that and continue to update that list. We can't photograph perpetrators in-dream and we don't know where they'll strike next. We could possibly remember their faces if we came face to face with them, but then you have to find them in the real-world population. Impossible.'

'We can't allow this abuse to fucking continue unchecked!' Justine pounced. 'If this were reversed and men were sexually assaulted and killed, we'd find an answer quick smart.'

'Perhaps there should be a financial compensation scheme funded by ZynnComm,' Jorma Despirito proposed, but quickly retracted. 'But that wouldn't work because there's no evidence.'

'Exactly, anecdotal accounts only. Users participate in DI at their own risk. It's there in the EULA every time they enter, and they waive their right to compensation when they hit start,' Kris stated.

'These women are being attacked and murdered in White rated experiences!' Justine reacted. 'These are unexpected, unanticipated attacks and should not be tolerated under any circumstances!'

'Of course, Justine. You are right.' Kris conceded.

'Jorma is right. How would victims prove their claims?' Ethan asked. 'What constitutes evidence? We only have their verbal recollections of their experiences, unless there was a witness, but finding that witness in the real world to corroborate their story would be difficult.'

'Not impossible, but yes, difficult,' Winston agreed. 'I did see some interesting research out of Canada reporting illicit substance use has declined by five percent due to DI, that's positive.'

'A study in Denmark has just concluded the retention of information during DI training increases seven percent over six months,' Kris boasted.

'Could that equate to women having a stronger retention of their traumatic experiences in DI?' Justine questioned.

Kris' gaze rested on her for a moment. 'Point taken.'

'Women need to be protected. I believe ZynnComm is working on technology to record memory,' Justine directed at Kris.

Kris hesitated before replying. 'I can say this. We have done some preliminary work in that area, but so have many companies.'

'Phase one clinical trials have almost concluded and the results are positive according to my source,' Justine challenged.

Kris smiled at her. 'Who would that source be, Justine?'

Justine returned his smile. 'I'm not at liberty to divulge my source. Is the information correct?'

'That's commercial in confidence, Justine. I can neither confirm nor deny that information.'

'The Glomar denial might be convenient outside this room, Kris,' Kit challenged. 'But if ZynnComm has the technology to help resolve this issue, we need to know.'

'This is up to Justine,' Kris told everyone. 'Tell me your source and I may offer some information on our research.'

Justine remained silent.

'I think we've found our first discussion topic, privacy versus safety,' Ethan proposed, resting his foil chalice on the table. 'I also think we keep our discussion and opinions within this room, until we reach a consensus on a topic and issue a media release.'

'Agreed,' Kris said. 'I propose we should always meet face to face,' he added.

'Why don't we use this location for all our meetings?' Professor Singh suggested. 'It's neutral and has ASO-C3 security shielding.'

The delegates agreed.

Enzo ate pizza at his workstation, entering data for his current project at the Port Augusta facility. A dialogue box popped up in the bottom right corner of one of his screens. *Remote access requested – yes – no.* Enzo clicked yes.

In Malmo, Sweden, Iminka watched her monitor intently. Sterling's Acid Spear Studios office was cluttered with electronic gadgets, folders, monitors and knick-knacks. 'It's happening,' she told Sterling.

Sterling walked over to see for himself. 'No detection?'

'Not as far as I can tell. Black Shield blocks external access, we're piggybacking off Enzo's login. We have a green light, we're in. My workaround has finally paid-off.'

'It's taken you long enough.'

'Fuck you!' Iminka barked. 'It takes as long as it takes. It was my fucking idea to leave the code on their system to allow access. None of your fucking overpaid geeks can do this.'

Sterling bent down and kissed her on the head. 'True. You are my golden girl,' he patronised. 'Have we got access across the entire network?'

'Almost there...the network defect hasn't been repaired. We have access and space, but we don't want to get greedy.'

'Maybe I have another use for this little bonus.'

Iminka looked up at him. 'What?' Her anticipation evident.

Sterling's idiosyncratic grin revealed nothing. 'Just a bit of fun. I'll keep you posted.' He returned to his desk.

'You don't want to do anything to jeopardise our access,' she warned as she exited the Norus network and put her computer to sleep.

Sterling frowned at her. 'You say some fucking stupid things sometimes. I'm not. Why would I risk our gravy train?'

'I'm just saying, don't do anything stupid.' She checked her PD. 'Almost midnight, time for bed.' She stood and stretched.

'You go, I'm still working on something.'

'Your Pleasure Principle paper?'

Sterling deliberately didn't look at her. 'Yes.'

'You've been working on it for a while. Is it almost finished?'

'No!' he growled, now eyeballing her. 'It will take as long as it takes.'

Iminka smiled as she left the office to sleep.

Hugo's taxi pulled up at the family home in Sydney a week before Christmas. His archived biometric scan allowed the autonomous vehicle access through the driveway gates. With bag in hand, and guitar slung over one shoulder, he studied the manicured drive. Time had passed by with little warning. Nothing seemed to have changed, everything was as he remembered it. The welcoming ambience of the yard was reflected in the smile on his face. Hugo was glad to be home.

'Hugo,' a voice called from behind him.

Hugo spun around, startled. An impressively sized Maori security guard stood in the doorway. 'Yes.'

'Do you need a hand with your gear, bro?' he asked, finishing with a beaming grin.

'Erm, no, no, all good. Thanks.' Hugo headed for the front door. 'Who are you?'

'I'm Benji. Welcome home.'

A middle-aged woman exited the pantry as Hugo threw his gear on the kitchen island.

'Hello, Hugo. I'm Ava.'

'Hi. Another new face. Everyone seems to know me.'

Ava pointed. 'Your photos are everywhere in the house. You have grown up!'

'Of course.' Hugo wandered out into the courtyard. Salt air flooded his nostrils as he gazed over sparkling Sydney Harbour.

Benji had followed him out. 'Your mother said you've been in Darwin?'

'I have, but it's good to be back.' His PD buzzed. 'Hiya, Mum.'

'You're home!' Margo exclaimed. 'Benji just texted.'

'I am.'

'Why didn't you tell us? We would've been there to meet you.'

'No biggie. Where are you? Where's Dad?'

'We're both in Port Augusta. We'll fly out within the hour. See you soon.'

That evening, after dinner in the courtyard, Hugo played his guitar as Saxon and Margo watched on.

'I can't believe you taught yourself the guitar in just 12 months,' Margo said.

'I didn't, I had a good teacher. I got lessons from a Spanish guitarist of an evening,' Hugo told them, putting his guitar aside. 'Cisco. Cisco Romero. He killed himself.'

Margo looked across at Saxon. 'That's...sad. Do you know why?'

'Nope. All the women loved his playing, true flamenco style...good looking guy too. One night he didn't come around for a lesson so I walked around to his place and there were an ambulance and police. They said he took sleeping pills, put a plastic bag over his head then sealed it with tape wrapped around his neck.'

The trio sat in silence before Saxon cleared his throat. 'I remember this surfer I used to know back in the early 20s, extrovert, always the life of the party, always off his face on something or other,' he explained. 'He was a damn good surfer. One night, he put his dog in the car and they drove off a cliff into the rocks and surf 100 metres below. They didn't even start looking for him until the next morning, when his girlfriend found his note explaining what he'd done.'

Margo frowned at Saxon. 'Thanks for sharing that little gem. So, how did you get to Darwin from Marree?'

'Hitched a ride in a van with a couple of Dutch backpackers. Kept a low profile in the van most of the trip, knowing you'd have the sniffer dogs after me.'

'What did you expect?' Saxon asked.

'Nothing less,' Hugo smiled.

'What did you do for work in Darwin?'

'You know, Mum, but I'll play along. Started out washing dishes and cleaning in restaurants, them got certified to work behind the bar–'

'What's Devil's Piss and a Raging Bull?' Saxon interjected, testing him.

'Devil's Piss is a nip of vanilla Galliano liqueur on ice and a Raging Bull is a nip of tequila and Kalua on ice,' Hugo replied without missing a beat.

'Correct,' Saxon grinned, looking at Margo. 'We used to drink those, didn't we?'

'Yes we did. Too many and too often as I remember. So, tell us, why do you want to join the family business?'

Hugo gazed squarely at his father. 'Because I want to be part of this amazing tech you've created. I want to learn all about it from the ground up.'

'Why the change of heart? I've been working on this for a long time and you've never really taken an interest?'

Hugo wrestled with that for a moment. 'I think it came down to choices. I think at first I didn't have a clue what you really did. I remember you took me to Port Augusta a few times in my early teens and showed me the equipment and labs. You tried to explain your research, but it wasn't for kids. I couldn't use it, so I switched off. Then when the Christine thing happened I saw your work as...more of an inconvenience, a problem in my life, so I wanted to distance myself from it.'

'And now?' Margo probed.

'I stayed away from the tech even after I turned 21, didn't want to know about it. Then, all my friends were progressively preoccupied with alternate realities, always talking about and sharing their experiences. Peer pressure sucked me in, I tried your tech, and it blew me away. I couldn't begin to imagine how you came up with the process, the tech that makes it all possible, and I needed to know how. It started eating away at me. But you know what the biggest kicker was?'

'You missed us,' Margo hoped.

'Yes, of course, Mum' Hugo feigned. 'I couldn't tell them you were my father and you invented the tech.'

'None of them recognised you after all that publicity?' Margo queried.

'A few people said I looked like Hugo Zynn, but I'd say, would I being washing dishes in Darwin if my parents owned ZynnComm?'

'Do you have any basic neuroscience experience?' Saxon questioned.

'I'm learning, I'm doing neuroinformatics at Western Sydney Uni.'

'What do you need to do for your prac component?' Margo asked.

'Research on spatiotemporal dynamics.'

'From what aspect?' Saxon pressed.

'My choice, as long as it fits with my research proposal.'

'Which is?' Saxon deliberately pushed to extract pertinent information from his son.

'Not sure yet. I was going to have a chat with you, Dad, and see what you recommend.'

Saxon glanced at Margo. 'Hmm. I'm sure we can brainstorm some areas you could explore, but let's kick it up a notch. If you want to come into the business, you have to know the product. The Academy will be running night classes starting next year, I think you should enrol.'

'I couldn't agree more,' Hugo grinned. 'I was going to ask you what my chances were of getting into the Academy, but this is even better, I can do both.'

'I'll make sure Kris holds a place for you.'

'Thanks, Dad, I appreciate it.' Hugo looked inside the house. 'A few things have changed around here...Benji and Ava for a start, and I noticed when you came home you had minders with you. Did something happen?'

'The pace of life has, let's say, intensified while you were away.' Margo explained. 'Your father and I are always on the go so Ava runs the house while we're away. You know we've always had security travelling overseas, Waylon thought we should boost local security given some of the...' she eyed Saxon, 'feedback we've been receiving lately.'

'What do you mean by "feedback"?'

'There have been death threats,' Saxon admitted.

Hugo contemplated his parents for a moment. 'That doesn't surprise me. We all know there are some twisted fucks out there.'

'You have your own trinity PPD as we call them,' Margo told him.

'Trinity PPD?'

'A 24-7 three-person protection detail.'

'Ahh, the hounds watching me in Darwin. I noticed them after a while. They always seemed to be there as far as I knew. Low key, blending in.'

'That's them. We knew you were on your way home, Waylon kept us posted, but we wanted to keep this as normal as possible, so we waited for your call,' Saxon admitted.

'Or a text message from Benji at least,' Hugo teased with a sly grin.

'Or that,' Margo smiled.

'I was wondering...I know this might sound like a dumb question, but you two are worth a trillion Nukoin–'

They both laughed. 'Nowhere near a trillion,' Saxon scoffed.

'Anyway, more than most. Why don't you have more houses or cars, or a megayacht like Pop?'

Margo flashed Saxon a quizzical look. 'Where did that come from?'

'Well, you see all these ultra-rich people in the media and online and they have half a dozen houses and fancy cars, helicopters, boats, an army of servants. But you are probably wealthier than all of them and you don't seem to, you know, flaunt it I suppose.'

'We don't need to,' Margo candidly admitted. 'Just because we have the means to buy all that stuff doesn't mean we need to.'

'Do you know how wealthy people stay wealthy, Hugo?' His father asked.

'Tax loopholes, good business managers and accountants?'

'Naturally, that's part of the equation. I'll let you in on how we, as a family, maintain what we have. Afterall, you're going to be playing an active part in all of this now. Most of what we have at our disposal is owned and maintained by Zynn Communications Corporation. This house, which I owned outright, was put up as collateral when Walt and I started ZynnComm, so now the corporation owns it and we lease it back for one dollar a week. The private jets, the apartment in New York, the cars are all owned by the corporation. Your mother and I receive a salary plus bonuses, which you will after you start working for the corporation fulltime.'

'So, Pop and you own ZynnComm privately, it's not traded on the share market?'

'Your mother and I own controlling shares, with the Tremaine Group owning the remainder. Correct, it's a privately held company.'

'Are there any plans to take it public?' Hugo asked.

'There were times in the past when we considered going in that direction, when the Tremaine Group owned majority shares, but Walt always found a way to convince his board to source funding for Tremaine and syphon it into ZynnComm research.'

'Your grandfather has a knack for getting people to do what he wants,' Margo added.

'My father was a self-made man, as is Walt. They were the driving force behind their wealth; their creativity is responsible for generating the wealth. I grew up with money most of my life, as did your mother, as did you. It is now our responsibility to maintain and grow that wealth. To retain the wealth we have to avoid excessive, extravagant overspending. Wealth creation versus wealth erosion. There is a theory, backed up by studies and anecdotal evidence across many cultures, which says the first generation builds the wealth, the second generation maintains the wealth and the third generation squanders the wealth. You are the third generation. Do you have any idea how much it costs to buy a decent superyacht, maintain it, moor it in Sydney Harbour and pay a crew?'

'No.'

'It was rhetorical, but far too much for the time we'd use it. I like sailing, so I'm a member of the Sydney Harbour Yacht Club. But for the few times a year I get time to be on the water, it's more prudent to hire a vessel. More houses means more tax, maintenance, and more people to run them. There are only three of us, this is more than we really need. Ava is all the help we need. We have a maintenance company looking after the pool and garden on a weekly basis, but any more is excessive. The more money you spend on unnecessary things the less you have. The idea is to use your wealth wisely or one day you'll wake up and it'll be gone.'

'Your father wears the same shoes to work every day and gets them resoled each year,' Margo revealed. 'That's his eccentricity.'

'Bullshit! I thought you must have bought dozens of the same shoe.'

'They are bloody comfortable shoes,' Saxon admitted in his defence. 'Makes sense to resole.'

'The lesson is to be frugal,' Hugo said.

'We, the three of us, have been born into a situation of privilege,' Margo reinforced. 'We had no control over that, but we do have a responsibility now that we're here.'

'I suppose we do when you look at it like that,' Hugo agreed.

'So, what's behind the original question? What do you want?' Margo grilled.

'No, nothing–' his eyes evaded hers.

'You still have your trust account money, don't you?' Margo persisted.

'Yes, well...yes, some of it,' he replied sheepishly. 'I didn't earn much behind the bar.'

'I knew this was going somewhere,' Saxon reacted.

'I'm sure we can top it up for you,' Margo offered.

'What? Why?' Saxon challenged. 'He'll be on the payroll soon enough.'

Margo rested her hand on Saxon's arm. 'A few reasons, darling. Because we didn't give him a 21st birthday present, he's our only child, and we have more than enough money to share the wealth.'

'On one condition,' Saxon threw in. 'You report your monthly expenditure to me for the next 12 months...and you promise to stick with your studies at the Academy and Uni.'

'That's three conditions,' Margo whispered to Saxon.

Saxon threw her a sideways glance. 'Three conditions.'

Hugo felt the urge to negotiate those conditions. 'Can I stay here rent free?'

'Of course,' Margo answered without hesitation or consultation.

'Can I use your...our accountant?'

'How much do you plan on spending?' Saxon asked a little bemused.

'Well, it's all getting very grown up and business like, so I just want to make sure I account for everything and get the right advice on education and work-related expenditure.'

'Wise guy,' Margo remarked with a grin. 'I'll text you her details.'

'I had to borrow a mate's DI device in Darwin. Do you think I could get my own, as part of ongoing research for my new role, with a debit account of say, 1000 Nukoin?'

A wide smile stretched across Saxon's face. 'You've got your grandfather's knack of pushing the envelope. Sure.'

'Done. I give you my word on all three conditions.'

'It's so good to have you home,' Margo glowed. 'You look so mature; you've filled out and got muscles! So different.'

'It felt good to be out of the nest and foraging for myself, but it's great to be home.'

'This isn't going to be as easy as working in a bar or kitchen,' Saxon warned Hugo. 'You will publicly become the heir to the throne. You'll be pushed outside your comfort zone, not just by me, but by Kris and Kurt at the Academy, and the media.'

'Oh, enough of that master's apprentice bullshit, Saxon, leave the boy alone. He's just gotten home,' Margo scolded.

Hugo gave his father a fixed stare. 'Dad, I promise this is what I want, and I will do my best to live up to your expectations.'

'Good.' A gentle, satisfied smiled emerged across Saxon's face. 'Welcome aboard.'

The Cloud Cab settled on the rooftop landing pad of the skyport, the rotors slowly coming to rest.

The attendantbot opened the glass entrance door. 'You're clear to board, Dr Kilroy,' it directed.

As Kris neared the autonomous drone, the cockpit hatch opened and he stepped inside. He buckled himself into the plush cabin seat.

'Destination please,' the drone requested.

'North Sydney CBD, Tremaine building.'

The drone rotors kicked over and gained power. Three more Cloud Cabs hovered, waiting their turn to land on the Western Sydney University Campus skyport as Kris' drone ascended.

Fifteen minutes later, Kris alighted the drone and took the elevator to the 20th floor. He was ushered into the Tremaine Group boardroom and took a seat beside Michelle Kronenberg, head of ZynnComm's legal team. Looking around the cavernous room, Kris felt small. He leaned forward to address Saxon, sitting beside Michelle. 'Thanks for the invite, but I'm not sure why you want me here.'

Margo, sitting beside Saxon, overheard Kris and leant forward. 'You're an integral part of the management team and we need the numbers,' she whispered with a smile.

Walt's image shimmered from the holoprojector, beamed in from his home on the Hawksbury River. 'Are we right to go?'

The last few meeting participants took their seats with coffee in hand.

'We are ready this end, Walt,' Alfred advised.

Three distinct camps were positioned evenly around the striking circular table: Tremaine Group executives, HBU Electronics senior management including their CEO, Lee Jung-Lee. beamed in from Korea, and ZynnComm. ZynnComm had the smallest delegation by far. Zelda Freudenstein dutifully sat away from the table, behind Alfred with PD in hand, poised to record the proceedings.

'Welcome everyone.' Walt's voice was raspy. 'This afternoon we will be discussing the possible sale, or partial sale, of Tremaine Group's share portfolio of ZynnComm stock to HBU Electronics. Tremaine Group will not make a decision today, but we would like to hear from both Lee Jung-Lee and Dr Saxon Zynn.' He paused to catch his breath. 'Lee, why don't you go first. Why should Tremaine sell part or all of our ZynnComm stake to HBU?'

The expected delay as the language translator completed its task added tension within the room. All eyes fell upon the holoprojection of Lee Jung-Lee.

Jung-Lee was a coat-hanger of a man in his mid-50s, his wiry frame draped in a suit as if it were still in his closet. He cleared his throat. 'Good afternoon. We don't want part of your 49 percent, Walt, we want all of it. We are here today to make an offer to the Tremaine Group valued at 170 billion Nukoin. This would be made up of 160 billion in Nukoin plus HBU stock valued at 10 billion Nukoin, giving you a three percent stake in HBU. Dr Zynn, we will make you an offer valued at 180 billion Nukoin. This would be made up of 170 billion Nukoin plus HBU stock for your 51 percent. Together, your corporations would own six percent of HBU which means a continuing revenue stream from your technology and a seat on the board.'

'With all due respect, our 51 percent is not on the table today, Mr Jung-Lee,' Saxon chipped in, 'but thank you for the generous offer.'

'No harm in trying,' Jung-Lee responded.

'I agree, a very generous offer, Lee,' Walt began. 'How would HBU improve on what we have already achieved?'

'We believe HBU can increase revenue by reducing device manufacturing costs by 25 to 30 percent, allowing a more attractive price point to a broader demographic. We have even toyed with the idea of giving DI devices away and charging a higher premium per experience. The whole world would jump on board and the revenue stream could grow exponentially after an initial loss.'

'Interesting strategy, Lee. How do you think you would manage being a subordinate partner to Saxon and his team?'

Jung-Lee turned to Saxon and his small cohort. 'ZynnComm has developed and delivered an astounding technology to the world. I think with HBU's experience and ingenuity, we will compliment ZynnComm, and together we will develop new products and markets.'

'Yes, I agree,' Walt said. 'I think HBU brings to the table decades of knowledge and is a trusted global brand. Together, the two organisations could be a dominate force, developing better products and new processes.'

Saxon squirmed in his chair, not enjoying where this was leading.

'What about you, Saxon, do you think you could work with HBU?' Walt probed.

Saxon took a breath. 'Mr Jung-Lee, I believe a partnership of this magnitude and nature would be a difficult marriage. As you have already stated, you want it all. That would always be in the front of my mind and the back of your mind. I would always be wondering if you were undermining ZynnComm in an effort to initiate a takeover in one form or another at some point. So, to answer your question, Walt, no I don't think it would be a productive merger.'

'Point taken, Saxon,' Walt concurred. 'As we are all aware, if Tremaine were to move forward with this sale, it would be one of the largest corporate mergers in history. We must also consider your history, Lee. HBU mergers and acquisitions over the past 20 years have been memorable, starting with Xerizon delivering technological convergence of smartphones with numerous medical devices to launch the biointuitive Personal Device market. This prompted HBU to embark on over a dozen catch-and-kill acquisitions of start-ups, followed by vertical, horizontal and congeneric mergers. Would that modus operandi change in future? I think not. When we take into account the additional income streams we've developed over the past year with accessories, merchandise, real-world media rights, advertising opportunities both in-dream and real-world, and future technologies based on the platform, we would be seeking at minimum 250 billion Nukoin for our 49 percent, Lee.'

Murmurs trickled through the HBU Electronics team. Lee Jung-Lee put his finger to his earpiece, listening intently, before the group fell silent.

'We have taken those revenue streams into account, Walt, but we fail to see why your market appraisal is so high given the financial data supplied to us and our risk profile of the sector,' Jung-Lee argued. 'If there is something we have missed or failed to include in our quite substantial offer, please tell us.'

Walt smiled. 'Lee, what you fail to understand is...we are the sector, Tremaine and ZynnComm, we dictate how this technology is rolled out. You talk about risk profile; What risk? This is the calm before the storm. Current market penetration is almost eight percent of the world adult population. DI will reach 30 percent within five years, from 740 million to 2.2 billion regular users. Those figures are pretty much set in concrete, Lee. HBU is one of the few corporations with deep enough pockets and technological expertise to compete against us in the near future, but you can't, that's why you're here, Lee. You are negotiating to own half of the greatest technology known to man. A technology that arrives once every three or four hundred years. Our latest breakthrough, Neurocoalescence, explores an entirely new use for the technology that will change the face of mankind in the coming decades, and you are not calculating that into your offer.'

'I understand, Walt. We will go to 195 billion. To recoup a further 20 billion Nukoin would add several years to our financial timeline.'

'We are at 250, you are at 195. I don't think we're going to move forward at this point in time–'

'Your shareholders will be disappointed if this merger doesn't go ahead, Walt. One final offer...210 billion,' Jung-Lee proposed, trying to resurrect the negotiation.

'Well, Lee, you managed to find another 15 billion in your pocket within seconds,' Walt teased. 'I tell you what, we'll meet you at 235 and you have a deal.'

The HBU team immediately plunged into discussion mode.

Kris leaned towards Saxon. 'Verdict?'

Saxon shrugged, wearing a concerned expression. Margo gently clutched his hand and squeezed. The faintest of smiles flashed across his face for her.

The HBU group ceased chattering. Their expressionless faces made it difficult to gauge a decision.

'You are a cunning negotiator, Walt; the folklore surrounding you rings true. You are a master of "no", to achieve your objective,'

Jung-Lee smiled. 'We can't make a deal at that price, Walt. It's over inflated and not good business for our shareholders.'

'If you walk away from this negotiation, the potential of this technology, your shareholders, your board, might be looking for a new CEO, Lee,' Walt warned.

Lee Jung-Lee remained straight-faced. 'We'll offer 220.'

'Thank you, Lee, but it's 235 or there will be no sale today.'

'Can we keep the dialogue open for a further six months and revisit the negotiations?'

'Lee, in six months our price will have increased. If you can't meet our price today, you won't meet it in six months. Although, we could discuss HBU manufacturing DI device componentry.'

'We will pass on that offer thank you, Walt,' Jung-Lee said, before barking, '225 billion!'

'No!' A HBU executive stood and yelled.

'Shut up!' Jung-Lee scolded through the translation. 'Take your seat.'

Every person froze, suspended by the tension now blanketing the room.

'You want a piece of the pie so badly don't you, Lee,' Walt teased sardonically. '232, my final offer.'

Lee Jung-Lee shook his head. 'No. I apologise for our poor behaviour, Walt.' The HBU executive resumed his seat.

'Don't apologise, Lee. The heat of the moment is what makes negotiating exciting.' He paused momentarily. 'So, as we were, as we are, as we will be.' Walt's image evaporated from the room, followed by Lee Jung-Lee.

'Fuck me,' Kris muttered under his breath, 'I thought Walt was going to buckle for a moment.' Everyone in the room began to scatter. 'So, business as usual.'

Margo smiled at Kris. 'There's no such animal at ZynnComm.'

At that moment, both Saxon and Margo received the same text message from Walt on their PDs. *'My mole told me Lee wasn't authorised to go above 210 billion. Buy as much HBU stock as possible.'* They exchanged looks.

Across the room, Alfred Nembo received the same text message.

Chapter Four

Hugo felt right at home in Rock Legends. Handpicked musicians from their prime peppered the hovering stage: Malcolm Young on rhythm guitar, Lady Gaga on keyboards, Jimi Hendrix on lead guitar, Ginger Baker on drums, Flea on bass guitar with Amy Winehouse and Tiffany Pickford on backing vocals. Tiffany was the latest to join the 27 Club. The experience was expensive, but he thought it was worth 150 Nukoin. Hugo stood beside the statuesque Tiffany, preparing to begin the 30 minute set when Elvis Presley, in his mid-30s, sauntered onto the stage eating a peanut butter, honey, banana and bacon sandwich.

'Sorry I'm late,' he mumbled, chewing his snack. He took his place behind the third backup singers microphone beside Amy.

'I told you not to fucking bring food onto the stage, Elvis!' Amy threatened.

Elvis stopped chewing and swallowed. 'I appreciate the reminder, Amy, thank you very much.' He offered here an apologetic smile and plopped what was left of his sandwich on the foldback speaker.

'Ready?' Hugo asked, without expecting a reply. 'Here we go.' He hitched his acoustic guitar higher on his shoulder as he walked to the centre stage mic. 'Welcome to Planet Clare everyone! Two, three, four.'

The 50,000 strong crowd surrounding the gently rotating stage erupted as the band, Hugo's Army, kicked off the set with the 2034 classic, Opal Eyes by Jed Gentry.

The anticipated text message from Wendy arrived on all their PD's simultaneously. *'All set. Meet in 10, link di.91.432564.UY - access code: AJ1029.'* Neither Margo, Kris nor Saxon responded.

Pink sand stretched on forever in all directions as a gentle breeze took the edge off the heat. Nibbles and drinks sat on the round table under the marquee where the clandestine meeting was taking place.

'This experience will be used exclusively for our discussions,' Wendy started. 'I haven't named it yet.'

'Lovely place,' Kris wryly noted, inspecting the landscape in all directions.

'Outdoors with no distractions was the brief,' Wendy replied with the hint of a grin.

'What we are about to discuss remains strictly between the four of us,' Saxon instructed.

'Do we have an agenda?' Margo enquired.

'Just one agenda item,' Saxon stated. 'How do we find this in-dream perpetrator in the real world and stop him from preying on users in White experiences?'

'Are you sure it's a single individual?' Margo questioned.

'I've been cross-checking assembled echo rapes and murders in all White and Yellow rated experiences with our database of women who have reported assaults to police worldwide. They're almost identical violent assaults. This predator is prolific,' Wendy stated. 'I've calculated he has raped or killed 58 assembled and live echoes so far.'

'Jesus,' Saxon exhaled deeply. 'Any luck following up unsolved real-world serial killings?'

'Not really, nothing like this. I believe we're dealing with the same individual based on location choice, modius operandi of assault, and because the timing of assaults are consecutive, never simultaneous. I've chronologically mapped the assaults. He started off cautiously, but he quickly gained confidence. He plays it very safe;

the pattern doesn't deviate from victim to victim, it's frighteningly habitual. I would say he has systematically reconnoitred these experiences well in advance of his assaults. He's refined his technique with deliberate, methodical focus, and his anonymity is empowering him above and beyond his appetite for rape and murder because no one's after him, no one's even looking for him.'

'Until now,' Saxon declared confidently.

'Could we send someone in with the sole purpose of remembering the perp's face then get a sketch artist to draw him and create wanted posters in-dream to warn people?' Margo suggested.

'Back to the wild west,' Kris grinned. 'I like it, wanted dead or alive.' His expression seeped from his face when he scanned everyone's reaction. 'Sorry to be so flippant, but that "someone" would have to be in the right experience, in the right instance and that is virtually impossible.'

'We've identified assaults across more than a dozen experiences based on complaints and assembled echo deaths. We need to narrow it down quickly, and DNA is the obvious starting point,' Wendy justified. 'It's all there on file. Kris and I think we've found a way in, using a vulnerability in the system. The DNAsafe algorithm protecting the DNA experience repository was created and is operated by Clearview Dynamics, which is out of our control. We don't know all of their system controls and they don't know all of Norus'. It will take time, potentially weeks to navigate our way through DNAsafe protocols undetected to extract the correct information.'

'Should we even try to access that information?' Margo questioned. 'If you're detected it could mean the end for ZynnComm.'

'I don't want to bring in third parties–' Saxon began.

'No, no, of course not,' Kris jumped in. 'Clearview Dynamics update Norus' DNAsafe code and firmware monthly using a machine learning program called ONL52. Norus is due for an update. We watch, we learn then we piggyback into the system off an error message probe to retrieve our information. Of course, there is a small chance Norus detects us and automatically reports the breach, but we're confident we can do this, Margo,' Kris reassured her. 'We've run five simulations so far and all but one was successful.

'Small chance? Twenty percent failure is high, Kris,' Saxon cautioned. 'If there's a breach notice sent, they'll know it was an inside job because Black Shield won't have been compromised and we won't have data files to prove otherwise.'

'We've isolated the issue,' Kris argued, looking at Wendy for support. 'At present, we're lost in the noise, the quantum noise,' he focused on Margo, 'that means errors. Errors increase the further we progress and we get swamped, we can't eliminate the noise. We could also fabricate bogus Black Shield breach alerts to automatically kick in if we do trip up—'

'We can, 'Wendy chimed in. 'We can recreate qware data signatures from our usual suspects, our state actors,' Wendy concentrated on Saxon. 'Kris and I were thinking the three of us could collaborate, using Neurocoalescence to solve the quantum noise problem.'

'Exactly, then I'm sure we can get our simulation success rate up to at least 98 percent. The more we do, the better we get,' Kris reassured them.

'We don't want to get good at this, Kris,' Margo warned. 'We just need it to be effective on a limited basis.'

'This predator will never go before a court because these crimes don't exist outside our heads and Gelchips. They can't be proven in the real world, there's no evidence,' Kris argued. 'Wendy and I carry out our Norus investigations quietly, get the DNA required, then the four of us make a decision how we proceed.'

'Effectively becoming a Star Chamber,' Saxon said.

Kris thought about the statement. 'Star Chamber, quite possibly, in one of the better iterations of the concept, yes, not what it evolved into. We need a solution to this problem quick smart. Veejay said it could get expensive, tens of millions, if it can be proven these women have suffered trauma. The DI Advisory Council know about project Rapid Sun too.'

'What! How?' Wendy asked.

'Justine Vanderberg, CEO of GeoSpace brought it up.'

'How did she find out?'

Kris shrugged. 'She said she had a source,' Kris explained. 'She wouldn't say any more.'

'After Saxon told me about what happened at your meeting, Kris, I did some digging,' Margo admitted. 'I know Justine, networking is her life. Dad has used her firm for equity funding on several projects. She's on the board of several businesswomen's organisations, I'm on one of them with her, International Businesswomen's Alliance. Ingrid McTavish is also a member.'

'Ingrid?' Kris queried. 'What does Ingrid do again?'

'She runs a not-for-profit charity called Sisters of Compassion that span 17 countries at last count,' Margo advised the team. 'It supports destitute women over 50 who find themselves homeless for one reason or another. Saxon and I are financial supporters. I spoke to Ingrid yesterday. She said she may have mentioned something about Andrew's research to Justine at a fundraiser.'

'That makes sense,' Kris commented.

'Can we use Andrew's memory recording tech? Is it ready? Is it viable?' Margo probed. 'I know you have reservations, Saxon, but this could be what we need once we narrow down the suspects.'

'Not yet,' Saxon immediately answered. 'I'm not ready to release this tech yet.'

'Can't we just use it in-house?' Margo challenged.

Saxon thought before he spoke. 'Possibly. Let's exhaust all other avenues before we have to.'

'The Council have no power to enforce anything do they? To compel us to use it?' Wendy wondered.

'No. But they have the ears of powerful people and government agencies,' Saxon said.

'If we can terminate this problem now, work out how to shut this individual down, this will fade into the background and we maintain the status quo,' Kris reasoned. 'We won't need Andrew's tech.'

'I think we've skipped a few steps before any of that happens,' Margo decided. 'We need DNA from our database to match it in the real world.'

The group fell silent as they contemplated the magnitude of the task.

'We'd need all DNA profiles from an experience after an assault has occurred,' Wendy insisted. 'We could do that retrospectively or wait until another's reported.'

'We've waited long enough,' Margo conveyed bluntly. 'I think we use a past experience. I also think we may need an in-dream security force.'

'We discussed having in-dream security very early on but held off to see how things developed. I think it's time, we need them,' Saxon agreed.

'I know we discussed this early in project development,' Kris said. 'But we always came back to the same obstacle, the same issue, who would give them their authority, their jurisdiction? Us? A government? If so, which one? Besides, White experiences can have upwards of 10,000 live echoes. That requires a lot of security.'

'We do it covertly,' Wendy proposed. 'They wear plain clothes, they blend in. They are well trained vigilantes, no badges, possibly weapons. We could have them everywhere.'

'Policing dreams will initiate a backlash from users, they'll ditch our experiences and go elsewhere–'

'Only if they know they exist, Kris,' Saxon countered. 'Only the four of us would know, and we trial them in White experiences only. We didn't anticipate this level of abuse early on; we glossed over the predatory nature of human beings–'

'Of men,' Wendy corrected him.

'That's still not going to identify this arsehole,' Margo argued. 'A security force sounds like a strategy moving forward, we could even utilise Lena's skills in our security detail, but that's not going to pinpoint offenders for us to track down in the real world now. We have to narrow it down to a dozen or so users, profile them, then get their DNA,' she clarified. 'How the fuck do we do that?'

'It's going to take imagination on our part.' Kris answered. 'We do this systematically, on several fronts. Wendy has started to cross reference the experiences where women have been attacked and killed based on complaints and assembled echo murders. Once we access the DNA info in Norus we cross reference all males present during all attacks across that narrow band of experiences. That will give us a short list of men to monitor in-dream. As you said, Margo, we meticulously profile those suspects in the real world, then we send someone to find them to confirm our DNA samples.'

'So, who becomes our bloodhound, perhaps our executioner in the real world?' Margo asked.

'Whoa, let's not get ahead of ourselves, we don't have to execute anyone,' Saxon cautioned his wife.

'We simply find them and block their DNA, prohibiting them from the platform, same as we have for other known perps,' Kris clarified. 'Problem solved.'

'That sounds too easy,' Margo reasoned, concerned.

The protracted quiet was broken as Saxon spoke. 'Believe me, it won't be easy. We'll be the only ones who know about this arrangement. Between us, what we initiate in here and the real world to hunt down perpetrators to keep users safe, will be known as Division Four. We'll utilise NCL to get our success rate up to at least 99 percent in simulation before we go anywhere near trying to infiltrate Norus. To handle the pointy end, the real world search, I suggest we approach Waylon privately, without involving Firerock. He'll be given a mission brief to find individuals, collect a DNA sample, nothing more.'

'I agree,' Margo seconded. 'He can be trusted.'

'Welcome to the Dream Chamber,' Wendy announced deadpan. 'This experience now has a name.'

The four sat motionless as the discussion weighed heavily upon each of them. To vocalise their concerns, rationalise their arguments, decide their course of action, seemed effortless, almost trivial, sitting in this surreal wasteland. Yet they all realised their decisions, these ripples, had the potential to gain momentum with enormous ramifications if discovered.

'We must do this to remain in control of the tech,' Saxon moralised. 'This is never to be discussed in the real world. We don't want anyone, and I mean anyone, Merlin, Miranda, Nikola–'

'Hugo and Walt,' Wendy tossed in.

'From discovering what Division Four is or does. Clear?' Everyone nodded. 'You never know who is listening or recording.'

'It's funny how ethical and moral safeguards can fly out the window so quickly,' Kris commented.

'It's sad this is necessary, Kris,' Margo responded. 'Not funny. It's twisted men with dicks who are the problem.'

'Here, here,' Wendy agreed. 'Let's face it, male humans have almost become redundant in traditional reproductive conception these days. More and more couples are using assisted reproductive methods. Here's an idea, we collect as much sperm as possible and put it on ice, then castrate all male children from 2050 on. Studies have proven castrated men live longer and are far less violent.'

'That's thinking outside the box, Wendy,' Kris complemented sardonically, before continuing. 'Not a very practical idea when you extrapolate all the consequences flowing on from where that could lead.'

'I don't see any issues with that scenario, Kris,' Wendy refuted with a grin.

'How many secret DI meeting's like this are going on everyday do you think?' Margo pondered aloud, changing the conversation direction.

'In the thousands, with backroom political powerbrokers leading the way I'd say,' Saxon replied.

'Secure Dream Meetings is a start-up targeting that niche market,' Kris said. 'Two of our London Academy graduates have created a basic off the shelf model with premium add-ons. Word is they're making a killing.'

'We'll make the Dream Chamber a weekly meeting until we get a handle on this,' Saxon recommended. 'Wendy, can you coordinate our calendars for the next month of meetings?'

'Will do.'

'Are we done?' Margo enquired. 'I need to get back.'

'I think so,' Saxon said. The others nodded in agreement.

'Heterogeneous,' Margo articulated with a smile before she was engulfed by the familiar red glow.

Saxon offered a hand wave. 'Jabberwocky.'

'Heading back?' Kris asked Wendy.

'No, I think I'll stay for the duration, and soak up the tranquillity. I need a break.'

'Nice for some, but the real world beckons. Rumpelstiltskin.'

After Kris left, Wendy relaxed back in her chair with a wine and olives, enjoying the solitude.

Arrow joined Merlin in his office and slumped into one of the chairs. 'Uncle Walt's experience is finished. Rendered and good to go.'

'Finally! I'll upload it to the network and text him.'

'Hey, it wasn't my fault the fucking delivery schedule blew out,' Arrow pushed back. 'You wanted edits, and that was before it switched from a simple one-off experience to a complicated continuing experience–'

'Did you run it through your new validation software?'

'That's another reason it took so long, the subsynaptic resolver took 26 hours. Aren't you going to get it checked?' Arrow questioned apprehensively. 'Just to be sure the validator worked?'

'Nope, we've done enough analysis, Arrow, it works. Kris, Wendy and Saxon have signed off on it, so now it's part of our everchanging production process. Your brilliant idea has decreased our postproduction time and saved two codesters three days of cross checking, so no.'

'You're the boss.'

Merlin searched for Walt's project folder onscreen. 'Computer, Walt Tremaine folder. He's been hounding me for days. Walt will tell us if he's not happy. There you are.' Merlin uploaded the WTv2.4.6 folder to the network backend, then initiated execution. He grabbed his PD and texted Walt the good news along with the link and access code. 'Finally done. Hungry?' He threw his PD on the desk.

'If you're buying,' she answered with a smile.

Walt pushed the door wide open to the opulent suite. Striding out onto the spacious balcony overlooking a turquoise Mediterranean sea, this opening scene from the draft versions had become familiar.

'I thought I'd find you here,' he said, leaning down to kiss Sylvia warmly, falling into her eyes. Walt hovered for a moment, taking in her unmistakable scent with a boyish grin on his face.

'Hello, darling, you're early. I thought you were still at Wildwood.'

'I missed you.' He ran his hand up and down her arm slowly. 'So I came early.'

She smiled up at him. 'It's only been a few days.'

'Feels like decades.'

'Is everything alright?' Sylvia's expression changed to concern.

'Could not be better,' Walt confided as he pulled a deck lounge across and sat close by her. 'Tell me, what have you been up to?'

'The usual, chasing money for our foundation. Monday I had lunch with the Hilderberg's, Marta Blackstone and Warren Schofield in London. Looks like all will be supporting the Mombasa orphanage project.'

'That's excellent news.'

'Last night I was in Barcelona for the Cutting Edge Benevolent Gala. New Planet Foundation announced they will come onboard as our partner for the New Science for New Minds project in Burundi.'

'Sounds like you've got everything under control as usual.' Walt stood and peered over the balcony to the sea. 'Look, I bought us a little runabout for a holiday.'

Sylvia got out of her deck lounge and spied the 80-metre luxury superyacht. 'Runabout my arse. That's a tinny!' They both laughed.

'I've cancelled all my meetings for the next few weeks and we're going to relax,' Walt revealed, putting his arm around his wife's shoulder and pulling her close. 'I think it's time I slowed down to smell the roses before I start pushing up daisies.'

'Don't be silly, you've got 30 years left in you. But I agree, you should slow down. I like the idea of spending a few weeks together. I'll call Carla and tell her to clear my calendar.'

'Do it on the boat.'

'Let me pack a bag at least.'

'No need, it's all on the tinny.' Walt took her hand and began to pull her towards the door.

Later that evening in Port Augusta, Merlin, Arrow, Wendy and Miranda got into Liam's vehicle. Merlin rode shotgun.

'I feel like driving on my birthday,' Liam said. 'I've only had a few beers.'

Arrow glanced at Wendy beside her in the backseat. 'You've been drinking, you can't,' she challenged.

Liam pulled his PD from his pocket. 'Breathalyser,' he told his device.

'Breathe onto the sensor for three seconds,' the app instructed him.

Liam took a breath and exhaled onto his PD.

'Your blood alcohol level is .06,' the PD reported. 'You have been blocked from driving this vehicle. Autonomous mode will be engaged.'

'Fuck!' Liam exclaimed. 'Who's up for a little Purple Spyder?'

'Where did you get Purple Spyder?' Miranda questioned. 'That's genetically crossed with psilocybin.'

'When I was in Sydney last month. I have a horticulturist mate who works at the Royal Botanic Gardens. He got it.'

'I'm in,' Miranda said. 'Haven't smoked that shit in a long time.'

'Let's go,' Arrow concurred.

'Merlin?' Liam pressed.

'Why not. Weekend tomorrow.'

'Destination, home,' Liam ordered his vehicle.

Merlin handed Liam a small gift on the journey. 'We got you a present.'

'We did?' Wendy questioned.

Liam was touched. 'A present? Thank you.'

'Actually, it was just me,' Merlin confessed.

Liam quickly unwrapped the gift and held up the limp rubber item for all to see.

Wendy and Arrow laughed as Merlin grinned.

'What is it?' Miranda asked.

'A Cock Sock,' Liam answered dryly. 'An Acid Spear Studios branded Cock Sock.'

'You just wanted to embarrass him on his birthday,' Wendy criticised Merlin.

'No, no, not all,' Merlin defended somewhat unconvincingly. 'He's a single man with urges and our technology can assist in that area.'

'It's not one of your old ones, is it?' Arrow jumped in, grinning at the girls.

Merlin turned around and gave Arrow a sly look. 'You are my–'

'Don't you fucking say another word,' she warned him with pointed finger.

'Its purpose?' Miranda requested innocently. The girls and Merlin turned to her. 'What?'

'She's knows her weed varieties, but she's a little naive in the cock department,' Wendy defended. 'It catches ejaculate when men are in-dream having lustful experiences.'

'Ewww!' Miranda squealed.

'Check this out.' Arrow tapped her PD to project a video feed onto the vehicle ceiling. They all leaned back to watch.

A young man, whose identity was obscured by pixilation, yelled something in a foreign language before the auto translator kicked in. 'We are the Dreamdwellers!'

'Dreamdwellers? A new band?' Liam wondered.

'These dream phaze users have managed to circumvent system protocols to stay in dream immersion for up to 98 minutes rather than the automatically enforced 33 minutes,' the voiceover informed.

'What the fuck! Where are they from?' Merlin demanded.

Arrow checked her PD. 'Uzbekistan. Uploaded 11 minutes ago.'

A young woman, also digitally concealed, explained. 'We just want to live in an alternative world, a better world than this oppressive dictatorship we live in everyday,' the translated voiceover said. 'Necessity is the mother of invention they say.'

A male voice speaking off camera in Uzbek could be heard before the English translation delivered his comment. 'You know the 33 minute time limit is for your own safety?'

'We've been testing this workaround for a few weeks and we seem fine,' the girl replied.

'Forward that video to Saxon and Kris,' Wendy directed Arrow.

'How do you think they beat network protocols?' Liam questioned.

Merlin shook his head slowly before answering. 'Fucked if I know. Someone tech savvy enough to know their way around compound quantum submatrices—'

'Maybe they didn't. Maybe they sublimated the geosyg algorithm on their devices before their cycle was up, to trick it into resetting somehow,' Arrow proposed.

'Saxon will want this fixed ASAP before the workaround goes viral,' Wendy said as

her PD buzzed. 'It's Saxon. Meeting in the R&D lab now.'

'Destination, work,' Liam instructed, altering his vehicle's route.

'Drop Miranda off on the way,' Wendy told Liam.

'Keep me some of that Purple Spyder, Liam.'

Liam pivoted the driver's seat 90 degrees and looked at Miranda and Wendy. 'You two make me dinner tomorrow night and I'm there.'

'See you at seven,' Miranda said without hesitation or consultation.

Ten minutes later, Wendy, Liam, Merlin and Arrow joined Saxon in the R&D lab meeting room on level two. Kris' image projected from Saxon's PD for the impromptu meeting.

Wendy ran her PD along her upper forearm. 'Muscle strain in extensor carpi radialis longus,' the Bioscanner app reported. 'Massage followed by heat pack to minimise pain.'

'What happened?' Arrow asked as she sat down beside her.

'Nothing serious, just too enthusiastic in the garden I think. The alcohol suppressed the soreness for a while, it's starting to twinge again.'

'How the fuck did they get past the network protocols, Kris?' Saxon questioned.

'We're not sure. There are no breach alerts, nothing,' Kris advised. 'I'm meeting with cybersecurity in less than five.'

'I want to be in that meeting. I want this patched immediately, tonight,' Saxon ordered.

'At least they aren't broadcasting the workaround,' Arrow told them, referring to her PD. 'Nothing on social media, even though everyone's asking for it.'

'I'm all ears,' Saxon prompted. 'Ideas?'

'Could we shut the network down in that part of the world, until we find a solution?' Arrow queried.

'We can do better than that,' Saxon remembered. 'The Network Integrity team in Sydney have been upgrading cyberthreat procedures, effectively isolating content distribution networks country by country if needed. We can turn Uzbekistan off at the borders.'

'Timing is everything,' Kris smiled. 'I'll tell the duty manager to cut them off and issue a systems maintenance alert. I'll get on to it now.' His image disappeared.

'I didn't know we could do that with Norus?' Wendy pondered.

'Upgrades were only finished this week. I don't want it broadcast business wide, keep it between us,' Saxon told the gathering. 'Might give us the upper hand in future.'

'I'll pull the country data and start searching for user cycle anomalies,' Merlin said getting up.

'I think we should check the geosyg algorithm on their devices too,' Arrow suggested, 'To see if it's been modified.'

'Liam, help Merlin,' Saxon instructed. 'Wendy and Arrow, find out who was in the video, who uploaded it and from where in Uzbekistan. I'll get Waylon and Firerock on the ground in Uzbekistan to follow up what you find.'

'Will do,' Wendy obeyed. Arrow followed her from the meeting room.

Saxon's PD buzzed. 'Kris, put the meeting on hold for a minute, I need to get Waylon and his team in the air.'

'I'll push it back five.'

'My Fast Chat tonight is with Brigit McKenzie,' Wagner Hussock introduced, 'and we will be discussing dream immersion trauma syndrome and her new movement, Stop Dream Violence. Welcome, Brigit.'

'Thank you for the opportunity, Wagner.' Brigit McKenzie's holoprojection occupied the chair across from Wagner.

Margo placed her mug of tea on the kitchen island to watch the interview on her PD in her Port Augusta residence. '*It's on*,' she texted Saxon, who was working on level two.

Saxon turned on a monitor in the developers' lab while he continued his work.

'So, Brigit, give me some background on how your Stop Dream Violence movement came about.'

'It evolved out of a discussion I had with women at a rape crisis meeting. We were discussing how unprepared we were. I didn't think about changing my pain threshold going into a White rated experience because I didn't think I'd be hurt in that environment, so it was off. White experiences are supposed to be where everyone has a great time. It was just lucky I had my safe word automatically set to active for all experiences I visit. Up until now VRXLR8 games and environments were our most immersive alternative experiences, but that was still pretend, still firmly in our real- world reality, they didn't physically hurt you. Sure, there are inertia and impact devices, but you never really sustained injuries. If they did, someone would be held accountable. Dream phaze is different, you can feel everything, even rape and death and no one seems to be accountable. Then our conversation moved on to the lack of support for DITS and that it wasn't recognised as a real condition,' she added.

'And why is that do you think?'

'There are several reasons. First of all, it's an emerging condition and there is virtually no research on the subject. I think the developers of the platform, ZynnComm, have chosen to bury their head in the sand in a hope the issues fall on deaf ears. They either underestimated or neglected to acknowledge this type of abhorrent behaviour could exist in White rated experiences.'

'And is that what you're fighting for, Brigit, some sort of policing in White and Yellow rated experiences? Because some users who visit Blue and Red rated experiences are joining your movement because of the impact violence is having on them.'

'Exactly, Wagner. We are asking for supervision in White and Yellow rated experiences, but yes, Blue and Red rated experiences are also having a negative impact due to the extreme violence. Society has been conditioned, been desensitised to violence through TV, films, VR and gaming for the last half century, but when you experience extreme violence or witness it, as you do in dream phaze, it feels entirely real and can damage people psychologically.'

'ZynnComm would argue that users are well aware of what to expect based on the colour coded rating system in place.' Wagner played devil's advocate.

'Yes they would, but again I would argue they have underestimated how realistic dream phaze experiences feel and the psychological impact they have on some people.'

'Have you been in contact with ZynnComm about your incident,' Wagner asked.

'I've made a complaint to the company and I've reported it to police.'

'And what did the police say? It's not something they can actually investigate, is it?'

'That is true, but they were very understanding. They took my statement and said they would look into it.'

'And have you heard back from them?'

'I've spoken to them and they admitted there is no clear procedure on how to investigate the incident or who has authority to do so. That's another reason why in-dream attacks sit in no man's land, there's no evidence or witnesses. It's my word against ZynnComm, so they have the advantage over anyone who has similar experiences to mine. The public has to stop this blind faith in big data, relying on big data to look out for us. They don't. Every one of us has to be aware of in-dream violence against women.'

'It's a real grey area when it comes to jurisdiction in dream phaze. I've spoken to several politicians and senior judges and no one seems to know where the power lies.'

'My rape may not have been in the real world, but it certainly impacted me, it has changed me just the same. I'm not the only woman to be raped in a White or Yellow experience and it's just not acceptable.'

'Perhaps ZynnComm doesn't have any urgency in addressing your issue because from a legal standpoint if you use their platform you forfeit all rights, ZynnComm has no liability, you participate at your own risk.' Wagner concluded.

'Yes. But any woman who chooses to participate in a White or Yellow rated experience does not expect to be raped and murdered in that experience. Something has to be done to safeguard women from this abuse.'

'I can tell by your tone how deeply this experience has impacted you, Brigit. So, how do you see your initiative tackling the problem?'

'Awareness and hopefully accountability, Wagner. I want to warn women, make them think twice before parting with their money. The issue is lack of accountability by ZynnComm for ignoring the continuing violence towards women in dream phaze. There must be measures put in place to make ZynnComm accountable for trauma experienced within their technology.'

'That will be difficult given civil liberty laws around privacy preventing disclosure of user dream preferences.'

'We need an intermediary. I did some research, and there was debate a couple of years ago over implementing a sort of dream investigation unit monitoring experiences. Maybe in light of increasing attacks it should be established.'

'I remember that, but it was squashed by authorities because it could impact civil liberties. They would have to identify in-dream users.'

'We have to start somewhere, Wagner, so I'm asking ZynnComm to think about how we tackle this problem so all women are safe. Can you imagine if men were being sexually assaulted and murdered in White or Yellow experiences? There would be an immediate solution.'

'Hang on, we have a beam-in,' Wagner reported. 'Gerda, welcome.' The holoprojection of a young woman appeared in the empty chair beside Brigit. 'What would you like to add to this conversation?'

'Hello, Wagner. I would like to say thank you and well done to Brigit McKenzie, for being brave enough to come forward. I was also raped, and then killed in a White rated experience but I was too afraid to speak out. I told a few friends. I have been getting counselling for the past few months and I am slowly coming to terms with the cowardly attack, but it is difficult.'

'Thank you, Gerda, for having the courage to say this publicly today,' Brigit congratulated. 'The more voices to join our movement the louder we get.'

'If you need a microphone you're welcome to come back, Brigit,' Wagner offered. 'Just one last question for both of you. Will you dream phaze again?'

In unison, they both answered. 'No.'

'That's all we have time for–' Wagner began.

Margo closed the interview window on her PD. *'Fucking Wagner keeps stirring the pot.'* She texted Saxon.

'Vindictive bastard. He won't change. We have another NCL session tomorrow. We're getting close. U may need 2 reach out 2 this woman & her movement,' he replied.

'Works for an advertising company. I'll get Selma 2 contact her.'

Kris' holoprojection glimmered into existence from his office in New York City via Saxon's PD.

'So, thoughts on the NCL session?' Saxon invited, dragging the drink coaster on his desk closer before picking up his coffee.

'How long have you had that coaster?' Wendy asked, watching him.

Saxon thought. 'Hmmm, about ten years.'

'I know it's been on your desk for the nine years I've been here.'

'You know the story behind the coaster?' Saxon assumed.

'Yep,' Wendy replied quickly cutting the conversation off.

'I don't,' Kris confessed, taking an interest in the coaster.

'I must have told you?' Saxon questioned.

'Yeah, he would have told you,' Wendy added trying to douse the banter.

'Nope.'

'Really?' Saxon gestured to Wendy to share the story.

Wendy let out a heavy sigh. 'Do I have to tell this story? It's so lame.'

'Maybe I don't need to hear the story.' Kris scrunched up his face.

'We can't move forward until Kris hears the story,' Saxon insisted.

'If I remember correctly,' Wendy sarcastically began, 'the architect who designed your house refurb picked up two timber offcuts from the dumpster and handed them to you. He asked you what they were, and you answered floorboard offcuts. He said no, they were architecturally designed industrial drink coasters. Virtually indestructible, last for centuries. Right?'

'Correct. I have one here and one on my desk in Sydney.' Saxon touched the 20 millimetre thick, 100 millimetre square blackbutt timber coaster.

'Show me the coaster,' Kris requested.

Saxon moved his coffee mug and placed it on the desk. He picked up the coaster and held it up to his PD.

'It's a piece of floorboard offcut. What makes it architecturally designed?' Kris questioned.

'The simple fact that an architect plucked them out of the rubbish and repurposed them with a new function. That's vision,' Saxon responded.

Kris gave Wendy an odd look. 'Fucking rubbish is what that is,' he volunteered.

Wendy and Saxon laughed at his comment as he placed the coaster back on the desk and his coffee mug on top.

'Absolute rubbish,' Wendy reinforced. 'Total bullshit.' The distraction lightened the tired mood. 'I will never tell that sorry again.'

'The Neurocoalescence,' Saxon paused looking up at the ceiling. 'Put your scrambler on Kris, I'll descramble my end.' He tapped his PD screen. 'Pause security camara and audio surveillance for 20 minutes. Authorisation code SZ677 alpha.' The tiny red light between the camera and microphone on the ceiling extinguished. 'The NCL session got us closer to solve the Norus access issue, but it'll take a few more sessions,' Saxon said.

'I'll run another simulation tomorrow with the amended interfractal T66 algorithm,' Wendy advised. 'Using multivariate polynominals with composite novar coefficients will certainly get us further.'

'We should've thought about focusing on the novar field earlier.'

'That's the beauty of NCL, Kris; between us, we did.' Saxon supressed a yawn. 'It's late, I'm tired.'

'Eliminating the graphox subroutine conflicts will get us beyond the Teliot barrier and into the main database,' Kris paused. 'I was thinking about our predator—'

'Kris, be very careful. Let's talk about this in abstract terms.'

'In abstract terms, sure,' Kris continued. 'After what Margo suggested in...you know. Can we give this fish a name? Something distinctive, so we all know which fish we're talking about. What about Griffin?'

Saxon shrugged. 'Sure.'

'We need bait to catch Griffin,' Kris alluded to the pair. 'Perhaps a Zen or Lena lure?'

Wendy turned to Saxon. 'How do you feel about that bait?'

Saxon said nothing for a moment, trying to think of a reason why he didn't want his sister's echo used in this way. 'It makes sense to use bait to hook...Griffin. Zen is in his target demographic, Lena is not, but she could shadow her. But to what end? How does that help us if they flush him out?'

'We would have to sacrifice Zen, so to speak, to isolate the experience, time and location of the feeding frenzy,' Kris proposed.

'Zen appears in many experiences, but only a few with Lena. We could load both Lena and Zen lures and link them together and monitor them in fishing experiences where we've had Griffin reports, and others that have similar demographics and themes, which could help isolate his feeding times,' Wendy suggested.

'Exactly,' Kris agreed. 'It will give us a baseline to start from and use for cross referencing.'

'It will. Let's implement that in the morning,' Saxon said.

'We need to start thinking about adding our in-dream...erm...fisheries officers to monitor Griffin too,' Wendy continued.

'We do,' Saxon concurred. 'But–'

'Reservists,' Wendy blurted out, 'That's what we should call them.'

'Reservists?' Saxon repeated. 'Reservists are usually military aren't they?'

'No, there are police reservists,' Kris insisted. 'In our case they would be fisheries reservists. We can program them with a variety of military, police and security tactics, so they can respond to any fishing situation.'

'That's an accurate description I suppose, civilians until needed,' Saxon agreed.

'Hiding in plain sight covertly monitoring fishing experiences,' Wendy added.

'That's something you and I can work on this week, Wendy. Enough chit-chat about that now. Oh yeah, before I forget to ask. That AFP agent contacted me again, erm, you know, Kosteska, and asked more questions about the Pleasure Planet experience. She has one of her men frequenting the experience to see if he can find a link to Konqwest. Have you had a look at it?'

'No complaints regarding the experience. I ran a diagnostic with the assembled echo expiration process and two female echoes have been killed, one in a vehicle accident, the other accidently hit with a cricket bat. I'll ask Liam if he can visit and have a look around if you like.'

'Okay, do that and let me know if he finds anything. We may be chasing the same fish,' Saxon shared.

Wendy thought about that proposition. 'There doesn't seem to be a link between Nugent's Luxury Plaza and Pleasure Planet, that's all speculation on their part.'

'Do I need to be across this?' Kris asked.

'No, I don't think so,' Saxon said. 'Home time.'

A white police van sat across the street outside a local bar in Mehrjon Street, Tashkent, Uzbekistan. Groups of young adults spilled out of the establishment and mingled outside the bar as the 11 p.m. curfew neared. A couple broke away from the crowd and began walking north. The police vehicle pulled up beside the intoxicated pair a few hundred metres from the bar and efficiently man-handled them into the transport without too much commotion.

Hours later, Saxon was entrenched in thought when the buzz from his PD brought him back. He picked up a lukewarm coffee mug parked on his architecturally designed coaster, leant back in his office chair and took the call. 'Morning, Waylon.'

Waylon's holoprojected head beamed from Saxon's PD. 'Hi, Saxon. Very early morning here, just gone 1:30 a.m. Just after 7:30 there, right?'

'Yep.'

'I hope I didn't wake you.'

'No, not at all. Been in the office for an hour. What have you found out?'

'We've interviewed all five involved and two individuals have been identified as the instigators. They're all first year software engineering students at the University of Information Technologies. The idea for the workaround was sent to all students who owned a DI device in their data structures and algorithms course, but only the two ringleaders acted on the anonymous email initially. They shared their devices with the other three. We're tracing that original email trail now. Unfortunately, it's bouncing around the planet, built around Kalmon mirroring techniques, it's quite sophisticated. The trail is pretty cold.'

'There are 31 students in that course with DI devices, correct?'

'That's right,' Waylon confirmed.

'Those 31 devices had a coding anomaly. Your five lab rats exploited that anomaly by tripping the geosyg algorithm to safe mode for a microsecond in two of the devices towards the end of their experience cycle, initiating a new cycle. They increased their experience cycles over a period of weeks. We've completed a hard reset of all 31 devices with an algorithm update and added an alert network wide for any similar breaches.'

'That's an extremely targeted coding attack,' Waylon said.

'Correct. Those five carried out an experiment created by someone else who didn't want to get their hands dirty.'

'Someone with access to the network's backend,' Waylon speculated.

'Exactly. Internal investigations have begun. Do you know if the workaround email went beyond that class?'

'Thirty-one students received the email and forwarding was disabled. Only the five experimented with it.'

'Makes sense. The workaround wouldn't have been any use to anyone outside that class. Only those 31 devices had the coding anomaly.'

'Someone with access to a current course enrolment list, cross referenced to those who own a device has manipulated those devices from within the network. We'll do background checks on the staff. It may be someone quite close to this group who knows one of your people.'

'Good idea. Did they say why they went public with this?'

'The video was taken when they were all drunk, as a joke, it was never meant to be posted. One of the group, a girl by the name of Larisa Zokirov, is prone to temper tantrums and was angry with the others, so she posted out of spite.'

'I'm glad she did. I'll get someone from Wendy's team to follow up with neuropsychological testing of the five, to assess how or if the extended sessions did any permanent neural damage.'

'I'll send you their contact details. My techs will continue to follow the digital trail and I'll keep you posted. Talk later.' Waylon ended the call.

Saxon felt apprehensive as he contemplated why this elaborate experiment was initiated, and by whom.

Chapter Five

The Great Tower of Babel painting by Pieter Bruegel in 1563 was the inspiration for the Romanesque building Merlin stood in front of, staring up. Multiple storeys of high stone walls, tapering towards the top floor, were punctuated with arched doorways and windows. He entered and climbed the uneven stairs. Reaching an old timber door, '*Hellfire Haus*' was crudely scratched into it. Opening the door, overwhelming aromas of cheeses gratified his nostrils. Camembert, Brie, Stinking Bishop, Munster, Stilton and Limburger cheese circles and blocks covered the 20 metre-long table. Intermingled between the cheeses were gourmet meats and treats, buckets of ice cold beer and bottles of wine, every type imaginable. As Merlin nibbled on double Brie and swigged Grolsch beer, he wandered onto a broad balcony overlooking a pink pool of water. The entire auditorium was intimately lit, with filtered background music by neo-futurist woodwind instrumentalist Du Yuan. A waterfall spilled from above, the origin hidden behind mist, into the pool populated with naked men and women of all shapes, sizes and colours, chatting, copulating and eating. Black and white porn films from the mid-20th century played on a massive screen suspended by fine gossamer cobwebs. A man approached Merlin from behind and stood beside him. The host echo introduced himself as Nimrod, the owner of Hellfire Haus.

'I was expecting something completely different. The name implies something darker, seedier, sleazier,' Merlin said.

'That was the idea, to pique interest,' Nimrod replied. 'But many of those who visit seem to return.'

'The entrance would certainly support a sleezy establishment catering for fetishes and such.'

'We cater for fetishes and all the deadly sins, including gluttony.'

'I noticed,' Merlin replied, before finishing off his cheese.

'Would you like to disrobe and join the pool party? What's your pleasure?'

Merlin offered a nervous smile before swigging his beer.

Below, a troupe of naked women appeared from a corridor and cartwheeled, backflipped and leapfrogged their way around the pool. Eight well-endowed men with metallic-looking penises, bearing a beautifully adorned palanquin, followed the female acrobats. A generously proportioned middle-aged nude woman sat atop the sedan chair, casually draped over the chair as it was gently lowered to the floor.

'Who's that?' Merlin asked.

'Lady Muck, a regular.'

Lady Muck alighted the human-powered transport and positioned herself on an assortment of cushions before her entourage began to fondle her, caress her, seduce her. A crowd gathered to watch the performance.

'She likes to put on a show,' Merlin commented.

'Very much so, that's her indulgence. Would you like to participate?'

'I'm an observer. I just wanted to see what goes on here.'

'Follow me, I'll give you a tour of our deadly sins suites. Something might float your boat,' Nimrod answered with a depraved grin. 'Voyeurism is high on the list for first time visitors, until they see something that piques their interest. More cheese and beer for the tour?'

Merlin chopped off a chunk of blue Camembert then grabbed another lager from the table. 'I might come back just for the food,' he joked as he dawdled after Nimrod.

'Of course you will.'

Iminka interacted with her PD as Sterling and Michael Santoro finished their lunch. Sterling's favourite restaurant, Blue Kitchen, at the entrance to the Casino Cosmopol in Kungsparken offered delicious portobello mushrooms atop steak and chips. Ideal for a chilly February day.

'Those fucking Uzbek students have opened a can of worms with their video,' Iminka complained. 'I knew we shouldn't have trusted them with the extension workaround. We should have used one of the Russian universities in Tomsk or Perm.'

'We needed guinea pigs, they served a purpose,' Sterling offered chewing his final portion of steak. 'We killed two birds with one stone. I wanted to evaluate the pinhole backend entry into the network with a small task, and the cycle extension code was the obvious choice, and both worked.'

'You said it was just a bit of fun,' she quipped. 'Fucking reckless if you ask me.'

'I didn't fucking ask you,' Sterling snapped. 'It would've been more fucking dangerous if we tested the extension code ourselves.'

'At least we wouldn't have broadcast it to the world. Now they've fixed the workaround and added an alert,' Iminka lambasted. 'Waste of fucking time.'

Santoro glanced from Sterling to Iminka. 'You sound like an old married couple,' the man of size observed as he placed his knife and fork together on his plate indicating his meal was over. 'Let's get to your apartment, I don't want to be late for the Wunderlust codester meeting and I want to discuss a few ideas with you beforehand.'

As their vehicle approached Sterling's apartment in the iconic Turning Torso building ten minutes later, Santoro couldn't help himself. 'I've always loved this building,' he drooled with admiration gazing out his window.

'Me too,' Iminka agreed, rolling her eyes at Sterling, knowing where this was heading.

'You know I own the white marble sculpture by Santiago Calatrava that inspired him to create this building,' Santoro bragged. 'Twisted torso.'

'Yes, you've mentioned that, about a dozen fucking times over the past year,' Sterling derided.

'I know, I just like to rub it in, you know, just how much money I have,' Santoro boasted with a sinister grin.

'I know exactly how much money I've made you over the past year, Michael; fucking truckloads.'

'Yes you have, Sterling, and Wunderlust Productions will make us even more.'

The streetscape bustled with naked people, young naked adults. Bright, oddly designed buildings gave the experience a cartoon-like feel that brought a smile to Liam's face. The architecture was based on Dr Seuss' illustrations from his books. Peculiar multistorey houses and buildings perched on weirdly shaped supporting beams, with external staircases, defied gravity. Not a straight line in sight. Liam's research on the experience was short and sharp. Created by the Kumar brothers, Pleasure Planet targeted university students, offering a chill space to explore their sexuality.

The unmistakable aroma of coffee and chocolate engulfed him. Liam paused to gawk along with a crowd watching a café group as they lathered each other in thick, runny coffee chocolate, licking it off each other.

'I've never seen a group event like this before,' Liam said to a young man with vivid red pubic hair.

'It's a thing, it started a few days ago,' the man replied.

'Coffeelickus it's called,' an entirely hairless woman said, looking Liam up and down. 'You a newbie?'

'A virgin you might say,' Liam smiled awkwardly, insecure in his nakedness.

'You look a little older than the usual demographic. Masters?' A woman sporting jet black hair with a platinum blonde pubic patch asked.

'Research doctorate,' Liam responded.

A bell rang in the distance. 'There's a game of Ginger Twister starting in the Pit,' the man informed Liam.

'Ginger Twister?' Liam questioned.

'You must have ginger pubes to play,' an auburn haired, hourglass-shaped girl wearing nothing but red wraparound sunglasses explained, taking his hand.

Liam scanned the small group. 'Most of your carpets don't match your curtains,' he joked.

Liam's new girlfriend handed him a can of red hair spray with a smile and pointed to his genitals. 'Want to play Twister with me?'

Liam entertained the thought of playing Ginger Twister for a few moments with his exceptionally attractive host but declined. He was here to work after all. He gave the spray can back and left them to walk over to a group of naked musicians playing in a plaza.

Liam wandered the exotic, crowded streetscapes for 20 minutes searching for anything out of the ordinary in a town of naked people seeking only one thing, pleasure. A young Asian man and woman, mutually masturbating each other on a park bench, grabbed his attention.

'It's not polite to stare,' a female voice behind him warned.

Liam turned around to a well-proportioned bronzed woman with a charismatic smile.

'Do you want to try that? I have a few minutes before I exit.'

'Erm, thanks, but I...I...I'm just looking today,' he stuttered.

'So I see,' she teased, glancing down at his semi-engorged penis. 'You seem to like what you see.' She reached out and gently took his manhood in her small hand.

Liam looked at his arm, *3 minutes 34 seconds* remaining. 'I suppose I could hand, I mean, hang around for a few minutes. What's your name?'

'More than enough time,' she smiled. 'Dalila.'

Margo picked at her fingernails while she watched the projection from her PD on the wall of the meeting room with her lawyers.

'I'm outside the newly refurbished and expanded maximum security state prison in Crescent City, California,' the reporter said. 'Where until yesterday Locky Slade, the man responsible for murdering Fundamental Purists founder and leader Jeremy Abernathy, was incarcerated. Last night, Locky Slade's body was found in a laundry skip with his throat cut. Speculation and rumour around his death have been rife. The official statement from acting warden, Stig Neumann, stated the federal Deaths in Custody Unit is investigating Slade's death. Slade is the fourth inmate to die at Pelican Bay prison in unusual circumstances in the past 12 months. Family of inmates and guards have speculated on social media that Slade was involved in prison gang infighting. Another said his death was payback for his wife speaking out about his role in the yet to be proven "organised" assassination of Jeremy Abernathy. While another rumour claimed that Slade was too outspoken about conditions in the notorious maximum security prison, initiating a hunger strike that spread throughout the prison and lasted four weeks.'

The door slid open. Selma Thurston entered the ZynnComm Sydney meeting room followed by a telepresencebot. Margo stopped the projection from her PD.

'Here you go. I'll be in my office if you need me.' Selma left the room.

'Call authorisation code required,' the telepresencebot requested.

'Call authorisation code MT941,' Margo replied.

'Holoprojection or wall screen?' The telepresencebot asked.

'Both.'

The obedient bot repositioned itself in the room and made the connection. Christine Knox and her legal entourage in Mississippi appeared across the table and on the wall monitor simultaneously. Christine was flanked by two middle-aged women and a younger man to her far right.

'Good morning. Thank you for agreeing to this meeting,' the woman on Christine's left greeted. 'My name is Penne Moreton, beside Christine is Shianne Redmond and Paul Stone.' On the wall screen, Amanda Voss could be seen sitting in the background, away from the table.

Margo leaned across to her legal counsel, Michelle Kronenberg, and whispered.

'Why is Amanda Voss in this meeting?' Michelle challenged the Mississippi group.

'Ms Voss is here for moral support; Christine requested her presence,' Shianne explained.

Margo whispered to Michelle again.

'She leaves or there will be no meeting,' Michelle stated bluntly.

'Ms Voss will not be participating in the meeting,' Shianne advised with a smile.

'Tell her to leave the fucking room or we cancel the meeting!' Margo barked.

Shianne and Penne quietly consulted behind Christine. Penne then turned to Amanda Voss and asked her to leave.

'I want her to stay,' Christine piped up defiantly, staring into the camera.

'We–' Michelle began, before Margo placed her hand on Michelle's arm.

'It's okay, Michelle,' Margo suddenly had a change of heart. 'Voss can stay.'

'Thank you,' Shianne said. 'Now, let's discuss how we can settle this before we reach the courts.'

'We have reviewed your allegations and this is pure supposition, you have no evidence to substantiate the claims made by Christine Knox,' Michelle announced. 'There will be no compensation and no public apology from Ms Tremaine. Plus, we have further information that was not forthcoming in your discovery documents.'

'What! What information?' Penne Moreton pursued with surprise.

'Quang, can you forward the file to Mississippi please,' Michelle directed her associate.

Quang tapped his tablet to send the document. 'Done.'

Time seemed to dawdle as the man in Mississippi circulated the file to screens in front of both Penne and Shianne. They skimmed the document.

'As you can see,' Michelle began, 'this is not the first time Ms Knox has had a pregnancy terminated. She has had two previous terminations, both under false names, one resulting in a so-called compensation payout. Basically extortion.'

'What happened in Christine's past isn't relevant in this case,' Shianne defended.

'There is precedence. Granted her first pregnancy and termination was the result of incest by her father, but the second was completely premeditated, not dissimilar to this case, so there is relevancy and precedence,' Michelle argued.

'Mute our mic Paul,' Shianne directed.

Penne and Shianne consulted with Christine. She listened intently to both women, her eyes flicking from one to the other as Amanda Voss approached and spoke to all three women. Their mic was unmuted.

'This is not going to play out well for you or ZynnComm in the media, Tremaine,' Amanda warned, standing behind Christine, her hands resting on her shoulders. 'It doesn't matter what Christine's life was like before you abused her fundamental human rights, violating her by maliciously removing her unborn child without her consent. That was a gross injustice. It seems to run in your family. Your father treated my husband like a common criminal which stressed his immune system, contributing to his death. I blame your father for my husband's untimely death.'

'Your husband was a first-class charlatan: his televised death was just another one of his scams,' Margo attacked. 'I'd say the bullet to his head killed your husband.'

'My husband was an honourable man, a revered man, a man who ultimately helped get your son back,' Amanda defended.

'Fuck off! I wrote that bullshit media backstory; he did nothing but whinge and whine. Abernathy was our insurance to get Hugo back unharmed. That twisted little cunt in front of you manipulated Hugo, herself brainwashed by your husband's fundamentally psycho cult. Then she breached her NDA by not keeping her mouth shut.'

'Anyone in Christine's position,' Amanda explained, 'who has been molested, raped repeatedly over many years by her own father, has deep psychological trauma, and we're working through that day by day.'

'My money is not paying for her therapy. Get her perverted father to foot the bill.'

'This isn't about money, this is about Christine claiming back her personal power, standing up to the powerful and privileged like you, Tremaine. You and her father forced Christine to do things she never wanted to do. She has been abused and now it's time for her to take back some control.'

'Fuck, she has you wrapped so tightly around her little finger it's not funny,' Margo patronised. 'Christine signed a document and accepted payment for the termination of the pregnancy. End of story. You're no stranger to terminating a child are you, Amanda? Your child would have been about Christine's age wouldn't she?'

Amanda remained silent, yet her stunned expression conveyed surprise.

'I think Christine is serving as the surrogate for your terminated child in '27. Was the father a client or an Oxford colleague?'

'You insensitive bitch. I terminated because the foetus was diagnosed with–'

'Motor neuron disease, I know, and you didn't have the time to care for a child with disability, you had a career and nothing was going to get in the way of that.'

'You know nothing about me.'

'On the contrary,' Margo held up a folder, 'we have extremely detailed intel on you, Amanda. You let nothing get in the way of your career. You and Christine are cut from the same cloth, you just went about it in different ways. Maybe you do deserve each other.'

'Fuck you! You were given everything your entire life. You were born into money; you married money and will die with money. Christine and I have had to work for everything we have, nothing was given to us.'

'Daniel Knox owns one of the leading dental practices in Sydney, Christine was never short of money. Morality and trust might have been non-existent in her life, but never money. You, Ms Voss, grew up in a working class household in Essex. Without ever having a part-time job or scholarship to get you through university, you managed to wear the best clothing labels and lead a highly active social life. Who paid for that, Amanda, or should I call you, Skye?

That was your escort pseudonym wasn't it?' She tapped the folder.
'It's all in here. I ask again, was it a client or colleague who fathered
the child? You had a large client base, so it was probably difficult
to determine. Junior lecturers at Oxford are so poorly paid, and you
had to keep up appearances.' Margo felt invigorated as the character
assassination continued. 'I remember meeting you once, early on in
Saxon's Oxford tenure. Do you remember?'

'No,' came her quick response. 'I do remember your husband as
an opinionated arsehole who was full of himself.'

Margo Laughed. 'Of course you don't. You only had eyes for
the men. We met at a faculty party. I remember commenting to
Saxon that you came across as more of a trollop than an Oxford
lecturer, fawning all over the men. You know what he told me? You
were known as the faculty bicycle. Many of the single male lecturers
had ridden you, even some of the married ones. He said you were
determined to sleep your way to the top. He had your measure, didn't
he?'

'We're not here to reminisce abou–' Shianne began.

'Shut-up!' Margo snapped. 'Your agenda, Shianne, is being
driven by Voss not Christine. You do know that, don't you? Voss is
paying your retainer. That malicious bitch is here to damage me, a
Tremaine, not help Christine. You heard her, she blames my father
for her husband's death and because she can't go after him, she's
pursuing the next best thing, me.'

'That is totally false you self-centred twat,' Amanda retorted. 'We
are here so you can admit the truth, the truth about what you did to
Christine and give her a public apology.'

Margo paused to regain her composure. 'You want the truth?
I was going to play this for Christine's benefit, to show her how
devious you are. Even sweeter with you here. How's this for a
concrete cold fact. Play the recording, Quang.'

Vision of Jeremy Abernathy, Amanda Voss and Locky Slade shot through a window appeared on the wall screen to both parties.

'Sorry about the scan and pat down, Mr Slade, but we can't be too careful,' Jeremy said. 'We have to be sure you aren't recording our meeting. We want to discuss a proposition that may sound a little weird, a little out there, but please, hear me out.'

'Turn it off,' came Amanda's small voice in the background. 'Turn it off!'

Margo gave Quang the nod and the video disappeared from screen. 'He had a mic in his glasses and the micro drone outside the window was flown by his wife. Looks like you weren't paranoid enough. We paid June Slade the fee you refused to honour in return for this recording. Money well spent. Sloppy way to tidy up loose ends, having Slade killed in prison. We just watched the story. A copy of your clandestine meeting could make the next news cycle if you want to keep pushing.'

'You are a fucking nasty piece of work, Tremaine,' Amanda spat out with spite. 'I want you to publicly apologise to Christine for your abhorrent actions.'

'There will not be a public apology,' Michelle cautioned. 'That's why we're here.'

Margo focused on Christine. 'Christine. Those three women surrounding you are still controlling what happens to you because they have an agenda. At this moment, after listening to and seeing what has transpired in this meeting, what do you honestly want?'

Christine stared directly into the camera for a long moment. 'For the past six years of my life I feel like I've been punished for something I didn't do. My life began to unravel when my father took advantage of me, to abuse me for his own pleasure. I want my father held accountable for his prolonged abuse, and my mother held accountable for being complicit, for...' tears ran down her cheeks. 'For standing by and allowing the abuse to happen year after year...and...I want an apology from you, here and now. Finally, I want all this to end. I want to stay here with Amanda and work for our community, our faith.'

'I can't do that, Christine,' Margo responded calmly. 'You agreed to terminate your pregnancy, you signed an NDA and you accepted Nukoin to do it. We have the video to prove that was your intention, which was our agreement. As far as I'm concerned, that's what you did, you terminated the pregnancy as agreed. You said in your statement that police took you from the busy street. That is your recollection, there aren't any witness statements or vision from street cameras. Nothing to corroborate your version of events. Did it really happen? If it did, perhaps your father organised it?'

'You agreed to meet me at Templeton's at eight. I didn't tell anyone about that meeting,' Christine challenged.

'I saw that in your statement,' Margo reacted. 'I didn't agree to meet you anywhere. I checked; I was in Port Augusta that evening.'

'We have PD text records stating the meeting was organised,' Penne confirmed.

'Not with me, not on my PD. I'll show you my PD text messages from that day if you like.' Margo continued without drawing breath. 'I'll tell you what I will do. I would like to help you get much more than a million Nukoin. I'll give you 50,000 Nukoin for legal expenses to prosecute your parents for the years of abuse they inflicted upon you. Make your father pay for what he did.'

Christine considered the proposal. 'Thank you, Margo,' Christine coolly replied, 'I accept your financial support.' She turned to Shianne, 'I want you to sue my parents as soon as possible.'

Amanda bent down and whispered. 'You should take some time to think about settling for Tremaine's superficial offer.'

'We can do better than this,' Shianne jumped in, clutching Christine's hand. 'You won't be allowed to speak out on this. She'll make sure of that.'

'I could make one call and shut your dream network down in minutes,' Margo threatened. 'That is the end game, you realise that.'

'On what grounds?' Shianne asked.

'Because I fucking can!' Margo retorted with a steely glare. 'Technical issues happen all the time and can take weeks to resolve. Christine, there is an NDA attached to this offer and this time you had better fucking honour it. If we see or hear anything, anything at all relating to this meeting or our agreement online or in the media, the Fundamental Purist dream network will be switched off and you lose nine million weekly subscribers. That will be on your head. Understood?'

'You won't see anything,' Christine obediently replied. She turned to Amanda. 'I think we're done here. Can we go please?'

Kris sat in his London office late on a Thursday afternoon reading through reports when his PD alarm hummed. He rolled up his left shirt sleeve exposing a tattoo of the Rod of Aesculapius accompanied by the word 'Anaphylaxis' on his inner forearm. Pulling out the narrow blood pressure ribbon cuff from the top of his PD, he ran it around his wrist and fastened it. It automatically inflated.

'Make a fist then raise and lower your arm please,' his PD instructed.

Kris followed the directions, then waited.

'Reading is 121 over 83,' his PD confirmed. 'Acceptable range. Data recorded and sent to Dr Grossman.'

The ribbon cuff deflated before Kris released it, allowing it to retract back into his PD. His PD buzzed and he read the text message from Wendy.

'*Meet in 10, link di.91.432564.UY - access code: EK9088.*'

Kris crossed his office floor embedded with a three-metre bronze disc that read, '*Somniare Aude – Dare to Dream*' and popped his head out the door. 'I'll be in a DI meeting for the next 40 minutes, Claude.'

'Sure,' his PA replied.

Kris locked his office door and made himself comfortable on the couch. He opened his custom DI device carry case and took a Thalpherycine wafer from the dispenser and placed it on his tongue. His PD buzzed, interrupting the ritual. 'Hey, Nik, I've got one more meeting then I'm outta here. I did remember we've got dinner with the Ma's tonight.'

'Gail just called, dinner's off tonight, she hasn't heard from Justin. He was supposed to fly back from Cleveland around two and she hasn't heard from him. She's worried.'

'He's usually pretty organised. Maybe something came up last minute. I have to go; I'll be home soon.' He tapped in the link and access codes.

Kris arrived first to the Dream Chamber and picked up a glass of wine.

Wendy, Saxon and Margo appeared almost simultaneously.

'Have you seen the advertising rumours circulating?' Wendy asked.

'So many rumours, so little time. Which one?' Saxon queried.

'An advertising agency has created an advertising echo squad that appears in multiple experiences tempting live echoes with real-world experiences.'

'Do they own the experiences?' Kris enquired.

'Nope. The advertising company pays developers a commission to include their spruikers in their experiences. The advertising echoes are promoting Virgin Galactic space flights, offering live echoes incentives to try it out.'

'Reverse experience exploitation,' Margo said. 'Users will be inundated with mindless advertising echoes. I'd heard some chat about this months ago. Which advertising agency?'

'Toshi Tawasaki out of Tokyo.'

Margo thought aloud. 'This might prove to be beneficial for us. We can promote our experiences as "advertising echo free zones". We'll stick with product placement.'

'Good,' Kris remarked. 'I don't want to be bombarded with damn advertising echoes and I think most people wouldn't.'

'Speaking of ad agencies, I've had Selma speak to Brigit McKenzie about her Stop Dream Violence initiative. Selma explained to her that her requests are outside our capacity to fix; Brigit wants dreams to be monitored. So, it seems Brigit's large PR network of colleagues and friends will be engaged to spread the word to recruit celebrities for her cause, expecting some government body to step in and take action.'

'Did she hint who that might be?' Saxon asked Margo.

'She didn't, but she did mention the agency she works for, Mogo, headquartered in Chicago, has some large US government accounts. Her Melbourne office has Ethan Tan's company Ethos as a long term client and she knows he's on the DI Advisory Council.'

'Good luck with that. Her request will fall on deaf ears there,' Kris assured them. 'I assume we haven't had any luck with Zen and Lena yet?' he quizzed Wendy.

'Not yet, it's early days. They've been deployed in all the known assault experiences and our Reservists are backing them up.'

'How many Reservists did you end up embedding in each experience?' Margo asked.

'It depends on the experience, but we're working on a ratio of one to every hundred users.' Wendy paused. 'I've been focusing on two previous assault cases occurring in our Vizador travel tours experience three weeks apart. Based on our last Neurocoalescence session, and several simulations, I've developed a variation on sequential encryption distortion which disrupts syntax for intermittent subroutines in Norus' deep subneural network. I've dubbed it opaque distortion interference, and guess what?'

'You've cracked it,' Kris offered in jest.

'Yes, I have,' Wendy admitted nonchalantly.

'Fuck off, I was joking,' he responded sceptically. 'Did you really get into Norus?'

'I infiltrated the DNAsafe code buffer and reached the raw DNA profiles for this one experience without anyone or any computer being the wiser.'

'Tell me you recorded your work and encrypted it?' Saxon implored, barely containing his eagerness.

'Of course.'

'Fuck yes! Well done, Wendy, fucking well done,' Kris congratulated. He raised his glass of wine. 'To Wendy,' he toasted.

The other three picked up their glasses and toasted Wendy.

'I knew there'd be a chink in the code somewhere and I was right. I've retrieved DNA profiles for all users during both assaults. I've cross referenced both instances of the experience and found 1,686 live echoes frequented both on those dates and times. Of those, 989 were eliminated because they were women. The remaining 697 males were aged between 23 and 91 years of age. Because we've already prohibited known convicted perps from DI, we can't cross reference this DNA with any real-world data. So how do we move forward?'

'This is brilliant news, Wendy, well done,' Margo praised, still getting her head around the importance of the development. 'This might be the game changer.'

'Exceptional work, Wendy,' Saxon commended. 'Now we need to work quickly; we need to duplicate this ASAP for the other experiences and get that list as small as possible before we dispatch Waylon.'

'Perhaps Waylon could make contact with the two victims on the quiet to see if there's consensus once we have that short list, with photos I mean,' Kris suggested.

'Maybe, but we need that short list. How long did this take, to get the original DNA list?' Saxon asked.

'The process took 34 hours from start to finish for a single instance of the experience,' Wendy elaborated. 'Sixty-eight hours for both instances.'

'How many assault experiences do we have to extract DNA profiles from?' Margo questioned.

'Last count was 24 extreme complaints,' Wendy said. 'I don't think we should run multiple retrievals concurrently in case we're detected. I think we should run them consecutively.'

'Agreed,' Kris approved.

'So, you've completed two, 22 more would take about a month,' Saxon calculated. 'As soon as you get back, Wendy, you need to get the process started, and keep it running in the background.'

'Will do. I'll cross reference as I go, and in theory, we should end up with our short list in a month.'

Late on Saturday night, Merlin and Arrow watched his PD waiting for coffee and pie floaters outside Harry's Café de Wheels in Port Pirie, an hour's drive south of Port Augusta.

'With the re-emergence of vintage games Grand Theft Auto, Assassin's Creed and Final Fantasy for the DI platform, today we're looking at who their target market might be and how they stack up against the big guns in DI,' the popular critic Godjoey explained. 'Jonny Fab has deemed all three titles hits in today's review for Hit or Miss which virtually guarantees them some success. Old gamers who remember these video and VR classics couldn't be the intended demographic, so who is the target audience for these gems? Having said that, there will always be diehard NBG's who'll want to revisit their gaming youth. Add to that a cutting edge immersive platform, and we have a renaissance of benchmark titles for a new generation of gamer. The company behind these classic revivals, Wunderlust Productions from Germany, acquired the DI rights to reprogram, rebuild and reimagine the titles with more sex, more violence and more action. The pedigree of Wunderlust Productions is bred from the successful duo behind Acid Spear Studios, Michael Santoro and Sterling Lindquist, responsible for the disturbing Sinnerverse network. These Wunderlust games are designed to break into mainstream markets for this pair of entrepreneurs, and let me tell you, they do not disappoint.'

'I played GTA a few days ago and it's one of the most twisted fucking games I've ever played,' Merlin commented to Arrow.

From out of nowhere, a small group of boozy troublemakers, singing and yahooing passed Merlin and Arrow, one of them knocking Merlin's PD from his hands to the ground.

'You're a small man,' Merlin barked at the sizeable scruffy guy in his late twenties.

Arrow panicked and tugged at Merlin's arm. 'Shut up, Merlin.'

'Merlin,' the thug mocked, looking around at his soused entourage. 'You a magician are you, Merlin?' He swayed closer to Merlin, towering over him. 'I think I'm slightly bigger than you, Merlin.'

'Small meaning what you've achieved in your life, arsehole.' Merlin snarled. 'You've accomplished absolutely nothing of any meaning, you've wasted your life. You won't be celebrated or missed when you're gone. You are a small, insignificant man.'

The drunk goon sluggishly processed Merlin's tirade with a confused expression, then scanned the faces of his inebriated followers. They evaded his gaze, knowing Merlin was right.

'All your friends agree with me from their body language,' Merlin goaded.

'Fuck you!' He swung his street hardened fist towards Merlin's face, but Merlin dodged the incoming knuckle sandwich.

Merlin snatched up his PD and Arrow's hand and ran towards a police cruiser pulling into the carpark.

'You are one lucky bastard,' Arrow panted through a smile.

Merlin stole a kiss from her lips. 'The main danger in life is taking too many precautions.' His belly grumbled.

'Boris needs that pie floater,' Arrow teased rubbing Merlin's tummy. 'You wait here and I'll get the food.'

Chapter Six

Wendy swung her leg over the hoverbike and started the engine. There were 3,841 other riders in this TranSprint experience instance and she was a neophyte. She waited for the signal to go, nervously re-adjusting her grip and her full-face helmet. The metal barrier in front of all riders dropped to the dirt unexpectedly, and veteran riders seized the opportunity over their competition and took off. Wendy fed her thrusters.

Dry, sparse terrain lasted for several kilometres before riders disappeared into old growth forest along well-worn tracks. Forked lightning strikes flashed as thunderclaps echoed in front of race leaders, wiping out many and sparking fires in the parched undergrowth. Wendy stuck close to the hoverbike rider in front who seemed to know what they were doing. Flames engulfed the track as her guide jammed on the throttle and accelerated through the blaze. Wendy followed with trepidation. On the other side, the landscape fell away sharply into a steep gradient with no end in sight. Wendy managed to stay upright, just keeping pace. A fluorescent magenta dust storm, fuelled by gale force winds approached at speed up the incline, reducing her vision and buffeting her bike. Two blue moons on the horizon immediately vanished in the haze.

No one had gone beyond 18 minutes 32 seconds, the current record for TranSprint. Wendy was determined to reach the 13 minute mark at least, the average for this game. The obstacles remained constant, but the order was unpredictable each time. Everything was unexpected for Wendy.

The wind eased and the grit settled, revealing a series of massive steel tunnels spread evenly across the landscape.

'Which one?' Wendy asked herself. She followed her leader into one of them. The gaping ten metre diameter pipe twisted up in gentle circles, getting narrower and narrower the higher she went. Thirteen

minutes ticked over on Wendy's dash. '*At least I'm average at this,*' she thought.

Wendy followed the incline, now barely wide enough for her crouched on the hoverbike, as a bright light engulfed her. She threw caution to the wind and trusted her gut instinct. She burst through a glimmering fluid membrane and found herself confronted by a maze of what looked to be stationary people in the distance. Her mentor, who had gained ground on her, rode into the labyrinth with confidence. Wendy needed to keep up or be left behind. She stopped abruptly, studying from afar. Left, left, right, left, left, right, left, left, right, left, left and finally left as her teacher successfully exited the muddle without hitting any human shaped obstacles. Wendy sped to the maze and entered. Left, left, right, left, left, right, but the corridor tapered. She slid into the next left corner at an angle she could not recover from and clipped the first figure, shattering it into shards of glass, propelling her and the hoverbike towards the next row of statues. Wendy's experience abruptly ended when she smashed head-first into a solid metal effigy. Game over.

'You want to try this?' Iminka said to Sterling, strutting into his office holding up a small brown nasal inhaler.

'What is it?'

'MD60.'

'That shit from Indonesia?'

'Microdreams, yep. It's fucking trippy.' She slithered up to Sterling's office chair and handed him the plastic inhaler.

'How did you get it?' He examined the unremarkable, unmarked dispenser.

'One of the codesters brought it back from her vacation in Padang.'

Sterling unscrewed the cover and went to smell it.

'Stop! One sniff and you'll be gone for 60 seconds,' Iminka warned him.

'That's all it takes?'

'One snort. That's it.'

'What was your experience like?'

'Make sure you're sitting or lying down. It knocks you out pretty much instantly. Intense ultra-vivid dreams and flashes of swirling colours like old kaleidoscopic and psychedelic thingy's, you know, films from last century, and if you're listening to music it syncs with drumbeats or guitar riffs, even people's voices.'

'Sounds interesting. Only lasts a minute?'

'Yep, 60 seconds.'

'Get someone to take it over to Gentek Pharma on Kabingatan. Tell them to ask for Kasper. I'll let him know it's coming. I want him to analyse it, I want to know what it is.' Sterling handed it back to Iminka.

'Poor man's dream phaze they're calling it. Fucking rife on the streets in Asia.'

'Highly addictive and people are overdosing on it,' Sterling added.

'They are, but come on, you have to try it at least once,' Iminka tempted, smiling down at him.

Sterling rose from his chair and took her petite face in his hands. 'You are a dangerous woman,' he whispered. Ajar, moist lips wrestled until both conceded and parted.

'Fucking dangerous.' Iminka went to leave.

'Wait,' he reached out an open hand. 'Once.'

'They have to be caramelised,' Hugo instructed, handing the onions to Margo.

'How long does this take to cook?'

'About 55 minutes to an hour, you'll love it.'

'So, you cooked this when you were in Darwin?'

'Only for myself. One of the chefs at a bistro I worked in showed me one day. It's shit easy and you don't need much, just pumpkin, onions, rosemary and pastry.'

Margo read the recipe on the screen. 'It says here we need maple syrup too.' Margo went and checked the pantry of her Sydney home. 'I don't think we have maple syrup,' she shouted.

There was no response because Hugo had heard something on the wall TV in the living room and had gone to investigate.

'We need...' Margo returned to an empty kitchen. She wandered into the living room to find Hugo watching a news report.

'...the trial of prominent Sydney dentist, Daniel Knox, who has been charged with the sexual assault of his daughter, Christine Knox, has been set down for May in the Downing Street District Court,' the reporter said. 'Heather Knox, Christine's mother, has been charged with–'

'Come on,' Margo took her son by the hand. 'Let's finish this pumpkin and onion tart. TV off.' They began to stroll back to the kitchen.

'What happened with your court case with Christine?'

Margo stopped. 'How do you know about that?'

He shrugged. 'You're one of the highest profile businesswomen on the planet. I don't know?' He mocked, dragging her by the hand back to the kitchen island.

'I thought I did a pretty good job of keeping that under wraps,' she admitted.

'Well?'

'Well, she was pressured into doing it by Amanda Voss, they didn't have a case so it didn't proceed. I offered Christine some advice, and I offered her some Nukoin to put to good use.' Margo pointed towards the living room. 'And I think she did.'

Hugo studied his mother for a moment before a smile emerged across his face. 'So, I believe we need maple syrup.'

The green spot from the laser wriggled on the wall as Saxon placed his PD on the bench beside his coffee mug. A projection of the room layout floated above his device. The measurement of *4008mm* was added to the 3D image. As he picked up his device, it buzzed; Walt was calling.

Walt's head sprung from the device. 'What are you up to?' His voice sounded surprisingly chipper.

'Just in the lab measuring up for a new piece of equipment. Happy birthday, you old bastard.'

'Thanks. No party this year, I have to take it easy. I don't feel up to it anyway,' he admitted. 'Not like last year, that was a fucking huge party.'

'Yep, it was huge, but you only turn 90 once.'

'I called because I wanted to thank you, Saxon. I wanted to thank you for Sylvia, for the reconnection. That beats any birthday party hands down.'

'That's right, you've had the experience a month now. I've been meaning to catch up with you about it. How's it going?'

'Fucking spectacular,' Walt gushed. 'It is...astonishing, awe-inspiring, fuck, it's just great to see her, feel her, smell her scent again after so long.'

Saxon grinned. 'Glad you like it. I'll pass your positive feedback on to Merlin.'

'Don't worry, Merlin knows how much I like it, I text him every second day with improvements and suggestions for future events and episodes. Merlin is my new BBF.'

'You know we have other experiences, Walt.'

'I do, but I'm happy with just one.'

'A little addicted?'

'A fucking lot addicted,' Walt brazenly admitted. 'That's not the only reason I called. Lee Jung-Lee has been given his marching orders,' he explained with a wry smile.

'That was expected.'

'It was. SkyCloud International buying in wasn't.'

'SkyCloud?' Saxon asked with surprise. 'Aren't they primarily a telco?'

'The Chinese multinational conglomerate has many tentacles. They negotiated a majority share in HBU Electronics, effectively taking them over. It won't be made public until tomorrow. Zam Chu has been redeployed to head up HBU.'

'Chu? Wasn't she heading up SkyCloud's North American division in Seattle?'

'She was, until she was recalled to Beijing yesterday and parachuted into HBU. To be honest, Chu is a fucking ruthless assassin. A businesswoman who'll do anything to win. I'm just giving you a heads up, she'll be coming after ZynnComm. She'll have to prove herself.'

'ZynnComm is privately owned between us, and we aren't selling,' Saxon assured him. 'And I hope you aren't either, Walt.'

'The board is standing firm. We aren't selling.'

'We own a few percent of HBU shares now. I'm surprised we weren't told about the takeover.'

'As do we, but nowhere near enough. SkyCloud did a deal behind closed doors with institutional shareholders, paid 12 percent above market value. If you thought Tremaine's pockets were deep, we're a pimple on SkyCloud's prick. Chu thinks outside the box, it's not all about business. She's ousted the executive management team and brought in her own people. My inside man has been given his marching orders.' Walt warned. 'Hang on.' He was distracted by offscreen chatter. 'Got to go, talk later.' Walt's image disintegrated.

Saxon thought about the SkyCloud International deal for a brief moment before his research assistant exited the elevator and trotted down the stairs.

'It's on its way up from engineering,' the clean-cut, 20-something man announced, heading straight to the goods elevator on the opposite side of the lab. Dixon Tarantola looked back at Saxon. 'Are you sure about where you want to put it?'

Saxon placed his PD on the bench and picked up his coffee mug. 'Yes. I've measured up and it fits perfectly now the third sleep pod has gone.' Saxon took a sip of coffee.

Dixon watched Saxon as he waited for the elevator to arrive. 'Wendy said I should ask you about the coffee coaster on your desk. She said it was an inspiring story.'

Saxon chuckled. 'Did she?'

Vincent Spencer left his New York office building and walked towards 14th Street Station. Spencer was a thin, stylish man in his mid-forties with silver grey hair. He was a leader, a clandestine leader. Looking at him, you would never guess where his motivations and allegiances lurked. For several years he has been the power behind United Storm Front.

As Spencer rounded the corner, a red RoboDrive branded taxi van pulled up at the kerb. The door slid open and a golden-haired man yelled, 'Vincent!'

Spencer didn't stop, he merely glanced at the man.

'Vincent!' came the call again. 'Shane sent me to get you,' he said with a slight European English accent and wide grin. 'Come on, get in.'

Spencer stopped and scrutinised the man. 'Do I know you?'

'Sorry, I'm Gerry, an associate of Shane's. He sent me to get you. Didn't he contact you? He's putting on birthday drinks at his place tonight.'

At that moment, a text from Shane McHawk, the USF Operations Commander, appeared on Spencer's PD. '*Sending Gerry to collect you for birthday drinks.*' Spencer strolled over to the taxi and held up his PD. 'Got it.' He prudently scanned the taxi as Gerry slid across seats. Spencer got in beside Gerry, placing his briefcase on the seat opposite. 'Well, let's get this party started.'

'Taxi, 345 South End Avenue, play music, cabin privacy,' Gerry ordered.

As the door slid shut, loud techno music flooded the vehicle and the side cabin windows tinted.

Spencer studied Gerry for a moment. 'Your face looks familiar,' his voice raised to be heard. 'Are you in the insurance game?'

'No, no I'm not. I play Hunters and Collectors in DI, like you.'

Spencer's expression turned frosty. 'I have no idea what you're talking about,' he hissed through stained teeth.

'You are Hunter One. Happy birthday, Vincent,' Gerry congratulated taking out a sizeable hunting knife. 'Here's your birthday present. The same kind of knife that killed Justin Ma.' He ran his finger along the stainless steel knife-edge before thrusting it into Spencer's left thigh, severing his femoral artery.

'Fuuuck!' Spencer yelled, hitting Gerry in the head.

Gerry jerked the blade left and right. Spencer's screams synchronised with Gerry's blade torture. 'Be still or I'll keep twisting!'

Spencer stopped immediately, heaving deep breathes.

Gerry grabbed Spencer's left hand and held it on the wound before he withdrew the knife. 'Keep pressure on it.'

'What the fuck?' Spencer bellowed, pulling at the door handle with his free hand trying to escape the vehicle.

'The door won't open while the vehicle is moving, Vince.'

Spencer grabbed his briefcase and slammed it into Gerry's face.

Gerry delivered a fracturing punch to Spencer's nose, dazing him. Gerry felt his lip and spotted blood on his fingers. 'You have between four and five minutes before you bleed out...or I can get you to a hospital and save your life. But first, I want you to admit your role in the murder of Justin Ma.'

'Fuck you,' Spencer slurred, struggling to find his PD in his jacket pocket. 'Shane will fucking hunt you down and gut you.'

Gerry grabbed the PD from Spencer's bloody hand and threw it in the front seat. 'Fat fuck Hunter Two, Shane McHawk, has been dead for hours,' Gerry responded with a smile. 'Okay, be like that.' He knifed Spencer in the lower abdomen cutting his common iliac artery.

Gerry texted his associate Hadwin. '*On our way.*'

Thirty minutes later, the RoboDrive taxi stopped at a non-descript warehouse in Brooklyn. The roller door opened and the vehicle entered.

Gerry dragged Vincent Spencer's limp corpse unceremoniously from the taxi by one leg, his head thumping the concrete floor. 'Grab his shoulders.'

'Problems?' Hadwin probed, looking at Gerry's swollen lip.

'Mosquito bite,' he deflected. 'Concrete ready?' he asked, looking at the mixer.

'Ready to go.' Wire-framed Hadwin grabbed Spencer's shoulders and they carried him to the edge of a large black plastic sheet.

Carefully, they rolled the body up in the plastic. Gerry grabbed a heat gun and proceeded to shrink the plastic around the body. The pair carried the snug cocoon over to timber formwork for a substantial concrete slab. Another black chrysalid was already waiting. They placed Spencer's casing on the sheet of steel reinforcing mesh a metre from the other. Both bodies were suspended off the floor inside the frame. Prefabricated rebar mesh footing cages were placed between the cocoons, and one on the outside of each. Hadwin and Gerry methodically wired the cages to the bottom mesh sheet. A final steel mesh layer was placed across the entire top of the formwork and wired to all three cages beneath. Finally, four bent loop lifting anchors were wired in place.

Gerry positioned himself with the concrete vibrator in one hand and the other directing the concrete delivery chute. He gave Hadwin a nod to lower the concrete mixer to start the process. The timber formwork filled in less than a minute. 'Screed it,' Gerry instructed. 'I'll start cleaning their PDs. When's the courier here?'

Hadwin checked his watch. 'In 15.'

'Okay, I'll clean Spencer's PD first. Where's McHawk's?'

Hadwin pointed to the top of the steel drum. 'I'll start rebirthing the vehicle once I've finished here,' he said. 'Which stamp do you want to use to finish the plinth?'

Gerry thought for a moment. 'The lotus flower.'

'Of course.' Hadwin began to meticulously screed the concrete smooth.

'About time,' Wendy snapped at Kris.

'Sorry. Just us today?'

'Both are tied up with meetings they couldn't move.'

Kris observed the Dream Chamber environment with a frown. 'What have you done to the experience?'

'I wondered if you'd notice,' Wendy replied with a proud expression.

'Of course I noticed, the sand has changed colour, and that smell...' he sniffed enthusiastically. 'Aniseed?'

'Liquorice sand.'

'Can I eat it?'

Wendy didn't hesitate. 'Taste it,' she urged.

Kris lent down and pinched up a small quantity of sand and put it in his mouth. 'Arghh, fuck!' He abruptly spat out the grains. 'It's just sand.' He kept spitting, before grabbing his wine glass. He swished the wine around and spat it, then repeated the cleansing. 'Ahhh.'

Wendy almost wet herself with laughter. 'Yes it is, Merlin,' she eventually managed. 'Wait till I tell Merlin about this. I pranked the great Kris Kilroy.'

Kris drank his wine. 'When you least expect it, expect it,' Kris warned in a low voice delivering a stink eye.

Wendy regained her composure. 'Hey, I learnt from the best. You told me it's the underplaying of the prank that sucks fools in. Okay, I've got three more names on our list, still working on the others. These frequented all assault experiences. I'll keep monitoring all profiles for DI activity against complaints until we pinpoint Griffin.'

'That's excellent, Wendy. We need to check all profiles with DNA databases, public and private.'

'Already checked most of the largest public databases, got cold hits on two profiles.'

'How do you know what a cold hit is?' Kris asked.

'I've watched my share of police forensic shows. I have names and last known addresses for those two. I have a photo and current location for another from a medical database. Waylon will have to search other databases. Then he can track them down to get a DNA confirmation. I've also run these profiles through our DNA sequencer. All have black hair and are Caucasian, which fits our very basic description.'

'If that's their correct skin colour. I don't think we can rely on that at all,' Kris warned. 'If we have names, we may be able to pinpoint their DI ISP point of presence locations.'

'Agreed. I'll pass this info onto Saxon and he can get the ball rolling with Waylon.'

In the Thaylean Bur region of space, located in the star dense Scutum–Centaurus Arm of the Milky Way, the Moojhan millennial war raged between multiple species. GalNexus was inhabited by a multitude of bizarre and aggressive lifeforms, the deadliest known as Species HB73. A technological civilisation of habitual liars with a complex hierarchical military structure. They ranked as the most advanced and ruthless antagonists within the charted galaxy.

The spider-like creature ambushed Merlin as he cautiously raised his head through a deck hatch. In a flash, Species HB73 discharged a purple wax-like compound at high velocity from its elephantine nasal cavity, coating the right side of Merlin's head as he turned away. His face immediately ballooned, resembling the most severe anaphylactic reaction.

'You fucking nerkle!' Merlin screamed as he melted three of his attacker's legs with his Griz-L-gun. That gave Merlin enough time to scurry back down the ladder. Species HB73 possessed fast regenerative abilities, its replacement legs began to grow almost immediately. Merlin tapped his comms earphone. 'I've got about a minute before I exit, the fucker snuzed me.'

'Get up here and help me!' Liam shouted into his ear.

Merlin staggered along a series of corridors and up another ladder to the engineering deck to find Liam cowering beneath two oversized arachnid Species HB73 bugs.

'Stand down, Commander,' the baritone voice from the larger creature instructed Merlin. 'Stand down, or he dies.'

'My head is killing me,' Merlin admitted, clutching the throbbing gristle his distorted head had become. Only able to see out of one eye, unsteadily pointing his Griz-L-gun in the other hand, he lost balance and fell against a control console.

Without notice, the smaller of the two aliens pinned Liam down. It positioned one limb with a narrow rotating appendage into his right nostril and methodically drilled up into his head. Liam screamed and writhed in pain, lasting only moments, as he escaped in a red haze.

Zen, accompanied by Tristan Grazer, arrived as Merlin collapsed to the floor. Zen sprayed each foe with micromites mist from her backpack cannister. The millions of miniscule predators instantly clung to their prey and went straight to work devouring both Species HB73 alive.

'Morris,' Merlin whispered loud enough for Zen and Tristan to hear.

Tristan Grazer immediately broke into enthusiastic Morris dancing, kicking, leaping and spinning, which brought a brief but satisfied grin to Merlin's misshapen face as he disintegrated.

Waylon Devereux sat in Margo and Saxon's residence in Port Augusta, his tablet device mirrored on the wall screen in the living room. With multiple windows open, he searched public and secure DNA databases worldwide, endeavouring to locate the men on the list Saxon had provided. DNA records for the men were found and plotted on a map.

Margo exited the elevator and walked over to Waylon. 'Made any progress?'

'Confirmed the five, profiling two of them now.'

'That's great news.' She sat beside him on the luxurious leather couch studying the information vista on the wall. 'Now what?'

'The information in these databases is the starting point. I need to collate names with countries, addresses, occupations and cross reference with relatives if I need to. Once I confirm all that, this information builds the basic profile to proceed.'

'How long will that take?'

'I've got a pretty detailed profile for these two already.' Waylon brought up photos of two ordinary looking men on screen. 'Based on their browser fingerprint, I know their PD brand, screen size, browser version, which apps they've downloaded, etcetera. Their social media profile has been fed into a Justann psychosocial algorithmic compiler, giving me their interests, hobbies, shopping habits and friends, even their general disposition. Neither has a police record. I've cross referenced their PD GPS signatures with ISP providers to locate their point of presence logons for their DI devices too.' Waylon pointed at the wall. 'The guy on the left, Ingmar Larsson, is a schoolteacher living with bouts of severe depression in Karlstad, Sweden. The one on the right, Enrique Garcia Vega, has narcissistic tendencies, is a police officer and he lives in Madrid.'

'When can you follow these two up?' Margo asked.

'I'll fly back to Sydney this afternoon. I fly to Spain tonight then to Sweden from there.'

'So, we might have DNA confirmation within days?'

'I certainly hope so.' Waylon glanced at the time on his tablet. 'I'd better makes tracks.'

'I'll tell Saxon the good news.'

'You sure you don't want to tell me why I'm collecting DNA from these men?' Waylon fished.

Margo searched for the right words. 'Because we trust you, Waylon. You have to trust us that there is nothing sinister in the assignment. The less you know now, the better.'

Waylon studied Margo for a moment. 'Okay. I'll be going.'

A frosty spring morning had steadily grown into a pleasant day by 11 a.m. Kris and Nikola walked past a media van covering the event. Kris did a double take and stopped when he recognised Hunter One's face from the Hunters and Collectors experience on a screen inside the broadcast van.

'What's wrong?' Nikola queried, stopping to wait for him.

A reporter, a few metres away, delivered to camera. Kris placed his index finger to his lips, signalling her silence, then pointed to the reporter.

'...businessman Vincent Spencer, CEO of Sundown Insurance here in New York, has been identified as a person of interest in the murder of Justin Ma. An anonymous source has told Murdoch Media, authorities can't locate Spencer. Spencer, described as a solitary, private individual, is said to be behind the website United Storm Front, a loose collective of white supremacist affiliates, including the notorious Aryan Crusaders and National Offensive linked to right-wing terrorism and vigilantism. Justin Ma, a prominent lawyer with the National Asian American Alliance, who is being honoured today at a dedication service at Willets Point Community College, was a fierce opponent of the USF website and was responsible for getting it taken down two months ago. John, back to you in the studio.'

'Come on, or we'll be late,' Nikola insisted, pulling Kris' arm.

Kris' mind raced as he obediently sidled up beside Nikola. Vincent Spencer, AKA Hunter One, has gone to ground in the real world and is linked to his friend Justin's death.

They walked towards the service podium near the entrance to the college when Kris locked eyes with a tall blonde man some distance away. The hairs on the back of his neck bristled as memories of the Hunters and Collectors experience washed through his head for the second time in quick succession. Kris strode towards the man with purpose, dodging and pushing people out of the way.

'Kris! Where are you going?' Nikola called, bewildered.

The blonde man took off, melting into the densest part of the crowd.

Kris pursued, standing on his toes to see above the throng. He didn't see the blonde man disappear down a stairway leading to a car park. Kris stood on a bench searching the gathering, until he spotted Nikola on the podium with Gail, Justin's widow, preparing for the unveiling ceremony. Reluctantly, he surrendered his quest for the blonde man. Kris joined Nikola and Gail for the formalities to uncover the bronze bas relief sculpture of Justin Ma, atop a substantial concrete plinth brandishing a lotus flower.

Walt's EA, James Hood, entered Walt's home office. 'Zam Chu has contacted your office and requested a meeting, Walt.'

Walt considered James for a moment. 'Wait.' He brought up the K-Metrics app on his PD, then held his thumb on the sensor pad. 'Can't Alfred handle it?'

'She has requested a meeting with you personally.'

'Kilojoule count is 2600,' his app informed him. '6100 kilojoules remaining.'

'When?' Walt asked.

'She's waiting.'

He threw his PD on the desk. 'Now! Fuck her. Tell her to call back in ten minutes. Get Alfred for me.'

'Yes, sir.' James left the office and closed the door.

Moments later, the telepresencebot rolled into place and Alfred was beamed into Walt's office.

'How are you, Alfred?'

'Well thank you, Walt. Yourself?'

'Not eating enough apparently, don't have an appetite. Zam Chu wants a meeting. What do you think she wants?'

'The same as Jung-Lee wanted, our ZynnComm stock.'

'I suppose so.' Walt paused. 'Do we want to take the call?'

'We should be cognisant of HBU's intentions,' Alfred advised.

'True, best to get it straight from the horse's mouth,' Walt agreed. 'Hang around, I'll get her back on the line.' Walt tapped his PD. 'James, get her back on the phone.'

'Yes, sir.'

'How's the board going?' Walt enquired. 'Faversham still being a pain in the arse?'

'Faversham is still...' Alfred chose his words wisely, 'trying to be the centre of attention in your absence.'

'I hope you're keeping him on a short leash.'

'Always, Walt, always.'

'Zam Chu on office audio, sir,' James announced.

'Hello, Mr Tremaine?' The female American voice queried.

'That you, Zam Chu?'

'Yes, sir. Thank you for returning my call.'

'What can I do for you, Zam?'

'Straight to the point, I like that,' Zam Chu sweet-talked.

Walt rolled his eyes at Alfred. 'That may be the last thing you like, Zam'

'Mr Tremaine, HBU is still very interested in acquiring the Tremaine Group's share of Zynn Communications. Are you open to listening to my proposal?'

'It can't hurt. Give it your best shot,' Walt encouraged.

'Thank you. We want to support your venture in Djibouti, specifically, your La Noor proposal in the northeast–'

'How the fuck do you know La Noor?' Walt gruffly interjected.

Alfred gave Walt a confused look.

'Due diligence, Mr Tremaine. Investment in Djibouti is gaining momentum, and you, Mr Tremaine, have a knack for having your finger on the pulse when it comes to shrewd investments. Tremaine's hydrogen production projects over the past 20 years in Africa are a testimony to that. But I believe you're facing some stiff opposition from certain political factions within the Djibouti government, holding your project back.'

'Nothing we haven't encountered before, Zam,' Walt replied in a confident tone. 'Why? What are you proposing?'

'HBU has influence in Djibouti. We have recently signed a 20-year agreement for communication infrastructure with the government. We could go into bat for you with the government and lobby for the project to get it over the line. Reciprocally, we will generously offer 250 billion Nukoin for your ZynnComm stock and take it off your hands.'

'That's a tidy sum, Zam.' Walt raised his untamed eyebrows at Alfred.

'That's a win-win for both of us. With an expanding infrastructure and growing demand for energy in that region, we estimate the La Noor facility has the potential to earn five to seven billion Nukoin per annum when fully operational,' Zam Chu asserted.

'You have done your sums, Zam. That sounds about right.' Walt paused for effect.

'Are you still there, Mr Tremaine?'

'Yes, Zam, I am. Tell me, what does a corporation, a conglomerate like SkyCloud International want with yet another electronics company like HBU? Why didn't SkyCloud come directly to us and pitch for ZynnComm? I don't understand the strategy behind it.' The dead air on the other end of the line hung longer than it should have, making Walt feel uneasy.

'SkyCloud International has many subsidiaries, not unlike Tremaine, just on a larger scale. HBU dominates a significant percentage of the electronics sector and also operates several affiliate companies, on par with the Tremaine Group, and we think

ZynnComm would be a better fit under our umbrella, than the mother company.'

'Fair enough,' Walt concurred. 'Thanks, but we'll pass at this point in time, Zam.'

'Will your Tremaine Group Board at least consider our proposal?' Zam pressed, with a hint of expectation in her voice.

'Nope.' Walt disconnected. 'They're fucking hungry,' he said to Alfred.

'Indubitably.'

Chapter Seven

Merlin stood on the highest point he could find, gazing towards the horizon. Twisted, entangled, junk metal piled high, stretched for as far as he could see. Cars, farm equipment, aircraft parts, building girders, industrial machinery, sections of cargo vessels, trucks, scaffolding, you name it, it was here in Metal Maze. He caught glimpses of people working their way over, under, through the junk yard in an effort to reach the major prize. The aim was to get from one end to the other in 30 minutes, with sponsored 'Easter eggs' containing shortcuts to incentivise and motivate players, to find the Vermilion Crystal Chest valued at 10,000 Nukoin. The game was only in its fourth week, yet already proved to be one of the most popular among 20-somethings craving the significant reward for what seemed like minimal effort.

Merlin made his way down from his vantage point, clamouring over oxidised blades of a submarine propeller when he heard the skin tingling screech of rusted metal surfaces sluggishly scrapping against each other in the distance, followed by an almighty crash, ending with distressing screams. He checked his time, *29 minutes remaining*.

A woman suddenly appeared behind him. 'Get out of the fucking way! Move! Move! Move!'

Merlin stepped aside just in time so he wasn't pushed into a metal chasm. 'Take it easy.'

'Fuck off, newbie. Get out of my way.' She scampered ahead of him at pace, leaping then swinging from loose metal cables hanging from an elevator car. The flat sheet metal she landed on immediately gave way and she fell into a pit of razor wire, writhing and screaming.

Merlin smiled to himself, deciding to take his time. He observed others as they navigated the course and cautiously followed the ones who seemed to know what they were doing, to see if there was method to the madness.

Waylon stood outside an apartment block in the Adriatic coastal town of Ortona, Italy, waiting. This was his ninth trip to gather DNA from suspects. His two previous trips to the USA and Poland proved fruitless for the Division Four team, as were all his efforts to date.

Anton Alfonso exited his apartment building along the path to the street and turned left. Waylon slipped on the DNA collection glove and approached Anton from across the street.

'Scusi, da che parte è Via dell'Oratorio?' Waylon asked.

Anton stopped, considered the African American before answering. He pointed. 'Alla fine di Via Medina, girare a destra.'

Waylon looked in the direction he was pointing. 'Grazie, grazie,' he said, offering his hand to shake.

Anton happily raised his hand and shook.

Back in his hotel room, Waylon placed a sealed plastic bag containing the DNA glove inside his suitcase. His PD buzzed; it was Saxon.

Minutes later, Waylon was sitting in the Dream Chamber experience with Saxon, Margo, Wendy and Kris.

'Thanks for coming at such short notice, Waylon,' Saxon acknowledged. 'Just a quick reminder that anything said here, remains here.'

'Where is here?' Waylon quizzed, looking around the barren landscape.

'This is the Dream Chamber,' Wendy told him. 'This is a private experience and only we know of its existence.'

'I was about to leave for the airport, on my way back.'

'Did you get it?' Saxon questioned.

'I did,' he responded, surveying the group, assessing up why he was summoned.

Margo passed him a glass of wine. 'You asked me why we wanted you to collect DNA samples from these men.' Waylon accepted the glass as he listened.

'We have a problem,' Saxon began, 'an in-dream problem and we're struggling to make any head way. The DNA samples you collected were from men we thought might be responsible for rapes and murders in White or Yellow experiences.'

'Those men, based on their DNA samples, have been banned from the platform, yet the rapes and murders continue,' Wendy added.

'We need someone to monitor in-dream, someone to shadow a couple of elevated echoes who are duplicated across multiple experiences and instances,' Saxon continued. 'They are our bait to catch Griffin.'

'Griffin? So, you know his name,' Waylon noted.

'No,' Kris responded. 'It's just a name we gave him so the four of us know who we're talking about. Unfortunately, we have no fucking idea who this prick is.'

'Are you sure it's just one man?'

'Yes. He is very clinical, very methodical,' Wendy offered.

'Does this have anything to do with the Stop Dream Violence movement?' Waylon asked.

'Yes,' Margo answered. 'We're trying to catch Griffin, but something is eluding us, we need skilled eyes and ears in experiences.'

'How do you know which experience or instance he'll be in next?' Waylon probed.

'We think we may have found a loose pattern emerging,' Kris explained.

'So, you've collated when the suspects' DI devices were used and when their DNA appeared in experiences on the platform?'

The group looked at one another a little puzzled. 'If the DI device is used, their DNA will automatically correspond in the system,' Wendy clarified.

'Have you done it?' Waylon pressed the point. 'Have you correlated the time of use in the real world for DI devices with their DNA in the experiences where the murders have occurred?'

'Forgive me, I'm a little confused,' Kris admitted. 'If their DNA is registered in the experience, then their DI devices must also be timestamped at that time.'

'That would stand to reason, but have you checked that's the case?'

Wendy and Kris looked at each other. 'No,' they both answered.

'I don't see your point, Waylon?' Saxon quizzed. 'Griffin would be using a VPDN.'

'I'm sure he would, but I'm not talking about concealing his location. I know this might seem like an unnecessary minor point, almost redundant, but what if a suspect's DNA has appeared in whatever experience, yet you find that their DI device wasn't used at that particular time in the real world?'

'How could that happen?' Margo asked incredulously.

'We've had uni students extending their experience cycles with a workaround. I may have just wasted the past month travelling the world collecting DNA. What if your perp, Griffin, has collected and replicated DNA, and has somehow fooled his DI device?'

'Fuck me,' Kris muttered under his breath. 'Waylon has a point. We've never thought about it from that angle.'

'Is that even possible?' Margo enquired.

A thought struck Saxon like a cold chisel driven into the back of his head. 'I'm loathe to say it, but yes,' he confessed. 'Amplify enough DNA cells, and you have enough to grow or bioprint functional skin for the forearm where the DI device sits.'

The small group pondered the implications of Waylon's scenario for a few moments.

'That wouldn't be easy, he'd need specialised equipment and skills,' Kris offered.

'True, but it could be done,' Saxon added. 'We need to reproduce this in the lab ASAP.'

'How could we miss this approach?' Kris wondered.

'Probably my fault,' Wendy admitted. 'I thought the DNA on file would be the logical starting point because he'd be using a VPDN to hide on the network. I under analysed and missed the obvious.'

'I wouldn't say this possibility is obvious, Wendy,' Saxon insisted. 'As Kris said, he would need specialised equipment and skills; a chemistry and biotechnology background.'

'So, it's not something just anyone could set-up in their garage or spare room?' Margo reasoned.

'I'm not ruling anything out,' Saxon assured the team. 'In hindsight, we should have done our due diligence and scrutinised both front and back ends of the process for all possibilities.'

'Okay, so there could be other reasons why we can't pin Griffin down,' Margo came back to the reason they were there. 'I still think we need Waylon in an experience Griffin might target next.'

'Of course,' Wendy agreed. 'We've run the numbers and we have three experiences where Griffin might strike in coming days.'

Zen and Lena made their way to the entrance for the ride. Waylon shadowed them 20 metres back. The ultra-high speed corkscrew rollercoaster experience, Dreamlooper, that hurtled more than a kilometre underground and a kilometre into the clouds was consistently in the top ten White rated experiences for the sheer exhilaration.

As Zen passed by an ajar service door for the ride, an arm shot out, grabbed her upper arm and reefed her into the stairwell. Lena was shut out as the door clicked closed and self-locked. Lena struggled with the door handle, pressing the security keypad multiple times before she withdrew a Griz-L-gun from under her jacket and silently melted a hole in the door beside the handle. She reached through and opened the door. In the unlit stairwell Zen and her captor were gone. Lena listened. She heard muffled screams echo from below, so she scrambled down the stairs. She saw Zen with her hands bound behind her back. A man, with his back to her in a black hoodie, whispered in Zen's ear.

'I love you, Janet,' Zen answered quietly.

'Get away from her!' Lena screamed, pointing her weapon at the man.

As the perpetrator spun around, he squirted pepper spray in her face. Lena momentarily recoiled, rubbing her eyes. She tossed her weapon and launched herself at the man and knocked him to the ground. Lena blindly punched, but the man took advantage of her compromised sense and pushed her off. He stood up, kicked Lena hard in the abdomen, pulled his hood over his head and exited the stairwell out another door.

'Are you okay?' Waylon asked as he arrived at the scene. He immediately cut the

zip tie handcuffs from around Zen's wrists. 'I saw what happened and came as fast as I could.'

'He went out...the door,' Lena panted, holding her stomach and sniffing, blinking madly through watery eyes. 'He's wearing a black hoodie.'

Waylon glanced at his forearm, *28 minutes remaining*. He left them.

Kris watched a news feed on his PD as he waited for all the members of the second Dream Immersion Advisory Council meeting to arrive. He adjusted the volume on his earfonic.

'Ex-fiancé of singer-songwriter Jed Gentry, Jasmine Le Serve, was found dead in her London apartment last night,' the news anchor reported. 'A time delayed social media post across several platforms left by Ms Le Serve stated she had never gotten over her relationship with Jed Gentry. Every time she heard his Grammy award winning song, Without You, written about her, she suffered bouts of depression. Jed Gentry was left at the alter by Ms Le Serve when she failed to show up on the afternoon of their wedding in July 2045. Her successful early career as the creative director and lead puppeteer for the innovative Giant Baby Marionette Theatre Company had all but faded in recent times as addiction, followed by multiple rehab admissions, took its toll. Jed Gentry has not commented at this time.'

'In other news, the Organic Dream Alliance has joined forces with the Fundamental Purists to lobby the International Psychotherapy Association for DITS, dream immersion trauma syndrome, to be recognised as a legitimate disorder and–'

'Good morning, Kris,' Ethan Tan greeted as he sat down opposite him. 'Morning, Jorma.'

Jorma Despirito nodded and smiled from the other end of the conference table.

Kris removed his earfonic and lowered his PD. 'How are you, Ethan?'

'I hate this weather,' he responded, removing his tablet device from his briefcase and placed it on the table. 'It was 20 degrees when we left Melbourne. Thirty-nine is too hot.'

'You must get the odd hot day in Melbourne,' Kris baited. 'It's not all rain and gloom.'

'We get our fair share of heat,' he countered with a grin, 'but we were just acclimatising to the cooler weather. My wife remarked that this weather just smacks you in the face as you get off the aircraft, and it does.'

'I'm with you, Ethan,' Jorma jumped in. 'I couldn't live in this climate. Give me rain and snow any day.'

'By the way, Ethan, Saxon wants me to set up a casual dinner meeting to discuss our revised procurement procedure and the upcoming Ethos contract renewal,' Kris said. 'We want to see if you can sharpen your pencil on your manufacturing costs,' he added sardonically.

Ethan snorted a small laugh. 'Not likely with rare-earth prices the way they are. I'll be in Florida for the next few days, diving a pirate wreck off the east coast. I'll be back in Australia next week.'

'Margo and Nikola will be coming, so bring Grace.'

'Send me some dates and I'll ask Grace to sort it out and I'll get back to you.' He took a Spacestix bar from his briefcase.

The conversation paused as Justine Vanderberg entered the room and sat beside Ethan. 'Good morning.'

A smattering of greetings ricocheted around the meeting room in Surat as the remaining members arrived. Pleasantries were short and sweet as the meeting got underway. Kris briefly reported on the number of DI units sold since their last gathering, and positive research from several reputable universities and institutions around the impact of the technology on certain demographics.

'You haven't mentioned dream immersion trauma syndrome in your roundup,' Justine challenged.

'The DITS numbers are very low in comparison to the number of users,' Kris responded matter-of-factly.

'What is being done to address the problem?' Justine followed up.

'Saxon is working with a team of psychotherapists, including Winston and his team, on finding a DI solution for PTSD, and that in turn could be useful for DITS. Do you want to elaborate on your work, Winston?'

'As Kris said, the numbers are quite small given the volume of use across the platform. Having said that, we have begun trials with test groups. Nothing I can report on yet.'

'There are fringe groups and civil libertarians exploiting the media, pushing for transparency,' Kris offered, 'which ultimately requires everyone to be tracked in DI. I don't think the majority of users would wear that; people want privacy in their dreams.'

'I'm with Kris on this, privacy has to be preserved,' Ethan agreed. 'The entire platform was built with that premise in mind, user privacy.'

'At what cost?' Justine challenged. 'Female users are still being attacked and killed.'

'I've been lobbied by the Central African Republic government,' Kit Bombo reported. 'Before they permit the DI platform in their country, they want the platform to be more transparent. They want to see where their citizens are in DI.'

'Why doesn't that surprise me,' Kris remarked in a condescending tone. 'Of course they do, they have an agenda. They'll be waiting a long time 'cause it ain't gonna happen.'

'What if we had an opt-in option for users? Users choose whether they are monitored?' Kit put forward.

'Would you opt-in to be monitored during dream immersion?' Kris asked Kit.

Kit glanced around the room at everyone. 'Possibly,' came his less then convincing response. 'In White or Yellow rated experiences I would.'

'We could introduce it in White rated only, where the incidents are taking place,' Jorma suggested.

'I doubt the majority would want to be tracked,' Kris decided. 'From whatever perspective you want to look at it, we can't ethically, legally or technically monitor an individual in-dream.'

'The evil bastards inflicting this grief are not going to opt-in to be tracked, and they are the ones we specifically want to track,' Ethan surmised, already busy crafting his chalice from Spacestix foil.

'There's no way to monitor anyone, anywhere in DI?' Justine cross-examined Kris.

'No, the platform isn't built for monitoring individuals. That would require a major overhaul, years of reconfiguration and new government agreements from every country that currently accesses the platform to abandon privacy laws,' Kris explained.

'Impossible,' Ethan added.

'And who picks up the tab for that?' Kris queried. 'It won't be ZynnComm I can tell you that much.'

'So, we come back to the proposition of an in-dream security force,' Kit said.

'Under whose jurisdiction?' Ethan pressed, growing weary of the conversation. 'We've been over this—'

'Us,' came Kit's quick reply.

'Us?' Kris questioned with a look of confusion. 'We are an advisory body, we have no authority, we have no power.'

'Well,' Kit began, 'I've had some informal discussions with several associates and they seem to think we could lobby certain UN bodies for endorsement to establish a collective security body.'

'You can't be fucking serious, Kit!' Ethan snapped. 'That was never the intent of this group. That's completely outside our scope of reference. We are not here to fucking police DI experiences!' Ethan stressed, looking around the table at everyone. 'We agreed our purpose was to maintain user privacy, not police experiences.'

'Granted the authority,' Kit continued, unfazed by Ethan's outburst, 'we could create a neutral security force without borders to maintain law and order in White rated experiences,' Kit explained.

'Whose laws would we enforce, Kit? UN Police mandates? US, UK, EU laws?' Kris challenged. 'It would be a political cluster fuck! Besides, there is no disorder in dream immersion, there are isolated incidents, full-stop. I know this is difficult, but–'

'No single body should have policing power,' Ethan reinforced. He slid his finished foil chalice towards Justine. 'For you.'

Justine was bemused. 'At present, we are an advisory body, but we could lobby to be mandated to establish jurisdiction with authority. Kit could write our constitution,' Justine rallied in support of Kit's suggestion.

'We are not here to police DI,' Kris reiterated.

'The idea has been floated that the platform should become a public utility,' Jorma offered. 'If that were the case, we could preside over a borderless security force.'

'What? Where did you hear that?' Kris asked in astonishment.

'Global Times had a story yesterday,' Jorma began, 'and–'

'The fucking Global Times! Propaganda sprouted by SkyCloud International because the Tremaine Group won't sell their ZynnComm shares to HBU. That's not going to happen,' Kris assured the group. 'They're trying their hardest to disrupt the platform to benefit themselves.' Kris paused to rein in his emotion. 'Over the past weeks, SkyCloud has denied claims of disrupting our DI platform. As you are all aware, they own the network infrastructure serving greater Asia. Just last week that network suddenly went offline for 16 hours. No one we have spoken to can verify the cause. Now this story appears in the Global Times calling for the platform to become a public utility. Arseholes.'

'As the honorary chairperson, given the low numbers for DITS, and that work is being done on how to support those women, I think we maintain the status quo and move on to other topics,' Ethan suggested.

'There is a ground swell against dream violence in general experiences and it won't go away with a little therapy. Stop Dream Violence rallies are being organised as we speak,' Justine said.

'You're marching?' Kris assumed of Justine.

Justine gave him a contemptuous glare. 'I will be supporting them, in an unofficial, personal capacity, yes.'

'As will I,' Jorma added.

'Here's a thought,' Professor Winton Singh piped up. 'I've been thinking that we need to be proactive in finding a practical solution. We need a scoping group to investigate possible solutions to minimise dream violence in White rated experiences. I haven't run this past Saxon, but what if we establish a scoping group from a DI Academy to investigate solutions?' he proposed.

'At our expense?' Kris pre-empted.

'I think it's only fitting given it is your technology,' Justine pointed out.

The idea quietly permeated through the group for several moments.

Kris took off his wire rimmed glasses, pulled a tissue from the box on the table, and began cleaning them. 'I'll run it past Saxon and Margo,' he finally agreed. 'I'll let you know.'

'The April 23rd public rally in four major cities worldwide has been orchestrated by Brigit McKenzie's Stop Dream Violence movement, with support from the Organic Dream Alliance and Fundamental Purists,' the reporter said on Saxon's wall screen as file footage played of previous Stop Dream Violence protests. 'Smaller fringe groups pledging their cooperation to get dream immersion trauma syndrome recognised as a real-world condition has added more momentum to the demonstrations. Failure to recognise and address issues arising from experiencing or witnessing terrifying events in DI has intensified in recent months from a small, well organised and vocal grassroots base. Experiencing traumatic events in dream phaze, impacting people in the real world and in natural dreaming, is no longer seen as insignificant. In fact, a think tank of psychologists, psychiatrists and ethicists known as Dream Qualia, based in Stockholm, has been conducting research into this development. The addictive nature of dream immersion has become–'

A "Breaking News" graphic flashed to screen accompanied by dramatic music before handheld video footage of a burning residence filled the screen. 'To breaking news,' the voiceover announced. 'Brentwood, the affluent residential suburb in Los Angeles, has been rocked by a series of explosions. Eyewitness reports are saying four residential houses have been targeted by militia groups armed with K64 revolver grenade launchers.'

'I saw this yellow van pull up, back doors flew open and a guy jumped out with a fuckin' massive weapon,' the excited witness explained to camera. 'He fired four shots at the house from this thing then jumped back in the van.'

'This is the third similar attack on residential houses in the city,' the voiceover continued over burning buildings footage. 'First in Bel Air, then North Beverly Park and now–'

Saxon's PD rang. 'Mute screen. Have you seen any news feeds?' he asked Wendy.

A distorted voice responded to his question. 'Hang on, just activating my descrambler.' Saxon tapped his PD screen.

'You mean the rallies?'

'What does she hope to achieve?'

'I'm going to add to our problems,' Wendy warned.

'Go ahead.'

'A female user was raped and murdered in the Dreamlooper experience a couple of hours ago. It gets worse. She was asked the Asimov question before the attack.'

'What?' Saxon sat stunned. 'Fuck...that means–'

'Griffin could be a codester, he has inside knowledge.'

'That would explain a few things. Have other women reported being asked the Asimov question?' Saxon wondered.

'Not to my knowledge, but we're only privy to interview transcripts from police. As well as reporting the incident to us and the police, the victim reported it to the Stop Dream Violence hotline. The media have latched onto it. It'll be everywhere in the next 24 hour news cycle and help bolster the rallies.'

'Great, that's all we fucking need.'

'It gets even worse. Waylon was there in the experience, following Zen and Lena. Zen was dragged into a stairwell, but by the time Waylon got to her Lena had fought off Griffin and was gone. Waylon lost him in the crowd.'

'Was Zen harmed?'

'No, Lena kept her safe. Waylon questioned Zen and Lena, and Zen told him Griffin asked her the Asimov question.'

'This is a dangerous development.'

'Sure is. He's only targeting live echoes now.'

'Why now? Did we get a description?'

'Griffin was wearing a hoodie...but Waylon got one from Zen and Lena. They told him he was Asian and possibly in his 30s.'

'Asian? I thought we were looking for a Caucasian man?'

'We all did. All the phenotype genetic markers indicated European ancestry. I've been wasting everyone's time, especially Waylon's.'

'Don't be too hard on yourself, Wendy, we still needed to isolate those DNA files and you did that.'

'I've checked the timestamps on our suspect's DI devices and they don't correlate with experience assaults. They weren't in use at the time. Waylon was right.'

'Do you know the locations of the bogus DI device logons for those experiences?'

'I'm running a point of presence search now, I should have them by morning, but I'd say he'll be connecting through a VPDN.'

'Probably, but he may be so brazen he doesn't use one. That may give us a location we can start from.'

'Or lead us down another fucking rabbit hole. I'll start sharing new violent incident reports with timestamps with Waylon as I work through them.'

'This latest experience might be the break we need,' Saxon enthused. 'We can pinpoint all users in that instance.'

'I hope so,' Wendy said despondently. 'I'll cross check all DNA with DI device timestamps until we find the odd one out. But we still won't have Griffin's DNA, just another false sample.'

'But you are reducing our suspect list,' he offered. 'Once we identify Griffin, tell customer service to reinstate those vindicated suspects to the platform. Tell them it was a glitch in the system and offer them a Nukoin voucher.'

'Yep. Any progress with the whole genome amplification process?'

'It'll be another few weeks. It's not a simple process cultivating functioning skin tissue from a smattering of donor cells mixed with stem cells. I've managed to partially accelerate the process using laser-assisted bioprinting and growth hormones, but it still requires time.'

'This will give us an indication of how long it takes to prepare samples. Our Griffin probably has several on the go at once.'

'Undoubtably, if it works. I bet you Griffin is a psychopath hiding in plain sight. He could be a codester or has a confidante who is a codester, that's how he knows the Asimov question,' Saxon speculated. 'He would need a secure, private location to carry out this type of work.'

'With biotech equipment. We need to start checking biotech equipment sales back 18 months at least once we have a location. That will take time.'

'It will,' Saxon agreed. 'Have you heard of a research group called Dream Qualia?' He asked, completely changing the tack of conversation.

'Dream Qualia? Can't say that I have.'

'Ask Liam to check them out. They're doing research we need to keep an eye on.'

'Will do.'

'I forgot to ask. Has Liam checked out the Pleasure Planet experience?'

'He's done more than check it out, it's a weekly routine. He said there's nothing out of the ordinary except everyone's naked and sex is plentiful.'

Saxon laughed. 'I hope he's not working too hard.'

'Her name is Dalila.'

'Dalila from Pleasure Planet.'

'No, she's a real woman. She's Caribbean, lives in George Town in the Cayman Islands. He's just returned from visiting her. He tells me her father's quite well off.'

'Good for Liam.'

'He's noted there's a strong Fundamental Purist's presence in the experience.'

'That doesn't surprise me,' Saxon replied.

'He's even bumped into a couple of work colleagues, but he won't say who.'

'Dreams are private, Wendy,' Saxon reminded her.

For the past month, Kris had made random visits to the Hunters and Collectors experience hoping to meet Hunter One, Vincent Spencer, or the blonde man he lost in the crowd at Justin Ma's dedication service. Kris was surprised he was still allowed to return at all after his maiden outing almost six months before. Kris assumed Spencer would return, even after he killed his echo and cut off his ear, because he commissioned the experience after all.

Kris' presence agitated some members of the group when they initially set eyes on him, recalling his first visit, and now unashamedly wearing the particularly white ear of Hunter One around his neck. But today most attention was focused on an ebony skinned man in his early thirties who was paraded around the clearing like a prize bull as this episode's quarry. Grunts and hoots of intimidation spread through the Neanderthal horde.

Kris surveyed the 60-strong mob. Neither Hunter One nor Hunter Two were present.

Instinctively, his hackles rose as he spied the tall blonde man on the opposite side of the pack. Adrenaline flushed through him as he stooped low and manoeuvred his way around until he was close. Kris stood behind the blonde man, holding the tip of his hunting blade hard against the small of his back.

'We need to talk,' Kris instructed in a low tone.

'I wondered when you were going to show up,' the blonde man replied calmly, remaining still.

'Move.' Kris pushed him to the side and followed him into the surrounding forest. They walked for almost a minute. 'Stop.'

The blonde man turned around. 'Wearing that with pride I see.' He gestured to Kris' ear necklace.

'Where is he?'

'Hunter One? He has disappeared.'

'To where?'

'I know who you are, Kris,' the blonde man disclosed with a slight grin. 'As I told you before I exited on your first visit, I'm with you.'

'What does that fucking mean?'

'My job is to flush out hardcore racist pricks in the real world.'

'Your job? Who do you work for?'

'Let's just say we're a group of concerned global citizens.'

'What's your name?'

'In here, I'm Hunter 1874. In the real world, I use Gerry, Michael, Seb–'

'What's your fucking real name,' Kris interrupted, frustrated with the pretence.

He hesitated. 'Wolf, Wolf Wynters.'

'Fuck off, what's your real name?'

Wolf began to laugh. 'That is my real name. Wolfgang Sebastian Wynters. Check when you get back. I live in Graz, Austria. Born October 12th, 2012. Check.'

Kris let down his guard and lowered his knife. 'Did you have anything to do with Justin Ma's murder?'

'None whatsoever. Shane McHawk lured Justin to the Emerald Ribbon Restaurant in Cleveland for a midday meeting under false pretences. As you know, Justin's body was found by the side of the Willow Freeway next day.'

'Who's Shane McHawk?'

'You met him on your first visit, Hunter Two. He was Spencer's right hand man in here and out there.'

'Was? McHawk's not here either?' Kris asked.

'Spencer and McHawk won't be back. They're dead.'

'Dead?' Kris was surprised. 'Do you know that for sure?'

'Did it myself,' he responded straight faced. 'They'll never be found.'

Kris contemplated Wolf through renewed eyes. 'Why did you run at Justin's dedication in New York?'

'Justin was a good friend. I didn't want you causing a scene and disrupting the ceremony.'

'What's your background?'

'German ex-military. I was with a special forces unit tasked with infiltrating and exposing far-right extremists in the German military and police.'

'Ah-huh. That makes some sense.'

'United Storm Front, the website Justin closed down, emerged from the shadows in recent months from being primarily an online intelligence gathering group to reinventing itself as the coordination faction controlling subversive militant hate groups. McHawk controlled one of those branches which is part of their insidious US domestic network, neutralising opponents, trying to boost its influence in Europe.'

'You infiltrate in here and track them in the real world?'

'We do. Dream phaze has been instrumental in infiltrating white supremacist and hate groups to identify leaders, putting names to faces in the real world, but–'

'That's great to hear,' Kris felt buoyed by the news.

'Don't get too excited. Your tech is a double edged sword. The platform allows them to meet, recruit, train and organise out of sight to become a more cohesive group. Thanks to you, membership has grown from just over 25,000 to 48,000 in the last year.'

Kris' effervescence quickly dissolved, worried by Wolf's insight. 'So, they're using the platform to recruit?'

'And train. Besides these general hunts, they conduct specific training sessions for invited members around the clock, and their network is expanding rapidly worldwide.'

'Fuck me, of course they fucking do.' Kris slowly paced. 'Everyone else is using it for training. That's a serious problem.'

'Yes, it is. In here, they aren't scrutinised by authorities. Using websites like United Storm Front they covertly recruit members. There were more websites Justin had his eye on, but that's all on hold as his team regroups.'

'How did you find Spencer and McHawk in the real world? You must have a lot of resources at your disposal?'

'We have a unique skill set in our team. We monitor ISP and VPDN traffic. We can see if they are connecting to a VDPN server, courtesy of their ISP. We approach the VDPN company and ask them to monitor an individual. We have methods to ensure VDPN companies cooperate and hand over activity logs. We use these logs to unscramble VPDN traffic to identify their IP connection and DI device, then we profile the individual. Biometric surveillance using gait, height, facial recognition confirms their identify in the field. It takes time, but it's effective. We've created a very comprehensive register.'

'I didn't think you could unscramble VPDN encryption?'

'There is tech available. It's expensive and restricted.'

'Why kill Spencer and McHawk, why not turn them over to authorities?' Kris probed.

'Those two pricks were particularly vile characters, and they had connections in high places. McHawk was ex federal law enforcement. Filth like them tend to fall through the cracks and walk free. Our way is permanent.'

Their attention was suddenly transfixed by someone running in their direction. The young victim popped out of the undergrowth with terror in his eyes when he saw the pair. Wolf quickly waved him on.

'Quick, kill me, take my ear,' Kris offered Wolf under his breath. 'It'll impress the rock apes. I don't need to come back here.'

'O-kay,' Wolf reluctantly agreed.

Waylon knocked on Saxon's office door on level two at the Port Augusta facility. 'Have you got a minute?'

Saxon stopped what he was doing on his computer. 'It will have to be quick,' he insisted, glancing at the time on his monitor. 'I've got a scheduled call shortly. What have you got?'

'Have a look at this,' Waylon said, walking into his office carrying his PD. 'This is why you and the family need security even on home soil.' He placed his PD on the desk and projected video onto the wall. 'This was taken last week and intercepted by my men yesterday.'

Rough video footage from a drone above Saxon's Sydney residence showed Hugo getting into a vehicle and exiting the grounds. It cut to footage shot from a vehicle dashcam following Hugo's transport.

'Where did you get this?' Saxon questioned.

'Two vehicles were identified following Hugo as he went about his studies a couple of weeks ago. We've been monitoring them and intercepted both yesterday. The men and a woman in these vehicles were Chinese citizens. This was discovered on a data drive carried by one of them.'

'Who do they work for?'

'They wouldn't say. But we did identify the woman from our files, she has links to SkyCloud International and now HBU.'

'HBU? Why doesn't that surprise me.'

'We handed them over to the Federal Police with a little evidence that will see them detained for 48 hours then deported,' Waylon confided with a grin.

Saxon's computer screen sounded an alert. 'This is the call I have to take. Timing is everything. As coincidence would have it, it's with HBU's CEO Zam Chu. Good work, Waylon.'

Waylon left as Saxon made himself comfortable at his desk to take the video call. 'Ms Zam Chu, I'm pleased to meet you. How are you?'

'Well thank you, Dr Zynn,' she responded enthusiastically. 'We finally meet.'

'Yes, yes. I was surprised to get your text out of the blue.'

'You're a hard man to get hold of. They told me you don't have a PA or secretary, so it took a while to get your number.'

'I like to organise the few external meetings I have myself. I'm in the lab most days. So, what is it you would like to discuss? Your text message was quite vague.'

'I know ZynnComm is progressing with the Neurocoalescence technology and I want to get in early to request that you consider HBU for procurement when you call for tenders for component manufacturing.'

'Ah, I see. Well, that's an unknown timeframe. We are still working through experimentation phases for certain components and then there are IP patent applications and processes. It could be years away.'

'I completely understand, believe me. I know how long prototyping can take on the road to commercialisation. But we would still like to have the opportunity to participate, whenever that may be.'

'We've overhauled our procurement program for current first-tier suppliers, which strengthens ethical management requirements, supplier diversity and environmental sustainability,' Saxon paused. 'Do you think HBU could meet our rigorous quality assurance processes to satisfy our high standards?'

'HBU has a reputation for quality, you know that, Dr Zynn. I think we would manage your manufacturing requirements quite well.'

'It's not the manufacturing side of your operations that concerns me.' Saxon thought about how he would approach the surveillance of his family. Finally, he threw caution to the wind. 'It's your management style that concerns me, Zam. The way in which you conduct your business.'

'In what way?' she asked somewhat surprised.

'My security personnel informed me of your surveillance team. They've sent your watchdogs packing, they'll be deported from Australia.' The delay in Zam Chu's response spoke volumes.

'I'm not sure what you're referring to, Dr Zynn?'

'Okay, Zam, play your games. Your request is denied with extreme pleasure. Now and forever.' Saxon disconnected, sporting a smile.

Chapter Eight

Turquoise ocean stretched to the horizon as immaculately shaped waves broke. The white water caressed the fine-grained sand along Echo Beach. Miranda, Wendy, and their friends, Hoss and Venice, relaxed on their towels drinking Margaritas under blue sky. Seagulls squawked overhead as Wendy tossed them dried anchovy flakes. The innate satisfaction of swimming and lazing on an idyllic, empty coastline made Echo Beach one of the most popular dream destinations for overcrowded city dwellers.

'I could live here,' Hoss admitted, stretched out on his back, eyes closed with hands behind his head. 'So far away from everything.'

'Far away in time,' Wendy quoted. 'As their advertising jingle suggests.'

'If only you had shitloads of money,' Venice commented. 'You could buy me a beach or island back home.'

'We'd have to give up our beautiful 29th floor apartment in Bogota,' Hoss jested.

'What's the population of Bogota these days?' Miranda asked, sipping her drink.

'Nudging 14 million,' Venice replied.

'Too fucking many,' Hoss added dryly, 'We are still trying to move to Australia, but visa conditions are strict.'

'Keeps the riff raff out.' Hoss missed Wendy's sly smile. 'What about the US?'

'Yeah, right. Three words, guns and domestic terrorism,' Venice said. 'Seriously, we could use your support,' she appealed. 'We could use someone on the inside.'

'Tell us what you need and we'll see what we can do,' Miranda reassured her. 'Won't we?' she looked at Wendy.

'Of course. Come on, I'm hot. Let's swim.' Wendy encouraged.

Perfect one metre waves ideal for bodysurfing, made coach Miranda's job easy, guiding the rest on timing and technique. Endorphins buoyed their adventurous spirit, each of them synchronising with the rhythm of the waves, like dolphins chasing pure enjoyment.

Saxon sat in his Port Augusta office reading through procurement tenders when his PD buzzed.

'Dipstick Sterling Lindquist has released an opinion paper,' Kris declared as his head projected from Saxon's PD.

'An opinion paper on what?'

'He calls it the Dream Immersion Pleasure Principle.'

'Geez. Is it debauched?'

'Surprisingly, no. It never mentions Acid Spear Studios or Sinnerverse.'

'So, what's the crux of it?'

'It has to do with the human desire for self-gratification and how DI feeds that desire. He proposes dream immersion could be extended to 60 minutes and is calling for more research to make it so.'

'Sixty minutes? We can't do that. Ballsy prick,' Saxon remarked. 'Where was it published?'

'On the Acid Spear Studios blog about 30 minutes ago. It feeds the Sinnerverse and Wunderlust blogs,' Kris explained.

'How did you get it?'

'Don't forget, I have a personal interest in Acid Spear. My alternative self is on the Sinnerverse subscriber list.'

'Ah, yes,' Saxon remembered. 'Should we be worried?'

'It'll be mentioned in the 24-hour news cycle, because of who he is, but ultimately, I don't think it'll have legs,' Kris downplayed.

'We need to discredit it. I'll ask Margo to look at a campaign through our usual media channels to talk it down if needed,' Saxon decided. 'I've been reading through the Ethos procurement contract,' Saxon changed the subject. 'They haven't sharpened their pencils; their prices are basically the same.'

'I wanted to speak to you about that.'

'There's also this matter of six unfair dismissals before the Fair Work Directorate. I've been doing a bit of research, and Ethos has a growing reputation for having a toxic work culture.'

'I think Ethan can be a hard task master at times,' Kris acknowledged.

'Hon Hai Industries are more competitive on price, and they have a better workplace reputation.' Saxon's PD buzzed. 'Hang on, Wendy's calling me.' Kris' holographic image blurred momentarily before splitting into two distinct light arrays, one dedicated to Kris' image and the other for Wendy. 'Hey, Wendy.'

'Hi, Saxon. Hello, Kris.'

'Hi, Wendy.'

'I just wanted to update you on the Uzbekistan students,' Wendy explained. 'We found negligible evidence of neurological, physiological or psychological side effects.'

'Bury that information, Wendy. Kris was just telling me Sterling Lindquist has released an opinion paper calling for extended immersion cycles.'

'You've read his Dream Immersion Pleasure Principle paper?'

'Where did you see it?' Kris quizzed with genuine surprise.

'Liam has his finger on the pulse for DI chatter, and this has gone viral. It's trending worldwide.'

'No legs hey, Kris?' Saxon commented sarcastically.

'Fuck me, that was quick.'

'Users want more time in DI,' Wendy said. 'This will be a discussion starter.'

'I don't want that Uzbek data publicly available to feed his agenda,' Saxon reiterated.

'I agree. Besides, we know from our own data 60 minutes for big dippers could be harmful over several months,' Wendy suggested.

'We don't want to feed the DITS lobbyists and aggravate the situation,' Saxon urged. 'I'll definitely ask Margo to start a media campaign using our research data to downplay it.'

'That's the other reason I called. Liam checked out the Dream Qualia group you asked about, Saxon. Guess who's funding them?'

'Zam Chu and HBU?'

'Nope. The Organic Dream Alliance. It's part of their strategy to force the International Psychotherapy Association to recognise DITS. It then becomes a medical disorder and therapy is covered by insurance which drives the IPA agenda for its membership.'

'Who's Dream Qualia?' Kris questioned.

'A research group in Stockholm,' Wendy replied. 'They're looking at DITS and they are also studying the growing issue of DI addiction.'

'Addiction? That's something Sterling touches on in his paper,' Kris pointed out.

'Dream Qualia are citing cases of people giving up work and counting down to their 33 minutes of immersion every day, followed by bouts of anxiety until the next time,' Wendy explained. 'Men are leaving their wives and families because they prefer their very short alternate life in DI. Uni students are abandoning their studies, building their waking lives around their favourite DI experience. Granted they are small numbers. There will always be addictive personalities.'

'When we aren't fulfilled, our psychological response is anxiety or tension. It happens with VR too,' Kris suggested. 'Thus, driving the addiction.'

'Even more so with VR,' Wendy agreed. 'People spend a lot more time in VR than DI.'

'They do,' Saxon agreed. 'Thanks, Wendy. I'll have a look at Dream Qualia, and Sterling's paper. What did you want to discuss about the Ethos procurement, Kris?'

'It was just something Ethan said at dinner last week–'

'I'll leave you to it.' Wendy left the call.

'We have upped our DI unit order by more than 25 percent and his rare-earth supplier has increased their price by 25 percent per kilogram. Ethan has absorbed his suppliers increase based on our volume increase, keeping our unit price the same. I've checked specific rare-earth prices over the previous 12 months and he's right, there has been a substantial increase in his raw costs.'

'Rare-earth elements are only a small component of overall costs,' Saxon argued.

'True, but the component he supplies is at the heart of the technology, it's vital. Without his Neuronic Reorganisation Actuator, production stops in its tracks. Ethan has a reliable rare-earth supply chain, and he has looked after us from the start.'

'Granted, he knows we can't do without him.'

'He could have increased prices, but he didn't. Besides, changing over to a new supplier for a few dollars would interrupt supply chains, unit production and perhaps quality.'

Saxon thought about those points. 'Okay, I'll have a chat with Margo, and we can discuss it in Chennai. But, I want you to go over both Ethos and Hon Hai Industries contracts. I want a thorough, commercially rational decision to take to the board.'

'Understood. See you in Chennai.' Kris was about to disconnect but baulked. 'Oh, that was the other thing. Has Winston Singh been in your ear about a scoping group to be set up inside one of our Academies–'

'To address dream violence? He has. I pretended you and I had discussed it briefly.'

'Sorry, I keep forgetting to add it to the agenda, not a high priority. If we do, I did think that Selma could use it for a media release to allay criticisms from the Organic Dream Alliance and Co.'

'I told Winston we are taking the issue extremely seriously and we've made it a high priority exploring solutions here at the Port Augusta facility.'

'That is true.'

'He was impressed.' Saxon thought about Kris' idea. 'I agree, let's make it formal. You inform the DI Advisory Council and then we'll send out a media release to demonstrate we are being proactive.'

Chennai was sticky-hot in mid-April. The new Dream Immersion Academy was the largest of the four Academies to date, by population. The Academy was a reimagined, refurbished 4-star hotel in the heart of Chennai, boasting 75 dorm rooms, 15 classrooms with adjacent developer labs, a dozen research labs, administration and meeting rooms, with a food court featuring numerous franchised eateries. Courses for the first 24 months were booked out and paid in advance, with those missing out going onto a long waitlist.

Saxon, Margo, Kris and Kurt mingled with the hundreds of dignitaries, invited guests and students in the glass-enclosed rooftop function centre. An hour before, in the main auditorium a floor below, the state Governor of Tamil Nadu had opened the facility to a worldwide audience, followed by Saxon's keynote address.

Margo sidled up to Kurt, who stared out across the smoggy metropolis of Chennai, handing him a glass of sparkling wine. 'Have you and Russell settled in yet?' She pulled a chair over to be at eye level.

'As much as we can,' he admitted. 'We've been here a few times, setting-up the Academy, but that was for a week at a time. Living here is going to take time to adjust to the bloody heat and air quality. Australia is hot, but this is a different kind of heat.'

'I said to Saxon when Kris put your name forward, we have to make sure you're happy with your digs. We went to quite some effort to find and fit-out your accessible, climate-controlled apartment.'

'The place is brilliant, thank you, Margo. Nungambakkam is so close to the Academy too.'

'Kris kept reminding us we had to set you up in the right place or you wouldn't take the job.'

'Correct,' Kurt mimicked Saxon.

'I'm glad you like it.'

'I appreciate the effort, Margo, honestly I do.'

'Believe me, Kurt, we think you're worth it. Kris has nothing but praise for your efforts developing the Academy Dream Team Program, making our Sydney Academy the gold standard for best practice throughout the industry.'

'I'll be the first to admit, we had our teething problems, but I think we're starting to see results with a higher calibre of student signing up for the Dream Team Program over the standard fee-paying courses. We're starting to see a stronger allegiance to ZynnComm, reflected in lower headhunting rates than in the past.'

'And that feeds back into our Academies. Employers want appropriately trained codesters from the people who developed the tech,' Margo added. 'The Dream Team Program is pure gold, Kurt.'

Kurt smiled at her admiration. 'You know, it's times like this when I'm glad I was a coward and couldn't go through with it.'

Margo looked confused. 'With what?'

'I haven't always been in a wheelchair. When I first became paraplegic, just after my 18th birthday, I was so close to pulling the pin, topping myself,' he explained honestly.

Margo gently placed a hand on his shoulder. 'Perhaps it wasn't that you were a coward, perhaps somewhere inside you knew you would overcome your obstacles at some point,' she suggested. A brief silence fell between the two before Margo finally spoke. 'If you don't mind me asking, Kurt, was it a sporting accident?'

'Kris has never told you?'

'He might have told Saxon, not me.'

'I wish it were a sporting accident, then I could blame someone. No, it was a dare, during a drinking game with my mates. We were in Robbo's backyard, by his pool, it was late, we were all pissed as maggots and the dare was to eat a slug for a slab of beer. I was a wild, unpredictable boy. I ate the slug. Turns out that slugs eat rat shit, rat lungworm larvae live in rat shit, and rat lungworm larvae can cause meningitis or paralysis in a small percentage of people.'

'Fuck, Kurt.'

'My immune system couldn't reject the nematode and I got a headache the next day then spent the next three months in hospital.'

'That is so unlucky,' Margo said.

'Not really, it was my fault. I made the decision to eat the slug. I remember picking it up, licking it, then swallowed it in one gulp. Now, I look at it being one of the best things that has ever happened to me–'

'How's that?'

'After I got over the initial self-pity, it made me slow down and I studied computer science. That led me to working for ZynnComm and now I run the largest Dream Immersion Academy on the planet.'

Margo's mouth curled at one end in a faint smile. 'Life's twists and surprises seem to make us more resilient.'

'I know it's an old cliché to say that I was meant to be here, doing this work, but when I dream, I have no disability. I'm still disappointed for a brief moment, even after 30 years, when I wake up in the morning to find that I'm still the same. I wish I could dream phaze more than once a day or for longer.'

'You're not alone there, Kurt. Have you tried exoskeletal supports or stem cell therapy?'

'I've used exoskeletal legs with neurodrivers in the past and they've worked, but I prefer my powerchair for ease of use. Because my paralysis is neurological, stem cell regeneration isn't available,' Kurt explained.

'Yet,' Margo offered. 'One day maybe.'

Saxon joined the pair. 'So, Kurt, how has our boy been doing at the Academy?'

'Visualise the phenomenon of raw energy entering through the soles of your glowing, golden feet, electrifying every cell in your body as it rises, before exploding from the top of your head into the universe,' the soothing female voice instructed.

Sterling felt connected to his surroundings as he visualised the energy surging up and through him.

'You have now finished the 20-minute guided meditation stage of the session,' the voice announced as Sterling Lindquist slowly opened his eyes. 'You will now enter the second and final stage, where you will release your anger.'

Sterling's platform, perched high on a mountaintop overlooking a sea of green forest, began to distort and swim as the transition of colours and shapes transported him to a residential neighbourhood. He instantly recognised the houses in Asbury Street, in the suburb of Rice Military. It was his old neighbourhood in Houston, Texas where he grew up. A group of four older male teenagers approached him. Sterling recognised them too.

'Look who it is, fucking weirdo Sterling Lindquist,' the largest one, Roden Goblet said, ruffling Sterling's bright red hair.

Sterling remained stationary; his aqua blue eyes focused on the ground in a submissive gesture.

'Where are you off to my little fuck knuckle?' the plump boy, Payne Hart, questioned.

Sterling cautiously removed a handgun from beneath his jacket and placed the muzzle hard against Payne Hart's chest. 'To your death.' He squeezed off two quick rounds into the boy.

The other boys scattered, but not before Sterling shot two boys in quick succession, felling both. Roden Goblet managed to disappear down a narrow path between two houses. Sterling walked over to one of the boys writhing on the footpath in a pool of blood, bent down and rolled him over. His left eye hung out, stomach in shreds, open heart pumping, no...he was dead. Sterling casually put a bullet in the back of the head of the remaining squirming boy as he walked by him in pursuit of his last tormenter, Roden.

'Come outside, Roden, I know this is your house.' Sterling walked between the houses into the backyard as light rain began to fall. 'If you don't come out, I'll come in kill your whole fucking family.' He waited for a moment before entering through the back door.

Inside, an older man walked towards Sterling brandishing a handgun. 'We don't want any trouble,' his left palm out in front of him as if surrendering.

Sterling shot the man in the face and continued to search for Roden. 'Your father's dead, Roden. Where's your mother?' Sterling caught a glimpse of movement in his peripheral vision in the kitchen. Without hesitating, he fired, hitting Roden's mother in the neck, her momentum carrying her forward, slamming into the refrigerator door before collapsing to the floor. 'Your mother's dead, Roden. Time to come out and play.'

Roden burst from a doorway with a machete raised above his head and swung down at Sterling with considerable force. Sterling felt the swoosh of air from the blade centimetres from his face as he pivoted and fired but missed. Roden turned and raised his arms for another go, but Sterling pumped three bullets into his chest propelling him backwards into a display cabinet packed with vintage porcelain Toby Jugs.

Sterling felt an immediate wave of emotional hostility effervesce from his being as he walked outside into the gently falling rain. Relaxing his head back with eyes closed, he felt wet kisses dampen his face.

'This dream immersion expressive therapy session has now concluded. Well done,' the comforting female voice congratulated. 'Your next session will be available in seven days. Thank you for using the Psychotherapy Institute of Brazil for Neurodivergent Expressive Therapy.'

Back in Port Augusta, five monitors surrounding Waylon displayed a multitude of visualised data. He had taken up residence in Kris and Wendy's old office on level 2.

Wendy entered the office and scanned the assorted data across the screens. 'I hope you can make sense of all that.'

Waylon pointed to the screen on the far left. 'These are all the ISPs the network identified during the 33-minute instance of Dreamlooper, showing all traffic. The next screen is isolating each VPDN tunnel by ISP, one at a time. That monitor,' he said pointing to the far right, 'is running a packet sniffer decoding each VPDN. The screen next to that is deciphering encrypted GT Protocol Secure Layer 3 data between the DI device and the Norus network. This monitor in the middle is aggregating snippets of data from each process which should isolate the real world IP address and eventually give us a timestamp and unique device identifier.'

'So, you managed to capture all the ISP traffic for that 33-minute window?' Wendy asked. 'Impressive. That's a lot of data from a lot of sources.'

'Yep. It isn't easy securing metadata under current privacy laws.'

'I've never seen programs that can reconstruct VPDN data before,' Wendy commented, intrigued by the sophisticated algorithms working behind the screens.

Waylon picked up a fist-sized chrome sphere from its claw-like power cradle on the desk and turned to her. 'Well, this isn't off the shelf tech. It was originally designed for VPN tracing, but with coding modifications, it works for VPDN's too. Only top tier inter-governmental security agencies have them—'

'Like GUESS?' Wendy suggested eagerly.

Waylon studied her face for a moment. 'You know about GUESS?'

'My brother was a journalist, he told me about their existence.'

'GUESS uses this tech,' Waylon answered quietly. He handed her the sphere.

Wendy felt the weight of the object. 'Wow, heavier than I thought. How did you get it?' she pried.

Waylon took the sphere from her hand and swivelled his chair back around to his array of screens. He placed the device back in its stand. 'Surveillance is my bread and butter.' He changed the subject. 'I'm surprised how many VPDN's were used during a White rated instance.'

'More and more people seem to be using them across all classifications. So, have you managed to pinpoint a location?'

'It takes time to restore encrypted information. At the rate it's processing, a few weeks and we should have an answer,' he advised.

'I think we need to code something into Norus to tag all DI devices, regardless of VPDN encryption, so we don't have to go through this again,' Wendy proposed.

Waylon's attention was piqued. He spun around. 'Like what?'

An impish grin spread across Wendy's face. 'Well, I've been working on a personal project. I've nicknamed it Spryt. It's a sort of exotic hybrid, a bit like a glint or specklePro cookie,' Wendy explained excitedly, relieved to finally tell someone. 'It's independent from the network, absorbs opaque distortion interference, automatically re-creates itself if deleted, it defies encryption and has a dormant mode until activated remotely.'

Waylon thought about what that might mean for a moment, before nodding in agreement. 'That would be a neat piece of coding.'

'I've created it, tested it in simulations, but...I have to muster the courage to broach the subject with Saxon, because, you know, it has serious privacy implications without user and government consent.'

'We're in unchartered waters, Wendy,' Waylon counselled. 'Pitch at the right time, in the right place, with support, and Saxon might be open to long term solutions.'

Wendy smiled at his encouragement. 'I'll keep it under wraps for the time being.'

Bhang sat at his workstation on level 3 as Merlin approached. 'How is the Havranek project going?'

Bhang jumped, slightly startled by his voice. He was absorbed in something on his PD. 'Just tidying up a few environmental elements.'

Merlin glimpsed the young blonde woman on Bhang's PD screen. 'Is that your girlfriend?'

'Are you kidding? As if. You don't know Jana Jenssen?' Bhang asked with genuine surprise.

'Should I?'

'She is trending off the planet. Jana Jenssen, the Danish model? You seriously don't know who she is?'

'Is she dead?' Merlin questioned.

Bhang offered him a confused expression. 'No, she isn't dead. Jana and four of her colleagues have launched a DI start-up, Danish Dream Girls, and it's rating off the charts. Millionaires, all of them, virtually overnight.'

'She's cute. Bit young for you, isn't she? She looks about 15.'

'Cute? She is fucking smokin' hot, Merlin.' Bhang tapped his PD screen to project her holographic image above his workstation. 'She's 19. I'm 34, her target demographic.'

'She isn't even old enough to access DI yet,' Merlin teased. 'What would you have in common to talk about? You're almost a generation apart.'

'Anything she wanted to talk about,' he said, ogling her. 'Curves that never end.' He flicked the projection with his hand, spinning her image slowly.

'Truly scrumptious,' Merlin agreed, his nostalgic reference lost on Bhang. 'I take it you've tried her experience.'

'I wish. I don't have a disposable 400 Nukoin at the moment,' Bhang sadly admitted.

'Fuck off! Four hundred Nukoin! Does that get you a seven-day pass?'

'Just 33 minutes with her,' he responded rather distantly.

'So, there's not a lot of story I take it,' Merlin commented deadpan. 'Twenty Nukoin will get you the same experience with women just as beautiful.'

'I know, but I think her appeal is...that she's not an assembled echo, she is flesh and blood living in the real world today,' Bhang quietly argued. 'There's a tangible reality to her.'

'O-kay' Merlin wasn't convinced. 'Let's get back to work,' Merlin suggested.

'There are already deepfake holoflix of her if you know where to look,' Bhang continued, with no regard for Merlin's request.

Merlin considered Bhang. 'I bet there are and I bet you have. When will I get the Havranek project?'

'Erm, I'll send it to the subsynaptic resolver in the next hour.'

'Perfect,' Merlin turned to walk away, but stopped. 'You know, I just had a thought. There's a very urgent project from a high wealth individual who didn't baulk at paying the expediency fee to fast track her experience. You will have to work your arse off to get it done in four days, but it comes with a 300 Nukoin bonus,' Merlin tempted.

Bhang gazed at Merlin through sceptical eyes. 'Are you yanking my chain? See if I'll bite?'

'No, no, not at all, I just remembered it. Came in late yesterday. I was going to offer it to Mercy, she likes the overtime. But it's yours if you want it.'

Bhang smiled. 'Bonus upfront?'

Merlin contemplated his request with apprehension. 'Sure, why not,' he said against his better judgement.

'I'll take it.'

Saxon donned surgical gloves before he removed a tray from the stainless-steel cabinet and visually inspected it. The four-square centimetre skin tissue looked perfect, complete with delicate fine hairs. He took the tray into his office and closed the door. He glanced up at the embedded ceiling camera. 'Pause security camara and audio surveillance for 20 minutes. Authorisation code SZ677 alpha.' The tiny red light between the camera and microphone extinguished. After rolling up his left shirt sleeve, he applied a dollop of shaving gel to the underside of his forearm. With a disposable razor, he removed the hairs from a portion of his arm, then cleaned up with an antibacterial wipe. A light spray of Skin Gloo over the area ensured the edges of the sample would adhere to his largest organ. Carefully, he lifted the freshly grown two-millimetre-thick skin patch from its receptacle with mosquito forceps and placed it on his prepared forearm, smoothing out any minor wrinkles with another antibacterial wipe. He precisely attached his DI device to his forearm, covering the foreign epidermal specimen. He switched it on and watched. The screen read, *'Access denied. Try again in 8 hours.'* Saxon cautiously removed the device from his arm and picked up his PD. 'Scrambler on. Call Wendy Setri.'

'Hi, Saxon,' she answered.

'Hey, Wendy. When were you last in DI?'

'Erm, about eight last night. Why?'

'I just tried your skin sample with my DI device and it denied access for eight hours.'

'So, it's possible, Griffin could have grown tissue to fool his device?'

'Correct. I'm going to try Kris' sample next, just to verify the results.'

'Well, that confirms Waylon's theory.'

'Someone has gone to a great deal of effort to conceal their identity.'

Wendy was called by someone in the background. 'I have to go.' She disconnected.

Saxon, excited by the discovery, exited his office and walked along the landing to Kris and Wendy's old office where Waylon sat in front of his workstation. Saxon checked that both the surveillance camera and microphone in the ceiling were still covered with tape with the word, *'disconnected'* written across it. Saxon stuck his left forearm in front of Waylon to gain his attention. 'The lab grown skin fooled my DI device.'

'Jesus,' Waylon moaned. 'I was hoping it wouldn't work. If this information gets out, the platform could be in real trouble.'

'Correct. This has to be our priority when we find this prick, completely destroy any evidence of this workaround.'

'With any luck he's a lone wolf, working in isolation,' Waylon responded.

'I've been thinking about that too,' Saxon admitted. 'If he has shared this info, we will have to implement a pretty thorough clean-up.'

'Understood,' Waylon replied.

Saxon stared at the streams of data on Waylon's bank of screens. 'Anything yet?'

'Well, I've narrowed it down to Australia as the place of origin.'

'Here? Really? That surprises me. I thought it would have originated in mainland Asia.'

'It bounced around there for some time, but the origins are here in Australia.'

'I'll get Wendy to check collating biotech sales here for the past 18 months. How much longer before you get a precise location?'

'Hard to say...a week.'

'I'll be in New York for a few days from tomorrow. We'll meet in a week or so and work through the logistics and resources required to eliminate Griffin quickly.'

'I've already nutted out a basic plan,' Waylon informed Saxon. 'We'll keep it simple and coax Griffin out of his comfort zone.'

'Good. I'll get Wendy to coordinate a DI meeting.'

Saxon stood outside his apartment building on Fifth Avenue in New York, waiting for his transport to arrive to take him to the Teterboro Airport. Saxon was a keen people watcher. He enjoyed observing people go about their business. A small 2030s model car pulled up beside the kerbside recycling bins. The driver and his passenger, a teenage boy, got out. Saxon's security detail stepped in closer as the driver opened the rear hatchback and pulled out two pairs of bright yellow rubber gloves. They quickly donned them while sizing up the number of bins on offer at the front of the café. Saxon's minders withdrew as the man and his offsider selected a bin each and proceeded to remove recyclable bottles and the like, placing them in heavy duty plastic sacks. Roaches escaped from both bins as they enthusiastically rummaged through them. The boy rubbed his eye with his gloved hand, apparently unperturbed by the filth and germs contaminating his PPE. Once their sacks were full, they took them back to their beaten-up red vehicle and grabbed another. He remembered his mother unsympathetically refer to these flotsam and jetsam entrepreneurs as street urchins.

Saxon had read about the streets of Manhattan in the 1830s, when thousands of pigs were allowed to wander the streets to consume garbage, until the aristocrats of Fifth Avenue put a stop to the practice. This in turn fostered a new industry, swill kids, collecting kitchen waste to sell to farmers for their now hungry pigs, and rag and bone men collecting for the burgeoning paper and glue industry. *'Turning street garbage into money was alive and well two centuries later'*, Saxon thought. *'The more things change the more they stay the same.'*

Saxon was mesmerised by the precision of the pair of bin skimmers as they methodically worked their way through four bins each before his vehicle arrived, disturbing his voyeuristic curiosity.

'Do it, or don't do it, trying is not an option!' Merlin berated Bhang. 'You took this project on knowing full well it was a fast turnaround. Should I hand it over to Mercy?'

'I know Merlin, I'm sorry, I had to make a quick trip to Melbourne, my mother is ill,' Bhang grovelled, sitting at his workstation.

Merlin looked at Bhang with a morsel of pity. 'I'm sorry to her about your mum, Bhang, but you don't have to contact the client and push the delivery back, again.'

'I'll have it finished by this time tomorrow, I promise. I'll even pull an all-nighter,' Bhang assured Merlin.

'I knew I shouldn't have given you the bonus upfront. Never again, Bhang.' Merlin left him and returned to his office.

Bhang could feel the other codesters staring at him. Turning around, Karl and Otto sat at their respective workstations craning their necks, before refocusing their attention on their work.

Merlin slumped down in his office chair, preparing to contact the client to explain yet another delivery delay, when he read a news feed scrolling across the bottom of his monitor. *'Sterling Lindquist, creator of Sinnerverse, releases data confirming longer dream phaze is possible.'* He clicked on the link and read the first paragraph. He picked up his PD and contacted Saxon.

'How the fuck would Sterling get his hands on your Uzbek data, Wendy?' Saxon pressed, pacing the dark sand in the Dream Chamber. Margo and Kris gazed at Wendy waiting for her response. 'I thought I told you to delete it?'

'You said bury, not delete,' Wendy reacted.

Saxon stopped pacing and glared at her.

'You did, Saxon. You said bury it,' Kris concurred.

'Okay, my mistake,' Saxon admitted as he continued pacing. 'So, who has access to where you buried it?'

'It's on a partitioned drive used for archiving projects. Only those in my division would have access. I changed the folder name, passphrase protected it, and didn't think any more of it,' she explained in her defence.

'Kris, I want a forensic audit of that drive. I want to know who accessed it in the past fortnight,' Saxon instructed.

'Sure. What's the folder name?'

'Telco reconfiguration 2045-47,' Wendy told him. 'Passphrase is 8, the numeral, MY, uppercase, breakfast, lowercase, SLOWLY, uppercase.'

'I'll get on it now. Rumpelstiltskin.' He vanished.

'The media are going to jump all over this,' Saxon bemoaned.

'Selina has managed the media around Sterling's call to arms so far,' Margo defended. 'I'll meet with her to see how we can control the damage.'

'Could we release selective early research data, you know, around the Brody Spark University trials.' Wendy suggested. 'That would reinforce our position.'

Saxon shot a concerned look at her. 'Tell me you're joking, Wendy?'

'If we redacted details, we could use it,' Wendy explained sheepishly.

'We will never publicly release any testing data from Brody Spark University,' Margo flatly stated. 'Never. Is that understood, Wendy?'

Wendy felt like she was being reprimanded back in high school. 'Understood,' came her meek response.

Later in the day, Wendy left work deflated, drained, waiting for the day to end. She exited the elevator into the ground level hangar in Port Augusta. She had deliberately switched her PD off, evading fever pitch social media hyping extended dream immersion. Wendy walked out to where her canary yellow Honda Hummingbird-12 flycycle waited on the tarmac. She unplugged the charge lead from the solar collector then placed her hand on the biometric security interface on the glovebox, permitting activation. Wendy mounted the beast, swinging her leg over the contoured seat, making herself comfortable. She attached the carabiner on her harness to the D-ring below the glovebox. She donned her helmet, then initialised the bladeless fluidic thrusters located either side, fore and aft, of the sleek carbon-graphene pod. She sat erect; her right thumb pressed on the throttle lever to ascend from the asphalt. Gaining height, Wendy eased the left thumb throttle forward pitching the thrusters to achieve forward motion above the scattering of sparse trees. She touched the cruise control button, leaving her day behind, and flew home.

Chapter Nine

Arrow looked across at the man sleeping in the driver's seat. The car was vintage, mid 1950s she thought. The traffic lights were red.

'Why is Dad asleep, Mum?' A young female child asked from the backseat.

Arrow turned around. 'Erm, I don't know,' she answered honestly.

The other child, a boy, piped up. 'He's playing.'

The lights turned green; the man remained asleep.

Arrow gazed out the car window and saw unconscious people laying on footpaths, on park benches, in store doorways, in other vehicles.

'Why is everyone asleep, Mum?' the girl wondered, peering out the rear door window. 'What's happening?'

'I'm not sure.' Arrow cautiously opened her door to get out.

'Don't go out there, Mum!' The girl shrieked.

'Whatever's making people sleep, it's in here too,' Arrow deduced. 'Dad's asleep.' She opened the door cautiously and stepped onto the road. 'You two stay there.'

'Hey you!'

Wendy heard the call but didn't know from which direction it came.

'Hey! Over here!'

This time Arrow saw the female caller and took a few steps in her direction. 'What's happening?'

'Get over here, and bring your children too,' the middle-aged woman instructed from the open store doorway.

Arrow studied the woman, not sure what to do. 'What's happening?' she called again.

'They will be coming soon, to collect the bodies. You must hide,' the woman urged.

Arrow turned when she heard noisy engines approaching from behind her, echoing along the street of high-rise buildings. She ran to the car to collect the children. 'Come on, get out. We need to hide.'

'What's happening, Mum?' The girl questioned.

'We're going to play hide and seek,' Arrow told her. She grabbed the hand of each child and hurried them across the street to the woman in the store. 'Quick, get inside.'

The women shuffled the children in and closed and locked the store door as trucks appeared at the other end of the street.

Arrow watched through breaks between curtains as tripedal beings loaded unconscious bodies onto the back of a truck. 'Where are they taking them?'

'I don't know,' replied the woman, watching through the next break in the curtains. 'You three must be immune to the sleep spores, same as me.'

'I suppose so,' Arrow responded. 'How long have they been here?'

'This is the third week of the invasion, I think. The spores started floating around late on a Saturday night and these creatures appeared the following morning. They never come out at night. I don't think their eyesight is very good.'

'Where's the military?'

'I haven't seen any soldiers, no aircraft. There's only a small group of us left.'

'Is–' Arrow began.

'Shhhh.'

One of the beings approached the front of their store to collect a young woman on the footpath. The mustard yellow creature stood three meters tall with a wide, elliptical shaped head. It had no discernible mouth. The eyes, all eight of them, were bright red and beady. Four tentacle shaped arms effortlessly picked up the woman.

One of the children knocked something over behind Arrow. She turned around in time to see the small boy morphing into one of the aliens. 'Fuck me.'

The middle-aged woman ran behind the store counter, pulled out a double-barrel shotgun, and blasted the creature in the face, spraying the young girl with blue blood and globs of yellow flesh.

The alien outside carrying the woman tried the door handle of the store.

'Where's the back door?' Arrow asked their rescuer with urgency.

'Follow me.'

Arrow contemplated the girl for a moment, before grabbing the girls arm and dragging her towards the back door. 'You had better not fucking change.'

Dappled sunlight reflected off the polished concrete floor of the Sunbaker Tavern in Culburra Beach as Saxon and Hugo picked up their schooners of beer from the bar and found a table inside. Thirty-three degrees Celsius was too hot to be sitting outside, even in April with a gentle breeze. One entire wall of the open plan pub was adorned with Max Dupain's iconic Sunbaker photo, taken over a century ago a few kilometres from where they sat.

'You used to come here for holidays with your parents, didn't you?' Hugo asked, sipping his beer.

'You remember that?'

'I remember seeing images of you on the beach.'

'We used to rent a house along Penguins Head Road, overlooking the beach,' Saxon reminisced. 'This pub wasn't here back then, neither was the estate as we drove into town, it was still being contested in the courts, it was all bush. I haven't been in Culburra for...almost 30 years I'd say.' Saxon thought. 'That's right, we didn't come down during the pandemic in 2020...that's when I stopped coming.'

'I've seen a doco or two on the pandemic. It changed the world.'

'Australia was luckier than most.' Saxon sipped his beer. 'This was always a great holiday, lots of surfing by day and playing games at night. Your grandmother wouldn't let us leave the TV on after the evening news. We had to play games like Jenga, Rummikub or cards, no electronic games.'

'You ever thought about elevating your parents to dream phaze?'

'Not really. No, I don't have a burning need to recreate them.'

'Mum needs to have some sort of contact with family, but you don't, do you?' Hugo enquired.

Saxon stared at Hugo for a moment before a smile grew across his face. 'Not like your mother, no. You know your mother grew up an only child, and when her mother died it left just her and Walt. She was very close to her mother. She doesn't have living aunts or uncles on either side.'

'And us, she has us,' Hugo reminded his father.

'She'll always have us.'

'That's why it's so difficult for her now. We have to look after her, Dad,' Hugo insisted.

Saxon was pleased to be having this conversation with his son. 'Yes we do,' Saxon agreed. 'I worry about her. She suffered bouts of depression when her mother died, but then we got the news about your imminent arrival, and that brought her back, she had something to focus on. Then...' he checked himself. 'This time it's going to be different. Elevating Walt would be easy, but it's different from being able to pick up her PD and call him any time.'

'What do we do?'

Saxon didn't have the answer to that question. 'I don't know. We'll have to play it by ear. This will be uncharted territory for both of us.'

'I'm an only child but I don't think I've missed that sibling connection or extended family environment.'

'Each of us are different. You're a product of your environment; you haven't known anything different,' Saxon smiled.

'Why don't I have a brother or sister? Why didn't you and Mum have more than one child?'

Saxon sat on the question for a moment. 'It's complicated. We should have this conversation when your mother's around.'

Hugo took the hint and together they drank.

'Pop grew up in foster homes, didn't he?'

'For about five years. His parents and only brother died when he was ten, in a house fire. Walt managed to escape. None of his relatives would take him in so he lived with several different foster families.'

'So where did his wealth come from if it's not family money?'

'You've read the stories or seen the documentaries on him. He invested some and gambled the lot.'

'I've read bits and pieces, but nothing comprehensive,' Hugo shamefully admitted.

'You need to research Walt if you want to be part of the business. You have to know where we've been to know where we're going. One day, your story will become part of our history.'

'Hopefully not all of my story,' Hugo answered with a crooked smile.

'We all make mistakes, fall on our face from time to time. Do you know how Walt got his initial break?' Hugo shook his head. 'Walt told me one night, during a drinking session, how a winning lottery ticket kicked it all off. You won't hear how he got the ticket, just that he won.'

'Tell me.' Hugo leaned forward eagerly, resting his arms on the table. 'Come on.'

'He left school when he was 15, got a job stacking shelves in a supermarket that bored him to tears. One weekend he disappeared from his foster home and caught a bus to Moree–'

'Where's Moree?'

'Northern New South Wales, an hour from the border. He worked on cattle properties doing odd jobs, learnt to ride, fence and muster cattle. He worked around the area until he turned 22, in 1980. One day, one of the other hands was supposed to go out with old Henry to mend fences, but he was sick, so Walt was told to replace him. Henry was in his late 60s and due to retire to Queensland in the next few months. While Walt was stranding wire, Henry was unloading hardwood fence posts from the truck when the load shifted and came loose. Henry was pinned under a load of posts, crushing his ribs and organs. This was way before satellite or mobile phones and they were kilometres from anywhere. Walt said he felt absolutely useless, he didn't want to leave him, but he couldn't help him either. He pulled the load off Henry but he was in a bad way, spitting blood, he couldn't move him. Henry was dying and both of them knew it. Henry told Walt to reach into his back pocket and get out three lottery tickets. Henry told Walt they were going to pay for his retirement. Henry insisted Walt take the tickets, but Walt refused. Henry finally convinced Walt to take at least one, so Walt picked one and put the other two back in Henry's pocket. Henry died out there in the bush with two worthless tickets in his pocket and Walt's ticket won him half a million dollars.'

'Shit! How fucking lucky was Pop? To replace the sick guy then pick the money ticket.'

'A man died that day and Walt has never forgotten him,' Saxon emphasised.

'Of course...it was unfortunate for Henry, but one man's misfortune is another man's opportunity.'

'And that's Walt, that's happened his entire life, being in the right place at the right time. He bought a small house near Rose Bay and a Chrysler GLX Valiant. With the remaining money he bought shares in Chrysler vehicles, because he liked them so much. He bought at $2.50 each.' Saxon took a break to drink his beer. 'He sold the lot two years later at the end of '82, for 18 bucks a share. He was now a multi-millionaire.'

'That's the year before he started the Tremaine Group. Right?'

'Yep. From the time he bought those shares to the time he sold them; he studied renewable energy technologies. In early '83 he gambled the lot and moved to California. He set-up his first engineering factory to manufacture wind turbines. Made money on that then moved back to Australia in '93 to go into solar power–'

'Pop had balls, to risk everything.'

'Believe me, he still does.'

'Mum said he hasn't been too well lately.'

Saxon remained quiet. 'He may not be with us much longer.' He sipped his beer.

Hugo reflected on his father's comment. 'That will be such a loss. I've been thinking about...do you ever think about the possibility of preserving a person's intellect, their accrued knowledge over a lifetime? To somehow code that into their elevated echo, to create not just a physical replica with similar mannerisms but an intellectually identical replica?'

Saxon smiled warmly at his son. 'Kurt told me in Chennai that your studies are going very well at the Academy.'

'Hey, I love what I'm doing,' Hugo admitted. 'Uni's testing me, the Academy is testing me, I seem to be thriving on it.'

'Good to hear. Now, back to your bloody good question, a question you could spend some serious time researching. I certainly think it's possible, and once you succeed with elevated echoes there's no reason to stop there, you could incorporate something similar into our assembled echoes. That's the sort of question you could use for your PhD thesis in a few years.'

'Yes,' Hugo pondered. 'Pop inspired me. Pop's had such a big life, and history will remember his achievements, but so much will be lost. He has so much experience and knowledge and when he goes...it'll instantly disappear.'

'It will, but that happens to all of us...until you find a solution my son.' Saxon raised his glass. 'To Walt.'

Hugo reciprocated by chinking his father's glass in a toast. 'To Pop.'

Wendy accompanied Enzo Fontaine into Saxon's office on level 2 of the Port Augusta facility.

'Sit down, Enzo,' Saxon's holographic projection directed him towards one of the empty chairs around the coffee table.

Enzo plonked himself down next to Wendy, across from Kris' projection. 'What's this about?'

'It has come to our attention,' Saxon began, 'that you are undermining our operations by covertly syphoning information to Sterling Lindquist. That is called industrial espionage and you can go to prison for that, Enzo.'

Enzo looked at each of them. 'What–'

Saxon raised his hand to stop Enzo speaking. 'This isn't an accusation, Enzo, it is fact. We had a forensic team preserve your network drives. Our techs, along with Kris, created forensic clones of all your drives and they methodically analysed them. We know your workstation has been a conduit for external computers accessing our network. Impressive Black Shield workaround,' Saxon complemented. 'More importantly, we know those external computers placed malware on Wendy's computer to record keystroke passphrases. We traced the source computers to Malmo, Sweden. That's how Sterling found the Uzbek data Wendy stored.'

'But I was told–'

'We don't want to hear it, Enzo. You will pack up your personal belongings and you will be escorted off the facility within the hour.'

'What about...' Enzo paused, realising it was no use arguing. 'Fine.' He stood and was escorted to the elevator by two security guards who had appeared by the office door.

'Now for Sterling,' Saxon said. He picked up his PD and tapped the screen. The PD buzzed. 'Speaker.'

'Saxon, what a surprise. I didn't even know you had my number,' Sterling Lindquist chattered in an upbeat manner.

'Our agreement has changed, Sterling. The percentage you will now pay ZynnComm per month has risen to eight percent of gross turnover for all your companies accessing our network, starting next month.'

'Eight percent! Are you fucking joking? Why would I pay you another three percent?'

'If you don't, we will deny access to the network until you pay. If you are late with your future payments, we will deny access until the payment is made.'

'Why? Why the fucking increase without negotiations?' Sterling pleaded.

'Because you are pond scum, Sterling. Enzo's on his way home, and I think it's time to stop pushing for extended dream immersion.' Saxon disconnected.

'That will hurt more than anything,' Wendy smiled, 'less profit.'

'Maybe we should have cut him off completely,' Kris suggested.

'Sinnerverse and Wunderlust are delivering revenue that will essentially cover all establishment costs for the Chennai DI Academy,' Saxon informed him. 'We are not sacrificing that sort of revenue stream.'

'I understand, but still...have you made a decision on renewing the Ethos supply contract?' Kris asked.

'Just waiting on the final rubber stamp from the board. We're meeting in a couple of days.'

'Good. Ethan keeps hounding me. I told him it's not my area, but he persists.'

Waylon knocked on Saxon's office door before opening it. 'Is this a good time?' He enquired, glancing at each of them in the meeting.

'Sure,' Saxon answered. 'Come in.'

'I have to postpone our meeting again, I'm so close but there's a technical glitch I've encountered,' Waylon explained. 'I've isolated–'

'That's fine,' Saxon said, putting his index finger to his lips to indicate silence. 'Let me know when you're good to go.'

'I will.' Waylon turned and left the office.

'The Mutsumo Aquatic Drone Challenge is now in the sixth hour,' the race commentator reported.

Hugo reclined on the couch eating cereal as he watched the wall screen in the Sydney house.

'Eight drones have completed 161 of 162 laps. A sloppy two metre swell whipped up by a 13 kilometre nor-westerly wind has claimed a record 31 causalities, all lost to the sea. Six have retired with equipment failure, with a further dozen having crashed into one another or into touchdown platforms or tubes. That leaves a field of 51 remaining.'

The vision switcher continually flicked between camera drones hovering high above the course and on-course cameras. The leading drone from the French team, DFX, was 20 seconds in front of the Polish craft, Elektro.

'DFX is coming in for their next touchdown on the sixth platform, a one-square-metre pad,' the commentator updated. 'The drone gingerly manoeuvres, waiting for a window of opportunity as water chop tosses the platform and spray covers the craft.'

One of the multiple displays along the bottom of screen, showed POV vision from the pilot adjusting for wind and the unpredictable nature of the bobbing platform.

'Here it goes.'

The drone skilfully descended onto the platform just long enough to register a touchdown. The display panel confirmed the landing as the DFX craft ascended and zipped off ahead of the Elektro drone, loitering, poised to negotiate the same platform.

'Next obstacle for DFX is the snaking 30 metre Y tube,' the commentator said. 'If they can manage one more lap at this pace, both DFX and Elektro will automatically qualify for the World Aquatic Challenge off Dubai in November'.

Hugo's PD buzzed. 'Mute screen.'

'*It's time*,' Margo's text read.

'*On our way*,' Hugo replied. Hugo knocked on Saxon's office door. 'Dad, Mum is waiting for us.'

A ferocious firestorm of poisonous vapours and molten debris spewed from the mouth of the volcano, slowly suffocating the inhabitants of the original sin city, the Roman resort city of Pompeii.

Ash fell, hot and thick, comprised of pumice fragments and blackened stones, charred and cracked by the heat.

Wendy briefly watched in awe as dense black plumes ballooned 30 kilometres high, concealing the afternoon sun, before she took cover from the hazardous conditions. Buildings shook with violent tremors, swaying to and fro as if they were torn from their foundations. Roof tiles crashed to the ground as dogs barked and howled across the city.

'We must leave while we can still see,' her man encouraged.

'Who are you?' Wendy questioned.

'Cassius, your slave,' he responded with a puzzled expression. 'You must have been hit on the head. You seem confused. Put this on your head.' Cassius placed a pillow on Wendy's head and tied it down with cloth as a protection against falling objects. 'We must get to the shore, to the ships.'

Wendy could hear the shrieks of women, the wailing of infants, and men shouting; some calling their parents, others their children or their wives, trying to locate them in the chaos. She could hear people lamenting their own fate or that of their relatives, and there were some who, in their fear, pleaded for death. Many desired the comfort of the gods, while others imagined there were no gods left, and that the universe would be plunged into eternal darkness forever.

The intense smell of sulphur accompanied the unfolding catastrophe, rousing Cassius into action. He snatched up a fire torch from a collapsed man, who was now being trampled by the terrified mob who ran blindly through the streets.

Wendy spat gritty ash from her mouth. It felt abrasive and unpleasant. Her eyes were irritated and sore.

'Wrap this cloth around your mouth,' Cassius told Wendy. 'Shield your eyes. We must get to the sea.'

Some who had stopped, in the hope that the nightmare would soon end, were overcome and buried beneath the weight of ash. Wendy checked her wrist, the green timer read *24 minutes*. 'Hell.' She grabbed Cassius' hand and followed.

Walt swam in the powder blue sheets of his king-sized bed, double pillows keeping his head from going under. The shrunken man was treading water, yearning for a final surge to take him.

Margo studied his craggy features as she stood watch. His etched wrinkles, his feral eyebrows, his flaccid discoloured skin beset with small scabs that refused to heal, his thin cracked lips, assigned him frail and fragile. He bore little resemblance to the father she knew as a girl.

Walt woke with a start, disorientated. 'Giggles...I have a confession to make.'

'You don't have to confess anything, Dad, there's nothing left to say.'

Walt searched his daughters face through tired eyes. 'You have a half-brother.'

Margo drew a quick breath of surprise, before confusion set in. 'A brother?'

'Before I met your mother, when I was still in the States, I was in a brief relationship and she fell pregnant. One day I couldn't contact her, couldn't find her, she just disappeared. About a year after I married your mother I received a letter from her, with a photo. She was living in Florida and she had a son, my son, your half-brother. She couldn't cope on her own and put him up for adoption in 1994. He was about 12 months old.'

'Where is he now?' Margo asked with an excited tone.

'He's married and lives in San Francisco. I've kept an eye on him over the years, a good family adopted him. I've never met him. I know that he runs a tech company of some kind,' he added.

'Did you keep in contact with his mother?'

'Carmel was killed by a drunk driver as she was crossing a road not long after I got her letter in '96.'

'What's his name?'

'Damian Ziffer,' came the fatigued reply, closing his eyes.

'Why didn't you...' Margo broke off the conversation when she heard Saxon enter Walt's lavish bedroom. There were so many more questions she wanted to ask. Saxon stood beside her, gently nestling her hand in his. 'Where's Hugo?' She sniffed, wiping her damp eyes.

Saxon glanced behind him. 'Coming. How is he?'

Margo hesitated, still processing what Walt had just disclosed to her. 'He drifts in and out of consciousness. How was your road trip?'

Saxon smiled. 'Great, yeah. It was good to spend some time with him outside of work and home.' He looked down at Walt and then at her. 'How are you holding up?

Margo contemplated Saxon with a faint smile. 'I think I'm good,' came her pseudo sanguine reply. 'Ask me in a couple of hours. We've been chatting on and off, we've said our goodbyes. He just told me–'

The door slammed behind them, severing the conversation.

'What the fuck,' Walt grumbled. 'Can't a man die in peace?'

'Sorry,' Hugo uttered meekly, as he joined his parents at the bedside. 'The wind caught it.'

Margo sat on the bed. 'It's alright, Dad, it was the breeze catching the door,' she reassured him, glaring at Hugo.

Through slits for eyes, Walt scanned his family. 'Ah, good, you're all here. Hugo, come sit on the other side of the bed.' His voice sounded raspy.

Hugo followed Walt's direction as Margo sobbed quietly.

'I have always walked to the beat of my own drum,' Walt paused on Hugo. 'The rhythm of our family is set by success, and there aren't many of us, so we have to maintain that rhythm. None of you need my money, but I'll leave most of it to you anyway to continue our family success. Most people are passengers through life, we are drivers, your parents and me. One day you will be too, Hugo. We make things happen, and in turn we make money. Lots of money. Lots of money in this world equals power. As the saying goes, with great power comes great responsibility. You'll learn what your responsibilities are as you get older. I didn't grow up with money or have a formal education like you. The world was my classroom. You know how I made my original money, Son?'

'You picked the winning lottery ticket from the three Henry offered you. Dad told me.'

'That's...almost right. I thought I'd take this story with me, but I might as well tell you.' Walt ran his tongue along his dry, cracked lips. 'Henry certainly had three tickets, and I took the lot. When Henry first showed me, I took one, out of courtesy. While I was sitting there beside his dead body, I figured he wasn't going to need them, so I reached into his pocket and took the other two.'

'Why did you tell me you only took one?' Saxon enquired, a little confused.

'The end result was the same, I just omitted a small detail,' Walt replied. 'Never let incidental facts get in the way of a good story. Picking the winning ticket sounds more dramatic, don't you think?' he asked Hugo.

'Sure does, Pop.'

'You all remember that when you're telling my story when I'm gone. How long have we got?'

Margo glanced at the wall clock. 'The doctor will be here in a few minutes,' she told him with a sniff. 'Are you sure this is what you really want, Dad?'

'Look at you with your mind spinning. I thought we'd settled this. Yes. Do you want to wipe my arse every day?'

'I love you so much, Dad, but I don't do personal care. I'd pay someone to wipe your arse.' They both laughed.

'I'm in that awful place. There's life and there's death, then there's that fucking awful place near the end where you just linger, hanging on, one sad fucking day at a time. That's where I am. I'm not enjoying the ride. I sleep too much and I'm still bloody tired. My body's worn-out. The painkillers make me numb, I don't want to eat and I can't drink whisky...I'm just waiting to stop, to die. It's my choice to finish my life when I choose.'

'I'm just checking, that's all,' Margo said. 'That it's the right choice.'

Walt ignored her concern and continued. 'We're told from the time we're little tykes, there's good and bad in this world, right and wrong, but you soon learn as you get older, they're all mixed up together and you have to unscramble them one day at a time, on so many different levels. I lost my parents and brother in a house fire...that I think I accidently started,' Walt admitted, a tear rolling down his cheek. 'I grew up in foster homes. I told myself for years that was my punishment. There was so much cruelty and very little love in those homes. I had to work through it by myself, one day to the next. Each day is a new start with new choices, I started to tell myself. The person you were yesterday is not the same person you are today or will be tomorrow. Everything changes, from the cells in your body to the relationships in your life, to the environment around you. No two days are the same. That's how I started to see it, and it's worked for me.' A gentle breeze nudged the curtains allowing mid-morning light to stream through the window and touch his bed, as a noisy black cockatoo screeched from the trees. 'Rain's coming. This is the right choice for me today. It seems like a nice day to say goodbye.' Walt managed a smile. 'Don't worry, Giggles, you'll see me in your dreams.' Walt patted Margo's hand. 'And your mother too, thanks to Saxon. The world will go on, it always does.'

'It's not too late to change your mind about humuration,' Margo said.

'I'll decide what happens to my remains thank you. There are nine and a half billion of us on this planet. Where do you think they put the 90 million that die each year? It's the most environmentally sustainable way to dispose of bodies,' Walt responded. 'I wanted you to take the helm of the Tremaine Group, but you declined, and I respect that. We all make decisions based on our values and priorities.'

'What's this about Tremaine?' Saxon's interest piqued.

'I've had second thoughts about–' Margo fell silent as a knock on the bedroom door initiated the beginning of Walt's departure.

'Do you want to get up, into your chair?' Saxon asked Walt.

Walt thought for a moment. 'Nah, I'm gonna end up on my back anyway.'

Into an awkward silence, Alfred, Walt's EA, James, and his physician entered the bedroom.

'James will record the event as a legality,' Alfred announced. 'Ready to proceed? We have to start with the paperwork, Walt.'

'That's one thing I won't fucking miss, paperwork.'

'It was announced today that Walter David Tremaine, the self-made billionaire businessman and Chairman of the Tremaine Group, decided to cease existing and was euthanised today at the age of 91,' the news anchor reported. File footage of Walt meeting heads of state, celebrities, captains of industry and sporting legends over his lifetime played as the commentator continued the media obituary with Merlin, Arrow and Wendy watching in Wendy's office. 'Walt Tremaine has choreographed his farewell as he did his business endeavours throughout his life. The man known for his business acumen and hardball negotiating style, will be given a private ceremony at The Calyx, Royal Botanic Gardens in Sydney before he is humurated. An hour later, a public ceremony will be held at the Parade Ground within the gardens before his remains are scattered across garden beds. His philanthropic work, begun by his wife, Sylvia Tremaine decades ago, has helped and supported tens of thousands of people. Large crowds are expected to turn out for his public farewell. This will be followed by an afterlife gathering back at the Calyx for dignitaries and friends.'

Two days later, after Walt's private ceremony had concluded, his body was gently lifted from the bamboo coffin and placed on the humurator insertion trolley. His clothes were respectfully removed and placed in a bag.

The stainless steel humurator sat inside a repurposed six metre shipping container situated in a screened off parking area of the botanic gardens. Since its development, humuration had gained favour as an alternative to cremation due in part to the decline of organised religion and their burial rituals, and that humeration was fast and cheap. Portable humurators had been developed by the Swiss company Finbon in the late 2030s. Finbon won the UN contract for energy efficient, rapid, hygienic body disposal. Mass fatalities from ongoing conflicts, natural disasters, and pandemics necessitated the request. The brief required the unit to operate in remote locations where electricity was unavailable.

'Confirming all prosthetics have been removed,' the senior technician said.

The assistant technician checked his tablet device. 'Undertakers report detected titanium left and right knees, removed. Two titanium plates and a dozen screws in right forearm, removed. Six implanted teeth, removed. Cochlear implant behind right ear, removed. That's it.'

'Good to go.' The senior technician touched the control display to initiate the process.

Electric motors inside the humurator whirred to life. The insertion trolley carrying Walt's withered naked remains began moving into the humurator feet first. At the same time, a blue roller shutter slowly descended severing the outside world once the trolley was completely inside. This initiated the trolley to tilt, raising the corpse towards an upright position before gravity took over, his body falling into the hopper. This was the fragmentation stage. It took just seconds to be shredded into chunks of flesh and bone by the twin revolving stainless steel shafts of the fragmentor. Discharged into an industrial sized metal bowl, the contents were then transferred through a series of high torque fine mincers. The resulting tissue pulp was flattened evenly across metal trays by drop-down rollers. Wafer-thin mesh lids snapped over the trays sandwiching the tissue, before being delivered to the vacuum pressure chamber for flash dehydration. Two minutes later, during the next stage of humuration, the agglomeration process, Walt's dried tissue was ground to powder before being tumbled in a rotary drum with fine sawdust and misted water. In the final process, pelletisation, the compound underwent thermal compression treatment resulting in centimetre long pellets deposited into a large urn, ready for the public scattering ceremony.

Humuration, the process of turning a human corpse into slow release fertiliser to create humus, took just 11 minutes from start to finish. This was Walt's way of giving back, decomposing and nourishing the garden.

After the public farewell, at Walt's afterlife gathering, Margo, Saxon, Hugo, Kris, Wendy, Merlin and Kurt sat chatting in a quiet corner of the venue.

'Well, I'm going to get back to the Academy,' Kurt announced. 'We've got a class doing their prac exams tonight. I want to make sure everything's ready to go.'

'I'm one of those, Kurt,' Hugo piped up.

'I know. It's against Academy policy, faculty taking students in their vehicles, but do you want a lift?' Kurt asked.

'I don't want to be seen breaking Academy policy in front of Kris,' Hugo responded light-heartedly. 'I think I'll stay a while.'

'Don't be late.' Kurt turned his powered wheelchair towards the venue exit. 'Bye, everyone.'

'Wait up!' Kris spoke. 'I'll catch a ride with you. I have work to finish back at the office. See you.'

'Remember, we want you at the meeting after lunch tomorrow,' Saxon reminded him.

'Sure. Then Kurt and I are flying back to Chennai.'

An assortment of farewells followed them.

Merlin rose from his seat. 'I'm off too. I'm going to meet up with an old school friend before we fly out tonight.'

'I'm going shopping,' Wendy proclaimed as she stood. 'It's Miranda's birthday soon.'

The pair left together.

'Why didn't you have more children?' Hugo raised out of the blue.

Margo met Saxon's gaze. 'We planned to have three children. You were the first and we planned the next one for '29. I miscarried at 12 weeks in '29 and at 11 weeks in 2030. We saw fertility specialists, who gave us every test there was, but no one could tell us why I was unable to carry a second child full term. We didn't try again after that; it was too depressing.'

'Why didn't you adopt?'

'We thought about it but decided not to. We decided to support orphanages instead,' Margo replied.

'And still do,' Saxon added.

'So, I'm one of a kind.'

'You could say you broke the mould,' Margo quietly remarked.

'That's a bit weird,' Hugo commented, twisting his face. 'None of us have siblings.'

'I do,' his father scoffed.

'Oh yeah...Aunt Lena. I forgot.' Feeling awkward, he picked up his beer and drank.

Saxon watched Alfred as he wandered towards their table with drink in hand.

'I was speaking with Roger Eddleston yesterday about Walt's will, he will be setting a date early next month for the reading. It will take a few weeks to finalise some paperwork. Will you be there?' he asked Margo.

'Of course,' she confirmed.

'I will organise a Tremaine Group Board of Directors meeting that afternoon. We will be nominating and voting on Walt's replacement as Chair. Will you be attending?'

'Yes, and Hugo will be joining us,' Margo said, reaching out to her son.

'Who do you think Walt's successor will be?' Saxon probed.

Alfred stared down at him wearing his aloof expression. 'I don't know, Dr Zynn, there are two candidates,' he answered cryptically, then turned and walked away.

Margo and Saxon looked at each other wearing puzzled expressions.

Chapter Ten

Wendy enjoyed procedural police dramas growing up. Her regular DI experience, State of Truth, set in the gritty metropolis of Reverberton, population five million, in 1991, ticked all the boxes as she played a detective solving gruesome homicide cases.

Detective Kevin Powers threw the file down on her cluttered desk. 'This just came in.'

Wendy went to open the manilla folder.

'Wait.' He placed his hand on the file before she could open it. 'Let me tell you about it first.'

Wendy was a little surprised but accepted the advice. She leaned back in her chair.

'A homeless guy found a suitcase two days ago by the side of the M21 Western Distributor heading to Sommerville. A woman's dismembered body was in the suitcase. As you may be aware, this is not the first woman in a suitcase, she's the third female victim concealed in a suitcase in the past six months. The luggage in each murder is the same model and brand, 74-centimetre hard shell Gypsylite deluxe. All the victims bought the luggage themselves.'

'This is an ongoing case. What are we doing on it?'

'Jinx and Graves were put on the Greystones murders this morning; we're taking over.'

'I hate inheriting old cases. That means days of scouring through piles of evidence to get up to speed.'

'Jinx believes the perp is one of Lomax's crew acting on his orders–'

'Lomax?' Wendy's interest instantly piqued. A chance to nail the evasive Zak Lomax.

'How the hell do you fit a body in a suitcase anyway?' Wendy wondered aloud.

'Gut them, sever the head and legs, then stick the head into the chest cavity,' Detective Powers answered very matter-of-factly. 'It all fucking fits.'

Wendy winced. 'Sorry I asked.' She opened the folder and stared at the macabre image of the squashed naked body folded into the suitcase. 'Fuck me. How does anyone do that to another human being?'

'Money, pressure, traumatic background, chemical imbalance in the brain like Lomax,' Kevin replied. 'Come on, we have to get to the morgue. Fisher's waiting to show us the girl unpacked.'

Wendy holstered her pistol. 'If these women bought the suitcases themselves, they must have been under the impression they were going on a trip somewhere.'

'Probably, an overseas trip,' Kevin surmised. 'Decent sized luggage.'

'Have these women got anything in common?' Wendy asked getting into the elevator.

'Raw Gristle.' Kevin pressed the ground floor button.

'Raw Gristle? The brothel above Hollowman's Bar?' Wendy had studied the backstory for State of Truth inside out to get in character.

'Yep, Christian Steinweg's place. The two other females were unidentified, until this last one arrived. The girl in the photo is Christian's 23-year-old daughter, Sheryl.'

'So, this is a turf war. What did Steinweg do to deserve this I wonder?'

'Jinx has a theory the other two girls were persuaded to leave Lomax's establishments. One from Club 88, the other from Colossus. Sheryl's murder was just sheer bloody mindedness on Lomax's part.'

'A warning. Let's pay Mr Lomax a visit after we see Sheryl unpacked,' Wendy suggested as they exited the elevator into a bustling foyer.

Margo, Saxon and Hugo sat at a meeting table in a Tremaine Group Sydney office for the reading of Walt Tremaine's last will and testament. Alfred Nembo was present, as was Zelda Freudenstein and Walt's EA, James Hood.

'Before we begin,' Walter Tremaine's personal lawyer and executor of his estate, Roger Eddleston stated, 'I would like to inform everyone that this version of Walt's will was created only a day before his life ceased.'

'When was the previous version written?' Margo questioned, before sipping her coffee.

'Several months ago,' Roger Eddleston responded. 'I would like to welcome Walt's son to the meeting now.' He tapped his tablet device.

Hugo looked at Margo with surprise. 'You have a brother?'

'Half-brother. He lives San Francisco.'

'So, he told you,' Alfred confirmed with a smile.

'The day he died.'

A middled aged man with a thin face, greying beard and receding hairline appeared on one of the large monitors in the office. 'Good morning.'

'Welcome, Damian,' Roger Eddleston said. 'Everyone, this is Damian Ziffer. Damian, I would like to introduce Margo, your half-sister, her husband, Dr Saxon Zynn and their son, Hugo. On the other side of the table is Alfred Nembo, Tremaine Group's Chief Operating Officer, his EA, Zelda Freudenstein and Walt's ex-EA, James Hood.'

'Hello, everyone,' Damian addressed.

'Hi, Damian,' Margo greeted. 'I'm pleased to finally meet you, I've been curious. Just out of interest, when did you find out Walter Tremaine was your father?'

'Hello, Margo. Great to meet you also. A week ago when Roger contacted me out of the blue. I must admit I was highly sceptical at first, until we met and he explained Walt's and my birth mother's story.'

'Surprised the fuck out of me when he told me on his death bed,' Margo declared. 'Welcome to the family.'

'Thank you.'

'You own Sentry Micronics, Damian?' Saxon enquired.

'Dr Zynn, I'm going to admit this upfront, I am a massive admirer of your work.'

'Please, call me Saxon, after all, you're my...' he glanced at Margo. 'Half brother-in-law.'

'Yes, Saxon, I started Sentry Micronics about ten years ago. We develop and manufacture rapid DNA authentication technology.'

'After Margo and I discussed your existence, I did a little research.'

'I didn't need to research you, I know exactly what you do,' Damian gushed.

'It's a small world. Your company's name rang a bell. I think I spoke to someone from your company about six or seven years ago when we were in early development for our DI wrist device.'

'Really? Back then we were prototyping—'

'I imagine Dad left something to Damian, that's why he's here?' Margo interrupted with her question to Roger Eddleston.'

'That's correct, Margo. Shall we proceed?'

Margo waved her hand in a gesture to go ahead.

Roger Eddleston cleared his throat. 'So, I won't go through all the preamble, I'll let Walt cut straight to the chase.' The lawyer touched his tablet again to activate a second monitor bringing up Walt's gaunt, haggard face.

'Hello, everyone. If you're watching this, I've well and truly fucked off.' His voice was gravelly. 'You will have met my son,

Damian Ziffer, by now. Damian, I'm sorry we didn't get to know each other when I was alive, but I did keep my eye on you. I even contributed to several rounds of seed funding through third parties for your start-up. I'm pleased you were successful. Okay, let's get this started,' he said, already a little breathless. 'Roger tells me as of today, my personal wealth is a smidge over 242 billion US dollars. That amount is based on my Tremaine Group shares, cash in my piggybank, the estimated value of assets that will be sold and my personal share portfolio. I've instructed Roger to gift 50 million dollars to both Zelda Freudenstein and James Hood for their years of committed service. Thank you, Zelda and James. To Damian Ziffer, the son I never knew, I gift 100 million dollars, and 20 million dollars to each of Damian's three children, my grandchildren. To Alfred Nembo, a life-long friend and business confidante, I gift 150 million dollars. Thank you, Alfred, for your tolerance, common sense counsel and your unwavering perspective that business is predictable. To my grandson, Hugo Zynn, a trust has been established controlling 250 million dollars which will be available on your 25th birthday. A three-million-dollar allowance will be released from the trust per annum between now and your 25th birthday. Enjoy, Hugo, but make sure you finish your studies.' Walt managed a smile.

Hugo's face said it all.

Walt continued. 'My little shack on the river, Wildwood, I'm gifting to my son-in-law and business partner, Saxon Zynn. I know you refer to it as Fortress Tremaine, Saxon, now it's all yours. Thank you, Saxon for your deep love for my daughter and grandson, I know you'll take good care of them. I am also grateful for your intellect and the phenomenal technology you have given the world. There are no words to describe what you've achieved, you are truly a man with unlimited vision, imagination and tenacious conviction.' Walt paused briefly to catch his breath. 'I'm gifting 40 billion dollars to various charities Sylvia and I were very proud to support during our lifetimes. Last, but by no means least, the bulk of my estate, the Tremaine Group shares, etcetera, will go to my darling daughter, Giggles, Margo Tremaine.'

Tears rolled down Margo's cheeks as she watched her father disperse the wealth he had acquired over nine decades of a complicated, yet rewarding, life.

'There's just one proviso, Giggles.' He paused. 'I want you as my successor. I want you to be Chairperson on the Tremaine Group Board of Directors for the next 12 months. Alfred and Zelda have both agreed to stay on and support you over the next year in any way they can. If you decline...you will forfeit your inheritance and receive nothing from me.'

Margo wiped her face as the sobering stipulation resonated within her.

'I know you don't need my money or the added pressure,' Walt continued, 'but I also think you, above anyone else, know how to run the business in the manner that it should be. There will have to be vote on the position, but Alfred and I think we have the numbers. Just 12 months at the helm, that's all I'm asking.'

Margo's eyes darted to Alfred. 'Why can't you run it?' Margo asked, speaking over Walt.

'It was Walt's final wish that you head up the business, Margo, not me. I will be there to help you, in any capacity. I see this as a great honour, a great privilege, Margo. Walt had absolute confidence in your business acumen and abilities, as do I.'

Margo considered Alfred's words for a fleeting moment. 'Fuck him!' She stood and stormed out of the office.

Finished with lunch, Hugo watched a news report in silence on his PD via a single earfonic.

Saxon saw Christine Knox on Hugo's screen out the corner of her eye and pointed. 'What's she up to?'

Hugo removed his earfonic. 'She's been awarded most of her father's money in a court settlement. Eighteen million Nukoin. He's going to prison for ten years. Her mother was found complicit and given a four-year community services order.'

'None of that will heal her,' Saxon offered.

'No...no it won't,' Hugo contemplated. 'Maybe I judged her too harshly given the level of abuse she had to put up with.'

Margo watched her two men chatting. 'Perhaps we both did. At least she stood up to him; he's been exposed and held accountable.'

Hugo considered his mother. 'Thanks to you in some part.'

Margo shrugged. 'I'm in two minds over that. I did what I did to protect you. I hope this helps her find some sort of closure.'

'I hope so too,' he agreed. 'I know you said you don't want to talk about what just happened...and you probably think I don't know what's going on...but if you run Tremaine they can't sell their ZynnComm stock,' Hugo blurted. 'We'd be solid for a year.'

A smile grew from the corner of Margo's mouth at Saxon, who raised his eyebrows. 'Yes, there are some upsides, but more downsides. I don't have the time or energy to run two multinational organisations. I told him that.'

'So, throw Alfred under the bus and leave the day-to-day operations to him, and you just weigh in on the big decisions,' Hugo suggested.

This time Margo couldn't help but snort out a laugh. 'Do you hear what I'm hearing?' she asked Saxon.

'Impressive,' Saxon commented. 'He has a point. Or you could take on James Hood as your EA, to be your finger on the Tremaine pulse, he knows how it all works from the inside, how Walt wanted it to work.'

'You t00?' Margo thought for a moment. 'James is now independently wealthy; he doesn't need to work.'

'So give him power,' Hugo pushed. 'Give him a huge salary with perks, give him a position with a seriously impressive title as your proxy for the day-to-day decisions, to act as a conduit between you, Alfred and the board.'

'Shit, what have they been teaching you?' Margo asked with amazement, before considering his reasoning.

Hugo exhibited a conceited smile. 'It's in my genes, Mum.'

'That it is.' Saxon looked at his watch. 'Come on, time to head up to the board meeting.'

Their security detail, sprinkled throughout the restaurant patrons, took their places at vantage points around the open plan eatery and secured an elevator moments after the Zynn's vacated their reserved table.

Fifteen minutes later, the Tremaine Group Board of Directors convened for their extraordinary meeting. At one end of the room, directors were beamed in from around the globe, at the other end, the remaining directors. Saxon and Hugo sat away from the meeting table with Mrs Freudenstein, who held her PD, preparing to record the proceedings. Margo was in quiet conversation on her PD as the meeting came to order, prompting her to disconnect.

Alfred tapped the table with his knuckles. 'Good afternoon, everyone,' he began. 'As you are now all aware, Walt has gifted his Tremaine Group shares to his daughter, Margo, making her the largest individual shareholder and newest member of our board. Walt also had another request that you are not aware of. It was also Walt's wish that Margo take over as Chairperson of the board for a 12-month period.'

Murmurs rippled through the 18 members.

'Congratulations, Margo, on becoming our largest individual shareholder, and welcome to our Board of Directors,' David

Faversham, CEO for the Tremaine Group greeted. 'With all due respect, I'm a little taken aback by Walt's wishes for you to take the Tremaine Group reins, after all, you have limited corporate leadership experience. Do you think you could survive the gruelling responsibilities of running a trillion-dollar private sector corporation?'

The room remained quiet as the members anticipated Margo's response. 'Thank you, David. Much has transpired over the past month. I'll be honest, I didn't anticipate the amount of grief and stress losing someone I have known, loved and respected for over 45 years could have on me. Sometimes I feel like I'm drowning in the quicksand of my thoughts...on those days I don't have much clarity.' She gazed at her son and Saxon. 'Fortunately, I have a fantastic support team. Today is not one of those vague days. Before Walt left us, I told him I didn't want the responsibility of running the Tremaine Group, I don't have the time. This morning Walt gave me an ultimatum, he wanted me to take over his role or forfeit all of my inheritance. I was between a rock and a fucking hard place. But at lunch today, I took counsel from my husband and son, and they offered me a solution that might work. David, I'm not a survivor, I'm a warrior, because that's what you have to be in corporate business. I believe I'm more than qualified to lead this organisation. My father never taught me anything, but I learnt everything about business from him growing up in this building. Now, together with my husband Dr Saxon Zynn and the support from my late father, Walter Tremaine, and this board, we have built the fastest growing tech company on the planet. I'm laser focused and know what has to be done–'

'What has to be done,' David Faversham interrupted before she got into stride, 'is a vote from the board members regarding who we think should head up this multinational corporation, Margo.'

Margo glanced at Alfred. He blinked slowly, indicating his support. 'Of course, David. What is the protocol in this situation?'

'We don't have a protocol, Margo. This is new territory, voting in a new Chair,' Alfred edified. 'But let us employ a simple protocol Walt liked to use when a serious issue was to be voted upon by the board. This will be a straightforward process. I will ask for nominations for the position of Chair, then we will have an open vote on those nominated. The nominees will not vote. Any objections?' Alfred searched the room. 'Good. Let the minutes show no objections were forthcoming. I now call for nominations for the position of Chairperson of the Board of Directors for the Tremaine Group.'

Venus Ezlander, a stylish middle-aged woman sitting beside David Faversham quickly spoke. 'I nominate David Faversham.'

In a slow and deliberate manner Alfred said, 'I nominate Margo Tremaine.' He paused. 'Any further nominations?' Again, he looked around the room. 'If there are no more nominations, we will now vote. Each of us has a single vote only, except for those nominated. Mrs Freudenstein will count votes for each nominee. Those voting for David Faversham, please raise your hand.'

Mrs Freudenstein stood behind Alfred and counted the raised hands. 'Seven votes for David.'

'Those voting for Margo Tremaine, please raise your hands,' Alfred directed, before he raised his own hand.

Zelda did a quick count. 'Nine votes for Margo,' she proclaimed with a smile.

'Fuck you people!' David Faversham snapped, as he slammed an open palm on the table. 'This will not pan out well for the Tremaine Group,' he warned before getting up and striding from the room.

'I would like to congratulate and introduce our new Chairperson of the Tremaine Group Board, Margo Tremaine,' Alfred announced with a satisfied smile.

Claps of congratulations from the small group buoyed Margo. 'Thank you for your support. It has been an eventful day. As we aren't all here, I won't say any more at this point in time. Meeting adjourned.'

Board members shook Margo's hand on their exit from the room, as the holographic directors called out their congratulations before disappearing one by one.

'The apartment on the 17th floor and the chopper on the roof are at your disposal,' Alfred informed Margo with a nod.

'James Hood will be utilising those assets, Alfred.'

'James?' Alfred asked a little confused.

'Before this meeting I engaged James as my Senior Executive Counsel if I were to win the nomination. He will be my eyes and ears on a day-to-day basis.'

Alfred stood firm with a respectful gaze. 'A warrior you are, Margo,' he agreed.

Saxon kissed and hugged his wife. 'Congratulations. We are celebrating tonight. Will you join us, Alfred?'

'Of course.'

Margo walked over to Mrs Freudenstein. 'You too Zelda. We need to wipe the slate clean and move forward together.'

'Yes, I agree,' Zelda said through a warm smile. 'It's what Walt would have wanted.'

'I'll invite James as well,' Margo added. 'The old team will be back together.'

'I'll reserve a table at The Banq,' Saxon announced.

The Dream Chamber was in session.

'I like this colour better than the dark,' Margo complimented. 'Is it grass green?'

'Neon chartreuse I call it,' Wendy informed her.

'I like it too,' Kris agreed. 'Does it taste like grass?'

Wendy smiled. 'Taste it.'

'So, Waylon, we finally have results,' Saxon got straight to the point of the meeting.

'We do. I'm sorry this took so long, but I thought there was a technical glitch and it made me question the data, so I wanted to make sure the data was correct. I've checked it twice to confirm my results and been working with Wendy to coordinate in-dream investigations. Griffin resides in Melbourne but travels extensively. He has wealth and power. He owns Ethos.'

'What!' Kris cried. 'No. Are you sure about this?'

'The data and evidence confirms it and so do eyes on the ground,' Waylon claimed. 'Once I confirmed the location of the DI device from the Dreamlooper experience, verified its unique device identifier, I put two of my team on the ground for a few days.'

'So, you are saying Griffin is Ethan Tan?' Saxon corroborated, still trying to wrap his head around the information.

'I find this hard to believe. Ethan Tan?' Kris checked.

'Ethan Tan is Griffin. Wendy gave me a list of biotech equipment sales in Melbourne stretching back 18 months. Koretech Imports was on that list. My men followed Tan to a warehouse complex in Oakleigh, a 15-minute drive from his home in Malvern, where unit eight is leased to Koretech Imports. Security around the warehouse is low key, basic, a few cameras and keypad entry. My men managed to gain entry through a skylight on the roof of the warehouse after one of Tan's visits. Tan has a dozen DI devices at this location and a biotech set-up with a bank of skin tissue samples. We have video evidence; all quantum ID codes for his devices and DNA from 63 skin samples. Every time one of his devices is activated, we track it. His last attack was Wednesday. One of his counterfeit DNA samples was used and the individual who owns that DNA was not active at that time. Wendy activated more Reservists to patrol the experience so no live echoes were harmed, but an assembled echo was killed. All the evidence supports he was there in the experience. He is Griffin.'

'It makes sense. He has the resources, the knowledge, opportunity and in all honesty, the personality. He's a risk taker,' Margo said. 'I've always found him to be an arrogant son of a bitch.'

'We've just renewed a half billion dollar contract with Ethos,' Saxon admitted quietly.

'He attacked and raped Brigit McKenzie,' Wendy stated firmly. 'She works for the advertising company Ethos uses. He's targeted woman he knows in the waking world. He's a predator.'

'Fuck,' Kris realised with astonishment. 'That's why he pushed to establish the DI Advisory Council, to protect himself,' he declared to Saxon. 'His personal agenda has driven him from the start.'

Saxon contemplated Kris' accusation. 'How many women, who have reported being raped or killed in White experiences, can be linked to Griffin?' he asked Wendy.

'Since Waylon gave me the QuID's for his devices and DNA samples, I've collated 87 that are categorically linked to Griffin,' Wendy told them. 'There are about a dozen extreme complaints I'm still following up. Then there are 51 assembled echoes I've found.'

'We need to stop him now,' Saxon stated with authority. 'Who he is, is irrelevant.'

'So where do we go from here? What would Walt do?' Margo mused.

'Send Waylon after him?' Wendy offered.

'Tan's out of the country at the moment and—' Waylon began.

'He's in Cyprus, diving wrecks off the coast for the next three weeks,' Kris informed them in an unenthusiastic tone.

'We've positioned a series of filament video cameras and motion detectors in the warehouse,' Waylon continued. 'We wait until he returns and strike when he's in DI.'

'Wendy, it's important to keep monitoring rapes or murders in White experiences from last Wednesday now we know he's out of the country,' Saxon instructed.

'Already on it.'

'Has he taken any of the DI devices with him?' Margo questioned Waylon.

'None have left the warehouse.'

'He could have others we don't know about?' Wendy suggested. 'Would he stop attacking for three weeks?'

'True,' Margo agreed. 'Why don't we take everything from the warehouse now?'

'He'll come back and know someone's on to him,' Waylon said. 'If we can take him and his equipment down at the same time, that would be safer.'

'Whatever action we take it has to be swift, we can't afford this workaround to be disseminated at all,' Saxon expressed.

'Perhaps we keep your team at arm's length,' Kris advised Waylon. 'We need to keep ZynnComm, and anyone associated with us clear from any collateral damage from what we're about to do.'

'What are we about to do?' Margo questioned with alarm in her voice.

Saxon frowned at Kris before he spoke. 'We can't afford this workaround to get out. We need to eliminate the source.'

'What do you mean by "eliminate the source"?' Wendy wondered.

'Kris, Waylon and I have spoken about whoever this individual turned out to be, wherever they were, they would have to silenced permanently,' Saxon told the group.

Margo looked from Saxon to Kris and back again with suspicion. 'So, what else did the swinging dick club decide?'

'It's not like that,' Saxon insisted. 'It was an informal chat over a beer. The situation has changed considerably from when we first sat in here and discussed banning individuals from the network. The problem is much more complex and requires a clear-cut solution to ensure this workaround never sees the light of day again. But...now that we know it's Ethan–'

'Your mate Ethan Tan, Kris. Are you having second thoughts?' Margo pressed.

Kris hesitated. 'I'll admit, I wasn't expecting it to be Ethan, fuck, none of us were.' He searched for the words. 'But regardless of who Griffin has turned out to be, I think we all know what has to be done. The rapes and murders must stop, and as Saxon said, we can never let this workaround go public. We can't just ban Ethan from the network. If we confront him, that won't work either, because he's integral to our product and services, our working relationship would be over. He has to permanently disappear, and we have to make sure there is no connection back to ZynnComm whatsoever. We, along with everyone else, must be ignorant to his whereabouts.'

'So, we really are a star chamber now,' Wendy remarked solemnly. 'All we need is our executioner.'

Everyone remained silent.

'I know someone who may be able to help,' Kris divulged in due course. 'I won't mention names because the less you know the better.'

'Who do you have in mind?' Saxon asked.

'Someone who can make Ethan disappear without a trace. Someone I met in Hunters and Collectors.'

'Can they be trusted?' Margo challenged, somewhat sceptical.

'Remember when Justin Ma was murdered?'

'Yes,' Saxon responded.

'I didn't think anyone was arrested for that?' Wendy alleged.

'No one has been because they can't be found. The two arseholes responsible for Justin's murder ran the Hunters and Collectors experience, as well as the real world hate website, United Storm Front. Justin was responsible for getting that website taken down.

Those two men, Shane McHawk and Vincent Spencer disappeared from the face of the planet and have never been heard from since. I know the guy who did that and I'm sure he would help us.'

'What happened to those men?' Wendy's curiosity got the better of her.

Kris smiled at her. 'He wouldn't elaborate. I can find out if he's interested in helping.'

'Ethan is a very high-profile individual, how does someone like that disappear without a trace?' Margo argued.

'Ethan has a secret warehouse where he covertly rapes and murders women at will, albeit in-dream,' Waylon replied.

'It feels real for the victims,' Wendy added.

'And for Ethan, that's why he continues to do it,' Waylon concurred. 'Ethan simply goes to his warehouse when he returns and is never heard from again.'

'Who knows what type of unsavoury merchandise Ethan has in his warehouse, on his computers,' Kris suggested with raised eyebrows. 'I can contact my man and Waylon and I could have a chat with him about how we proceed.'

Each of them looked at one another, unsure of sanctioning Ethan Tan's demise.

'Does Ethan have children?' Wendy asked.

'No, that might be a positive,' Margo said. 'I like Grace. I don't know how she ended up with Ethan.'

'If nothing is done, in-dream violence in White experiences will continue,' Waylon reminded them. 'He could also disclose his method to others.'

'What if we set him up, had him arrested and he spent years in prison?' Wendy proposed. 'We could easily do that.'

'And what if he published his workaround while in prison on social media?' Saxon reacted. 'Can you imagine how this type of information could impact the platform? A black market in skin tissue would spring up in months and chaos would follow if people knew they could get away with anything and we couldn't control it.'

'We can't let that happen,' Kris agreed. 'If he remains alive there will always be that threat he'll distribute the information.'

'There is a way we could keep tabs on all users,' Wendy piped up with a sideways glanced at Waylon.

'How?' Kris asked.

'I've been working on a type of exotic hybrid cookie we could load onto the network that would keep tabs on all devices. If we need to identify a device in future, even those using VPDN, this cookie could be activated.'

'That's a step too far, Wendy. That would be a blatant breach of privacy,' Saxon warned.

'Only we would know it existed,' she countered. 'It would make it lightning fast to pinpoint individual units for future incidents.'

'I'm with Saxon on this, Wendy,' Kris agreed. 'Although it would be a great tool to have in our arsenal, all it would take is some techno-geek to stumble upon it and the word would be out. We would be crucified.'

'I think you'll need something like this long term to track devices,' Waylon threw in. 'I wouldn't rule it out completely.'

'I think Wendy and Waylon have a point,' Margo chimed in. 'Never say never. We should keep an open mind.'

'Let me be clear,' Saxon was blunt. 'I will not allow tracking cookies on the Norus network. We succeeded in solving this issue, and if something like this occurs again, we will manage. We can't risk compromising our ability to deliver private experiences to users. Understood? Governments and users expect nothing less,' he paused to let his edict sink in. 'I think Waylon and Kris should have a discussion with his contact tomorrow. We have three weeks to solve this problem.'

'I think they should have the discussion and then distance themselves so Kris' mystery man can finish the job,' Wendy decided. 'The further we are all away from this the better.'

All eyes fell upon Margo. 'So, let it be done. I don't want to hear any more about this until I see it in the media.' Focusing on Waylon and Kris she added, 'Just make sure there is no paper or electronic trail and all conversations are away from recording devices.'

'I'll organise an in-dream meeting tomorrow,' Kris said.

The group fell silent as each contemplated the magnitude of what they were about to be a part of.

'This is the right thing to do for the victims,' Saxon's jaw was set, 'and the business.'

'I can confirm, based on our research, an hour in DI is achievable. I think it would be beneficial for users and for ZynnComm,' Saxon Zynn stated. 'Users could enjoy their favourite experience for longer and we would charge a higher premium for the privilege, win-win.'

'You were opposed to extended DI up until recently, what changed your mind?' Stark Green asked.

'The surge in public opinion wanting us to make the change caught us off guard, Stark. We didn't appreciate that people wanted to spend more time in DI, in recreation. We thought 33 minutes was enough time, but we were wrong.'

'And you've also acknowledged DITS, dream immersion trauma syndrome, is an actual condition with real-world implications for victims,' Stark confirmed.

'I know DITS is real, Stark, because I have the condition,' Saxon acknowledged.

'Fuck,' Kris muted the video on his PD. 'We need to squash this quick smart. I'm amazed it fooled Digimarx 3...a lot of AI and money has been thrown at this.'

'Margo and Selma are on it with a media release,' Saxon told him. 'They've contacted Stark and he's agreed to condemn it tomorrow on his show. Synthetic media propaganda isn't easy to remove once it goes viral, even harder to find the ring leaders.'

'Deepfake has been illegal on the network for decades, making this a sophisticated variant.' Kris swiped his PD screen to remove the video. 'Probably commissioned on the darknet. It fooled tamperproof creation authentication and PD distribution display protocols.'

'Darknet media creators are always one step ahead it seems.'

Both men took a sip of coffee as they scanned the buzzing lunchtime crowd in the Sydney DI Academy cafeteria. Students eating and chatting at other tables were aware of Saxon, sneaking glimpses of him. Saxon's minders were sprinkled throughout the room, keeping a close eye on the herd.

'Who would gain from posting this? Definitely Sterling,' Kris speculated.

'Zam Chu,' Saxon responded. 'SkyCloud?'

'Even state actors wanting to disrupt the status quo.'

'Alfred even contacted me and asked when I recorded it.'

From out of nowhere Hugo approached their table. 'Is it true? Are you extending DI?'

'Take a seat,' Saxon urged, pulling out a chair. 'No, it's not true. It was a deepfake video.'

'I fucking knew it!' He turned to a table of fellow students eagerly looking his way and gave them a thumbs down. He sat tentatively on the edge of the seat. 'I told them it was bullshit, even after I watched the interview.'

'Seems it's done a damn good job of convincing people it was actually your dad,' Kris said.

'It's a bloody convincing deepfake. Who made it?' Hugo asked.

Saxon raised his eyebrows. 'Your mother is trying to find out.'

'I've got a class. I have to go.' He returned to the table with his friends, sharing his news.

'This bullshit around extending DI is going to be harder to smother now,' Kris grumbled, looking at Hugo and his friends. 'Fucking slimy individuals have fed the fire. You know, we could always create our own deepfakes of Sterling and Zam, have them ready to go when we get to the bottom of it?' he suggested.

'We are not slimy individuals, Kris. We will not stoop to their level. We have to reinforce why 60 minutes in DI isn't sustainable,' Saxon resolved, watching Hugo and his classmates leave the cafeteria.

The alarm on Kris' PD buzzed. 'Time for the meeting with my contact.' He finished his coffee. 'I'll be in my office.'

'I'll come up in about 45 minutes. I'm meeting with Margo and Michelle Kronenberg to discuss legal avenues for this damn video.'

Chapter Eleven

Liam awoke to a child crying in another room. A woman slept soundly beside him. His gut feeling told him to investigate, to find the crying child. You never knew what to expect in Astounding Experiences, and that kept Liam coming back for more. He cautiously got out of bed, pulled back the curtain and peered out the window to flashes of ground-to-cloud lightning strikes and the sound of distant thunder. From the silhouetting, he guessed the house was in a rural area on cleared land sprinkled with trees.

The child cried out again, drawing Liam from the bedroom. He wandered down the hall following the cries. As he opened a bedroom door a burst of lightning lit up the room. There was no floor, just a black abyss. Liam's momentum made him teeter, he lurched forward, still gripping the doorknob, first with one hand, then with both. A cold updraft carried the tormented cry of a child from below. Liam struggled to hang on. Manoeuvring his hands, he gripped both knobs, front and back. His weight on the door initiated the separation of the top hinge from the narrow door frame. Something from below wrapped around his left ankle, pulling gently at first, testing his resolve, gradually increasing. His sweaty hands lost grip on the metal door knobs and he fell into darkness, the child's cries echoing in his ears. Liam whiplashed back and forth until he came to rest dangling upside down from the tether that gripped his leg. He focused in the direction of the child's sobs. A lightning flash revealed a small child wrapped tightly in the many legs of a massive house centipede.

The child's head was exposed. She seemed to compose herself when she saw him. 'Please help me,' she begged.

The sizeable, elongated creature bristling with numerous hirsute legs appeared to be fixated on Liam. He reached up, struggling to untie the fibre around his leg, but failed. Hand over hand he pulled himself upright. Liam peered up into the darkness to see the source of the binding. Another lightning flash showed he was held by a single strand of web from the spinneret of an impressively massive spider. A sudden series of lightning flashes followed, illuminating the walls busy with life. Hundreds of smaller house centipedes ran rampant.

'*How the fuck do I get out of this?*' Liam pondered.

The Mediterranean Sea off the coast of Cyprus was calm and quiet. The balmy halfmoon night had devoured the familiar gem-blue water of the day.

Forty metres below the sea surface, Ethan Tan glanced at his wrist dive computer, '*1124 kPa*' remaining. 'Hey, Chrissy?' There was no response through the wireless comms of his dive helmet. He halted and looked behind him but couldn't see the beam from his dive buddy's lights within the sunken wreck. Ethan switched off the tri-beam lights built into his helmet, watched, and waited. No lights, pitch black. 'Chrissy?' Abruptly, he felt immediate changes in water pressure. As he flicked his lights back on, everything around him was visibly shuddering, sediments clouded the water. 'If you can hear me, Chrissy, I think it's an earthquake. I'm in the engine room on my way up.'

Quickly working his way through the barnacle encrusted steel girders, massive pipes and long-seized engines, his light fell upon the opening into the lower cargo space. The wreck stopped shivering. Ethan remained motionless as he checked his wrist computer; the water pressure had returned to normal. The graveyard of cluttered, creature-encrusted trucks littered the port side of the vessel. This had been the wreck's bottom since it sank almost seven decades ago with 108 fully laden lorries onboard. As Ethan swam through murky water over slowly decaying relics, his mind raced.

Quickly and quietly an arm slipped out from between truck cabins, knife in hand, and severed the air hose at the rear of his helmet, spewing an endless spray of bubbles. In the poorly lit effervescent confusion, the muzzle of a PPS-N2 underwater pistol was pressed firmly against the soft underside of Ethan's jaw and fired. The tip of the four centimetre stainless steel dart penetrated through the top of his helmet, releasing a fine plume of blood that dispersed into wet darkness. Ethan went limp.

Saxon and Margo sat at the kitchen island in their Port Augusta residence, eating dinner. Saxon ate mouthfuls of cheesy tuna pasta while working on his tablet device, as Margo watched her PD and listened via an earfonic.

'Look!' Margo exclaimed, quickly mirroring her PD screen to the living room wall display.

'...tech guru, Ethan Tan, the CEO of Ethos and inventor of Swipe Charge technology, is feared missing off the coast of Cyprus near Larnaca in the Mediterranean Sea,' the news voiceover reported over footage of search craft and divers. 'Tan and friends had been scuba diving sunken wrecks in the Mediterranean for the past two and a half weeks until yesterday. Yesterday evening, Ethan Tan and his dive partner, Christina Stavrinou were reported missing after their dive boat captain lost audio contact with the pair as they explored the lower cargo deck and engine room of the MS Zenobia. During their dive, a 4.5 magnitude earthquake at a depth of 55 kilometres was recorded between Cyprus and Syria. Christina Stavrinou was located 40 minutes later after initiating her rescue GPS, but Ethan Tan is still missing. In a statement, Ms Stavrinou said she was following Ethan one moment and then something hit her helmet and her dive lights went out. She lost communications with the boat and Ethan and then the earthquake hit. She became very disorientated in the dark.

Night dives off Cyprus have gained in popularity in recent years and Ethan Tan, considered to be a highly qualified and experienced diver, liked to push the limits with adventurous night dives. The search for Ethan Tan was called off last night due to several aftershocks and resumed at first light local time.'

Margo muted her device and turned to Saxon. 'Do you think...it could be–'

'The fickle finger of fate? I'd better call Ethos and see if there's any news,' he suggested unemotionally.

'I'll give Grace a call and see how she's holding up.' Margo left her meal on the island bench and walked across the room, sitting on the living room couch.

Saxon's PD buzzed. Kris' head projected out of his device. 'We just saw the news about Ethan. Have you heard any updates?'

'I called Morino at Ethos and she's on her way to Cyprus,' came Kris' response. 'It's about one in the afternoon there now and still no sign of him.' Kris paused. 'We have another problem. I'll send an invite for DC.' He disconnected.

An hour later, the Dream Chamber was again in session. Kris, Saxon, Margo and Waylon were in attendance.

'Wendy didn't respond,' Kris told them.

'What's the problem,' Margo asked.

'Waylon,' Kris gestured for him to begin.

'Forty-five minutes after the first news of Ethan's disappearance broke the motion detectors and cameras in the Koretech Imports warehouse were activated. I had men there within 15 minutes, but by the time they arrived the eight DI devices and all the skin samples were gone. His man had tidied up.'

'Any idea who it was?' Saxon asked.

'I've analysed the footage many times and it's a heavy-set man, wearing a hoodie, dark clothes and gloves. That's all I know.'

'Did they follow him?' Margo pressed.

'He was in and out in three and half minutes, they weren't there to see him leave.'

'The security cameras. Can you access them?' Saxon questioned.

'We have several access applications lodged, but they'll take days to approve,' Waylon informed them.

'We never factored in an accomplice,' Margo thought aloud. 'Shit.'

'There was no evidence or intelligence there were others involved,' Waylon said.

'The good news is Ethan won't be found,' Kris divulged.

Margo gave him a quizzical look. 'How can you be sure?'

'My man confirmed the kill,' Kris bragged. 'Ethan's body was kilometres away before the first search and rescue boats were dispatched. And we were lucky enough to have the diversion of an earthquake to coincide with our mission.'

'So, this diving accident was the plan?' Margo asked incredulously. 'The plan to eliminate Ethan?'

'You said you didn't want to know about it until it was in the media. Waylon and Wolf...' Kris instantly tried to recover from his slip of the tongue. 'Let's call my man Wolf.' Saxon shared a smirk with Margo. 'Okay, his fucking name is Wolf,' Kris snapped, angry at his disclosure. 'Anyway, they decided it should look like an accident because there wouldn't be any loose ends.'

'We have one massive loose end now,' Saxon added.

'We should have gone in and dismantled the warehouse when we got word from...erm,' Waylon glanced at Kris, 'Wolf, but we weren't expecting visitors.'

'Cunning bastard,' Saxon ruminated. 'I wasn't expecting a plan B either. Does Ethan have security?

'No,' Waylon answered.

'I thought one of them might fit the bill for our new mystery man.'

'We can still track the devices,' Waylon reassured them. 'We'll get the security cam footage. We'll find this guy.'

'Tonight, we have the dream master, Dr Saxon Zynn, with us,' Ivy Lane announced to her live audience. 'Welcome, Dr Zynn.'

'Thanks for the opportunity to be on the show, Ivy.' Saxon sat in his office in front of the telepresencebot, his holographic image projected into the chair in the New York studio.

'There has been fierce debate in all media recently about extending dream immersion to 60 minutes. There have even been deepfake videos of you extolling the virtues of extending DI and the acknowledgment of dream immersion trauma syndrome. What is your opinion on both of those subjects?'

'Let me state categorically, Ivy, we have a duty of care to our customers, and it would not be in their best interest to increase dream immersion to 60 minutes. Dream immersion for 60 minutes is highly dangerous. Let me explain why. We developed this technology, we've researched the optimum time to be 33 minutes, any longer and users could run the risk of inducing seizures, stroke or developing short term psychosis. We all dream for about two hours each night when we sleep, and the brain is quite active during dreams, enabling creativity and providing emotional restoration, tiring the brain. Now consider, many users are big dippers, they dream phaze every day. We knew that would be the case as users became accustomed to the platform. If we added an additional 27 minutes to each immersion, taking them to 60 minutes every day, week in, week out, brain fatigue would manifest as psychological problems in the real world—'

'Along the lines of DITS?'

'Well, we're still analysing the reports of people who are understood to be living with DITS. Trauma can mean different things to different people and manifest in unique ways. You must remember, Ivy, we have over 34 million unique users per month on our platform. I've seen research claiming around 935 users per month are impacted by DITS, that is .0000275 percent of all users, all users, not just White rated experiences. That figure is across all classifications. Some people are not paying enough attention to ratings and inadvertently entering experiences that are far more violent than they anticipated.'

'Women experiencing rape and murder in general public experiences say it feels very real, very traumatic, and what they experienced deeply impacts their waking life,' Ivy argued. 'They live with those memories.'

'Don't get me wrong, Ivy, I'm not dismissing their claims. I believe these women have suffered horrific violence in White rated experiences, I do. We're researching the correlation between PTSD in the waking world and the impact of extreme violence against women in-dream to map the similarities. But you have to understand how difficult it is to anticipate where future attacks may occur, they are random. We have established a senior research team to look at ways of minimising in-dream violence in White and Yellow rated experiences, and for the last month extreme complaints are in decline.'

'And what has caused that, Dr Zynn?'

'To be honest, Ivy, we aren't sure yet. It could be several factors, perhaps the media attention in recent months, but continuing analysis over time will give us a better understanding.'

'Any decline in violence in White rated experiences is positive.'

'Of course, Ivy.'

'It's been a week since Ethan Tan was last seen, and from expert reports there could be a number of possibilities for his disappearance. There are hypotheses of equipment malfunction, being caught in wreckage during the earthquake, there are even conspiracy theories that he faked his own death and he's been seen in South Korea. Regardless of what has happened, how will ZynnComm move forward? Because Ethos is a major component supplier for your DI device, and you've recently renewed a half billion dollar contract with the company.'

'You know, Ivy, Ethan is a very experienced diver, with hundreds of dives to his credit, all over the world, but the ocean or sea can be an unforgiving environment for anyone, earthquake or not. It's been an especially difficult time for Grace, Ethan's wife, over the past week; my heart goes out to her. These unsubstantiated stories of sightings on social media only exacerbate her angst. It's also hard for his work colleagues and employees to come to terms with. It's not about how this impacts ZynnComm, Ivy, it's about us supporting Ethos through this difficult and uncertain time. Ethan has worked closely with us from the start, and we'll maintain the status quo, maintain stability for everyone. We've had meetings with Ethos this week and our working relationship will continue unchanged. We will support them and work with them to get through this episode. I think that's what Ethan would want us to do.'

The inaugural Ultimate Warrior Knockout was in the closing stages of the fourth of seven consecutive days of competition. Sixty thousand plus users entered the event, Wendy was one of them. Just under 20,000 remained.

On a dry barren landscape, in the heat of day, the remaining competitors wearing singlets, shorts and runners encountered the Wall of Barbed Wire. Stretching on for as far as the eye could see in either direction, the seven-metre-high obstacle could be tackled in one of two ways, climbing over or cutting through. Wendy briefly watched the competitors trying to climb the malicious barrier. Some contestants took off their singlet and shorts and wrapped them around the hands and went gung-ho over the wall as quickly as possible, slicing themselves to shreds in the process. Wendy decided on the second option. She wrapped her flame red hair in a tight bun so it wouldn't get caught. She struggled to cut the mess of rusted spiky wire with her mini bolt cutters. Her sweaty palms lost grip on more than a couple of occasions, slicing up her knuckles. 'Fuck!' Pain thresholds for all competitors were enforced, set at four, so she felt everything. Wendy didn't stop. Painstakingly, she severed the strands before cautiously bending back the wire onto itself and tangling it up. The opening through the metre deep wire obstacle was now large enough to contort her way through. Screams and cries from opponents warned Wendy of her imminent fate. As she gingerly eased herself into the hole arms first, a rogue strand sprang back and punctured her thin singlet, wedging in her belly flesh. Wendy couldn't move forward or backwards without being wounded. She tried to reach back to remove the offending prong but her forearm got snagged on pointed metal. Gritting her teeth, Wendy deliberately dragged herself through the crude gap as sharp steel effortlessly carved a nasty gash deep into her stomach, initiating her guttural cries. Wire claws punctured the back of her head and grabbed her hair several times. Her only choice was to tear wads from her scalp.

On the other side of the wire wall, burdened with arm, face and leg cuts, she collapsed. The deep laceration on her abdomen was bleeding profusely as she got to her feet. A referee wiped blood from her upper arm and registered her entry number. Wendy's arm readout showed seconds remained in the instance. She had made it through to the fifth day of competition.

'Is this worth 50,000 Nukoin?' A woman suffering serious slashes across her face, entangled in a crude cavity a metre off the ground, called out.

'I–' Wendy began, but the familiar crimson glow engulfed her and she was gone.

The third Dream Immersion Advisory Council meeting convened under melancholy circumstances in Surat, India.

'I'm sure everyone here is feeling...feeling like they don't want to be here,' Kris broke the silence. 'Ethan was a friend to everyone in the room and the situation surrounding his disappearance two weeks ago is difficult to accept and will be for some months.'

'I still have the foil chalice he gave me at our last meeting,' Justine Vanderberg mentioned softly.

'So, nothing at all has been found?' Jorma Despirito questioned Kris.

'I've been in contact almost daily with Yumi Morino, the Chief Operating Officer at Ethos, and she said they're still searching, but nothing has been located.'

'You would think something would be found, equipment, body parts...you know, if a shark attacked him,' Jorma finished awkwardly.

'Shark attacks in the Mediterranean are few and far between, Jorma,' Kit Bombo told her.

'I've seen vision from the search and rescue teams and there are trucks piled on top of each other all over this sunken ship,' Kris informed the group. 'This geographic region has half a dozen earthquakes each year. The most logical explanation I've heard is he's been trapped beneath one or more of these trucks, shifted by the earthquake. He may never be found.'

'I saw Saxon on Ivy Lane's show last week, Kris,' Justine shifted the direction of the conversation, 'discussing in-dream violence. He mentioned serious violence was decreasing in White rated experiences. Can you quantify that?'

'Don't quote me, I don't have the exact figures with me right now, but on average between 10 to 14 rapes or deaths have been reported per month for the past six months, then this last month just a handful of assaults, no rapes or murders. We collate information from several sources regarding extreme complaints in White and Yellow experiences. We have our usual reporting and feedback channels from DI users, the international police reporting portal and our team also works with and collects information from the Stop Dream Violence movement. From those three sources, in-dream violent incidents have declined significantly over the past month.'

'Saxon said you don't know why,' Justine continued.

'Not really, we know there has been a steep decline in reports over the past month, but can't explain why yet—'

'That's a sudden decrease,' Professor Winston Singh threw in. 'I've discussed this with Saxon and it sounds like someone has possibly stopped entering DI. The perpetrator may have been imprisoned or died for example.'

'One individual wouldn't be responsible for that sort of number, surely?' Jorma Despirito queried. 'It would have to be several individuals.'

'Throughout recent history, individual serial rapists and murderers have been responsible for literally hundreds of rapes or murders.' Kit Bombo recalled. 'They flew under the radar for years. Remember Amari Selassie?' Blank faces around the table conveyed ignorance. 'You know, that nightclub in Johannesburg, called RePublic. It was back around 2027, maybe 28. I remember the female and male toilets were inappropriately signed "Holes" and "Poles". Anyway, they employed a bouncer, a security guard named Amari Selassie. He raped and killed 267 woman over five years before he was shot dead by one of his victims.' Still the vacant stares surrounded him. 'Maybe I remember it because my cousin was a detective on the case, she helped unravel Amari's trail of destruction. But my point is, one man could easily be responsible for a dozen rapes or murders per month in dream immersion, especially when an individual's identity is protected.'

'I take your point, Kit,' Jorma agreed.

'Whatever the reason, I hope they don't return,' Justine said.

Kris watched the oscillation of the conversation with some relief, knowing the real culprit was dead. 'We won't know if this is an irregularity until next month's figures come in,' he pointed out.

After the meeting, Kit Bombo waited until all the other members had left the room before he spoke to Kris. 'May I have a quick word, Kris?'

'Of course, Kit.'

Kit got up from his chair and moved closer to Kris. 'I just wanted to discuss a proposition.'

'A proposition? Has it got anything to do with your private in-dream security force?' Kris asked sarcastically.

'No, no. A separate matter. Have you heard of the Human Egalitarian Law Party?'

'Yes, of course I have.'

'I'm a senior member in the Angolan branch and we are expanding exponentially since we launched there and simultaneously in Ethiopia, Nigeria, Egypt, South Africa, here in India, Brazil and Indonesia. We are now seeking candidates in Australia, the United States and the EU.'

'Let me stop you there, Kit. I admire what the HELP has achieved so quickly and I believe it is an international political movement that is long overdue, but I don't have the time to take on that sort of responsibility. I couldn't represent the HELP adequately.'

Kit gave him a polite smile. 'With all due respect, Kris, it was not you we were thinking of.'

'Oh...oh, okay,' Kris accepted, somewhat deflated.

'Sorry, Kris, I haven't explained myself clearly. We were thinking of approaching Alfred Nembo to assist in establishing our HELP offices in Australia.'

'Alfred? Of course Alfred.'

'We aren't looking for candidates just yet, there is a process. You know Alfred and we were wondering if you could solicit a meeting with him to discuss his involvement.'

'Surely you have enough influence to just call him and set up a meeting?'

'Possibly, but that is not how the HELP operates. We like to take advantage of casual, person to person networks, where there is familiarity. We have found this personal approach much more authentic and effective.'

'Okay, sure. I could have a chat with Alfred when I get back to Australia.'

'Thank you so much, Kris.' Kit got up to leave.

'By the way, interesting story about that Amari fellow. It put things into perspective.'

Selma Thurston approached Brigit McKenzie in the carpark under the building where she worked in the Melbourne CBD. 'Brigit!'

Brigit looked up from her PD as she walked to her car. 'Yes.' She gazed at Selma, processing her face. 'Selma? Selma Thurston?' Brigit recognised her from their video chats.

'Yes. I know we haven't met in person. I thought we should.'

They shook hands. 'Down here? Why didn't you make an appointment?'

'Let's just say I have some news that should be conveyed privately,' Selma explained.

'News about what?'

'Come, I have a vehicle over here where we can talk.' As they walked over to a white van the central door unlocked and slide along the vehicle.

Brigit hesitated when she saw Saxon and Margo waiting inside. 'What's this about?'

'Hi, Brigit,' Margo greeted. 'Please, come and sit down. We have some news you might like to hear straight from the horse's mouth, so to speak.'

'Hello, Brigit. I'm Saxon and this is Margo.'

'I'm well aware of who you both are.' Brigit sat opposite them and Selma beside her. The door slid closed.

'So, why the clandestine meeting?' Brigit began sarcastically.

'Would you like to know who raped you in Nugent's Luxury Plaza?' Margo proposed.

Brigit looked at Selma, then back to the power duo. 'For what purpose?'

'Everybody serves somebody,' Saxon admitted. 'We serve the governments who allow us to deliver dream immersion safely by adhering to privacy and customer wellbeing.'

'You seem to be getting half your responsibility right,' Brigit mocked.

'We think we've resolved the risk of rapes and murders in White rated experiences, Brigit, and we wanted you to know how that came about. We want to give you some closure,' Margo insisted.

'I'm listening,'

'We know that you've worked with Ethan Tan's Ethos company,' Saxon said.

'I have. Mogo handles advertising for them.'

'He is the man who raped you in-dream,' Margo stated coldly.

Brigit remained silent, weighing up the information. 'Ethan Tan? How do you know that? I thought privacy restrictions prevented anyone from being identified?

'They do, and they will continue to do so,' Saxon explained. 'We collate reports of in-dream violence from several sources, one of course, being your Stop Dream Violence movement. We had our suspicions when a few red flags were raised, so we began an investigation into Ethan. You, along with almost 100 other women, were his victims. Ethan Tan was a serial rapist and murderer.'

'He had a warehouse where he set-up a sophisticated system with multiple DI devices to assume other people's identities,' Margo continued. 'I won't go into detail, but if you check your complaints register since his death, there have been zero rapes or murders in White experiences.' Margo concluded, letting the information sink in.

'Where's this warehouse? Can I see it?' Brigit pressed for information.

'It was dismantled soon after his disappearance,' Saxon said. 'It was in...'

'Oakleigh,' Margo finished. 'Not just anyone could have done this, Brigit. He had in depth knowledge of the platform, unfettered access and deep pockets.'

'So why haven't you gone public with this?' Brigit questioned. 'Tell the world what a fucking abomination this man was.'

'We don't think it would be in our best interests to publicise the matter,' Selma reacted.

'It would be in my interest. How did he do it?'

'We won't reveal vulnerabilities in the system,' Saxon replied. 'But the oversight has been rectified.'

'We don't want you discussing this information with anyone, Brigit, especially anyone in your movement,' Margo requested.

'Good luck with that,' Brigit boldly proclaimed with a laugh. 'Of course I'm going to tell the world, I'll sing this from the rafters. This man was a predator in every sense of the word and I will tell anyone and everyone online and off.'

'We thought you might feel like that,' Selma asserted, reaching for her PD. She opened the device and tapped a video. It automatically projected and played on the interior van door.

'I'll bankroll this project but you have to agree to my terms,' Iminka said, sitting around a café table with Brigit and one other.

'You tell me what you need and we'll do the rest,' on screen Brigit agreed.

Selma paused the recording. 'We could give this to the authorities and Brent's and your career would be ruined, your lives would be over.'

'Where did you get this?' Brigit queried, ashen faced.

'You've been on our radar for quite some months, Brigit,' Margo informed her. 'We know you, Brent Lurmington your AI syntheneer at Mogo, and Iminka Korhonen were behind the deepfake videos of Saxon. You can go to prison for deepfake distribution in some jurisdictions. Did you know that, Brigit?'

Brigit was visibly incensed, her body language shouted frustration. 'You expect me to just to roll over after your fucking organisation has sat on its hands over dream violence? That's why I made that video, to make you sit up and take this shit seriously.'

'To the contrary, Brigit, we've had a team analysing and researching this extreme violence issue for over six months,' Saxon defended. 'We have much more to...' he hesitated.

'Lose, you were about to say lose, weren't you?' Brigit suggested. 'Well, I'll fucking tell you what I've lost.' She turned to Selma. 'You talk about losing my career and my life. I lost my life as I knew it seven months ago, when I was forcibly raped and violated in a dark alley. I lost my boyfriend and my friends through emotional, physical and social isolation. It took me months before I could function and work again. It totally fucking ruined my life.' Tears rolled down her cheeks. 'I still have nightmares about the abuse; I have since it happened. That is PTSD. That's what I've been diagnosed with after visiting your fucking entertainment network, Saxon and Margo.'

Selma handed her a tissue.

'Look, Brigit, this in-dream abuse hit us without warning too,' Margo explained. 'Ethan was a rogue element we weren't expecting, we didn't know how to fix it, but we never stopped trying. Now we need your help to get things back on track.'

'How do you know he was the only one, there could be more?'

'The reports of extreme complaints have ceased. He worked alone,' Saxon promised her.

Brigit sobbed, contemplating her response. 'I won't say anything to anyone,' she uttered quietly. 'You have my word.'

'We have more than your word, Brigit, we have video,' Margo reminded her matter-of-factly. 'We also want you to slowly dismantle your Stop Dream Violence movement over the next six months. Most of your supporters and allies aren't victims, just vocal sympathisers. You have no reason to keep banging that drum now that Ethan Tan is gone.'

'Did you do that?' Brigit challenged the pair. 'Were you behind his disappearance?'

'What! No, that was just good fortune on all our parts,' Margo chortled. 'He's rotting at the bottom of the Mediterranean for all we know. As far as anyone is concerned Ethan Tan had zero to do with in-dream violence and we want it to stay that way. We just want a smooth, uneventful transition back to normality.'

Brigit thought about Margo's request to wind down her movement. 'I'll check the reports from the time he went missing, and if there are no more rapes and murders in White or Yellow rated experiences over the next six months I'll dissolve the movement.'

'Thank you, Brigit,' Margo expressed with a genuine smile.

'You seem to get along with Iminka pretty well,' Saxon suggested.

'She's okay, I suppose.'

'We want you to develop and nurture that relationship,' Margo said. 'Of course, we'll bring you on board as a consultant, a confidential consultant, off the books, so no one is the wiser.'

'You want me to get information from her about Sterling Lindquist, don't you?'

'Sterling is also under our umbrella,' Saxon confided. 'On the fringes, but still under our umbrella. We own a percentage of everything he creates, but he pushes the boundaries and we want to keep a closer eye on his activities.'

Brigit considered the proposal. 'And if I decline?'

'That is your choice,' Margo advised. 'If you want to turn your back on 5,000 Nukoin a month, that is your prerogative. But, you could do your job at Mogo and quietly be our consultant as well.'

'Five thousand you say?' Brigit reflected for a moment. 'Eight thousand and I'm there, but no face-to-face meetings.'

Margo didn't blink. 'Eight it is. Selma will be in touch. You just keep in contact with Iminka and we'll set-up a secure in-dream meeting room. Is that acceptable?'

Brigit looked to Selma. 'Sure.'

'Thank you for meeting with us today, Brigit,' Margo said. 'We understand what you've been through and the impact that it's had on your life. We hope we can work together towards a mutually beneficial future.'

'Just one more thing before you go, Brigit,' Saxon added. 'We are about to launch Dream Immersion Neurocoherence Training, a DITS recovery program, in partnership with Harvard Department of Psychology. I would be honoured if you would participate, it will help you.'

Brigit studied him for a moment. 'If it helps my state of mind, why not.'

'Thank you,' Saxon responded sincerely. 'We've had great outcomes with PTSD sufferers.'

'And remember, this conversation never took place,' Margo reminded her.

The Banq restaurant, high above Barangaroo in Sydney's entertainment precinct, was one of Margo and Saxon's favourite restaurants. Offering a degustation 10-course menu of fine dining against the city's most spectacular backdrop guaranteed a pleasurable experience.

'Congratulations, we hit a billion unique users this week,' Saxon boasted, offering his glass in a toast.

'That's ahead of schedule.' Margo reciprocated.

'By two months.'

'Alfred suggested an interesting proposition at yesterday's meeting,' Margo tempted before sipping her wine.

'I'm all ears.'

'It's almost a month since Ethan disappeared. Alfred said it might be in ZynnComm's best interest to acquire Ethos. Vertical integration provides security with continuity of supply, reduces our base costs and creates greater brand value.'

Saxon chuckled at the suggestion.

'What's so amusing?'

'You beat me to the punch. I had a similar conversation with Kris. I spoke with the bean counters and we have the capital to do it without external financing.'

'The Tremaine Group can always chip in if needed. Alfred advised we should make a bid sooner rather than later; the vultures will be circling.'

'Agreed. We own the intellectual property, so it makes sense to consolidate part of the manufacturing and reduce costs. Adding Swipe Charge technology to our list of patents would also be a feather in our cap and improve our bottom line.'

'Should we bid publicly or in petto?'

Saxon contemplated their options. 'To make a move publicly would be premature. Too soon. Nothing is going to happen for months until the court investigates and rules on his disappearance. His assets will be frozen until that time. I would imagine Grace will inherit the majority of Ethos. In the meantime, you should reach out to Grace and plant the seed of the benefits of a sale, to us. What do you think?'

'Saxon Zynn, you never cease to amaze me.' She raised her glass to toast.

Saxon met her glass with a gentle chink. 'To our...magnetism.'

'No, I think intoxication is a better word,' Margo corrected with a seductive smile.

Chapter Twelve

The front of Merlin's body thumped the rubbery pavement with force as he landed. He stood, expecting damage to his naked frame but was unhurt. *'What an odd way to enter an experience,'* he thought, *'falling from the sky naked.'* As he gained his bearings, Merlin witnessed a young woman dressed in military fatigues shoot an unclothed man in the head at close range.

'Sorry,' she feigned. 'You fucking real world hump!'

Another young woman, dressed the same, pushed a flyer into Merlin's hand. 'What were Isaac Asimov's last words?'

Merlin quickly scanned the headline, *'Death to all live male echoes!'* Merlin looked at her. 'I love you, Janet,' he answered.

'He's one of us,' she yelled to the shooter.

The woman with the handgun gave Merlin a prolonged stare before running towards another man who had just fallen from the heavens and landed on the pavement. 'Hey!'

'What's this about?' Merlin held up the flyer to the woman.

'Fucking live echoes come here to rape and kill us, not anymore.' She ran off after the shooter who had caught up with the other young man. He was shot three times.

Merlin dropped the flyer. 'Is this normal?' Merlin asked a middle-aged man passing by. 'People being executed in the streets?'

'I don't know if this is normal for a Blue rated experience. You saw the flyer, it's only men,' the man said. 'It's a virus in the assembled echo code. They didn't shoot you?'

'I gave her the answer to her question.'

'Me too. You're not an assembled or elevated echo are you?'

'No.'

'You must be a codester. That Asimov question was a stroke of genius on the developers part.'

'Thank you. That was my idea.'

'You? You work for ZynnComm?'

'I do.'

'What's your name?'

'Melvin Tripidakis.'

'I've read about you. They call you Merlin.'

'I don't think this is a virus,' Merlin suggested, disregarding the man, still watching the violent women on their rampage. A couple of naked women fell from the sky, but they were ignored. 'The code for assembled echoes is...' He turned to see the man had been joined by two very elderly women, waiting for him to finish the sentence.

'What were you going to say?' the old woman wearing a metallic pink skin-tight unitard asked.

'Who told you it was a virus?' Merlin quickly changed the subject.

'Someone in another experience,' the man replied.

'That's odd information for another user to know,' Merlin noted with some concern. 'Erky perky. What's that stench?' He pegged his nose with thumb and finger.

'What did you just say? Erky perky?' the other elderly woman wearing a metallic blue skin-tight unitard quizzed Merlin, laughing.

'That stink, what is it?'

'Burning bodies,' the man answered, pointing to a plume of smoke a short distance away. 'They collect the bodies and burn them. You'll get used to it.'

'Who the fuck says erky perky?' blue unitard woman commented to her friend amused.

Merlin surveyed his surroundings. 'Is this the Magical Mystery Tour?'

'I think you've taken a wrong turn at Albuquerque,' pink unitard woman derided.

Merlin considered the woman. 'That's a strange turn of phrase. I like it.'

'This is Purgatory,' she announced.

'Purgatory?'

'Welcome to Purgatory, Erky Perky,' blue unitard woman greeted. The two women strolled off cackling to each other.

'Purgatory is one of 20 tours on offer for MMT,' the man informed Merlin. 'It's totally random where you end up. As I said, someone in the Martian Histories experience, another in MMT, told me yesterday it was a virus. The same thing is happening there. MMT is a Petroc Brothers cluster and I wanted to find out more.'

'Petroc Brothers? Don't know them.'

'You might want to get some clothes on,' he recommended, looking Merlin up and down, 'I'm Captain Blaq,' he held out his hand. 'B-L-A-Q.'

'Captain Blaq? I've heard of you. You created AssassiNET! I love that experience.' Merlin shook his hand.

'Thank you. Follow me.'

'What's the point of Purgatory?' Merlin enquired as they walked towards a building.

'The point? This is my first visit too, I've been here,' he checked his arm, '22 minutes. From what I gather so far, there are some extremely dangerous, obnoxious and annoying individuals here. Expect the unexpected, I think.'

'See you later, Erky Perky!' blue unitard woman screeched from across the street.

'Yep,' Merlin agreed as he waved to the guffawing women.

'Look out!' Captain Blaq yelled, pulling Merlin by the arm. A man fell from the sky and almost hit him. As the nudie gradually got to his feet, the old women shuffled across the street towards him. Blue unitard woman brandished a large handgun. Pink unitard woman asked him the Asimov question, but the man was ignorant. Blue unitard woman didn't hesitate, she shot the man in the face.

Merlin watched, perplexed.

'Merlin brought this issue to me yesterday so I thought we should meet and discuss it immediately,' Wendy informed the group of Kris, Saxon and Merlin via a secure video call. 'Tell them, Merlin.'

'I was in Purgatory yesterday, it's one of the experiences under the Magical Mystery Tour cluster developed and produced by the Petroc Brothers,' Merlin explained. 'Anyhow, assembled echoes were asking the Asimov question on arrival and killing men who didn't know the answer.'

'Who are the Petroc Brothers?' Kris questioned.

'Petroc Brothers is a company name; they aren't actually brothers,' Wendy clarified. 'Nessa Sharp, Zeek Luschwitz and Haze Munster are the company directors. They're a small start-up located in Seattle, Washington.'

'I met a guy in the experience named Captain Blaq,' Merlin went on. 'He told me he visited another experience in the cluster the day before called Martian Histories, and the same thing was happening there.'

'What data do we have on deaths in this Petroc produced cluster?' Saxon directed to Wendy.

'No assembled or elevated echoes have died in any MMT experiences. But we've received complaints from live male users suffering quick deaths in that cluster. It started a few days ago.'

'I visited Galactic Trading Post about an hour ago, one of the other experiences in the cluster, and it's the same there,' Merlin warned. 'Normally it's a trading market offering spaceships, weapons and tech, today there was a militia of female assembled echoes killing live male echoes.'

'What rating are their experiences?' Saxon asked.

'All Blue,' Wendy confirmed. 'I must also tell you that Nessa Sharp is a very vocal supporter of the Stop Dream Violence movement.'

'Her way of revenge?' Kris offered. 'How many Gatekeeper of Dreams units do they manage?

'A dozen,' Wendy said.

'Tell Sydney to deny platform access to the Petroc Brothers cluster immediately,' Saxon told Wendy. 'When they contact us let me know and we'll have a chat.'

'Consider it done,' Wendy acknowledged.

'Dream Phaze has reached the number one worldwide entertainment medium this month for the first time,' the reporter announced. 'Holoflix came in second, just nudging out VRXLR8. DI has also officially become the fastest adopted entertainment technology ever.'

Saxon muted the wall screen in his Port Augusta residence as his PD buzzed. 'Waylon.' A garbled voice emerged from the speaker. 'Hang on, just activating my descrambler.' Saxon tapped his PD screen. 'Are you there?'

'Hi, Saxon, how are you?'

'Can't complain. I've been meaning to ask you; how did Josh go with his application for Global Disaster Rescue?'

'Passed the psychometric, the physical, the exam and his degree in fire science has got him to interview.'

'That's great! That must make you proud.'

'He's a good boy, I just wish his younger brother was more like him.'

'He's a musician, yeah?'

'A struggling musician.'

'We all have our specialities,' Saxon remarked.

'So true.' Silence punctuated a change of subject. 'We think we've finally found the person who beat us to Griffin's lair.'

'Someone already on our radar?'

'No, but he does work for Ethos.'

'Have you found the skin samples?'

'No. He drove to Sydney immediately after his salvage exercise in Melbourne. His name is Jett Zeelander.'

'What does he do at Ethos?'

'Biotech research.'

'Makes sense. What now?'

'He has a house in Sydney but shares his time between Ethos labs in both Melbourne and Sydney. We've been watching him for a couple of days. He lives alone with several large dogs guarding the premises. We can intercept him between home and work if you like?'

'I'm in Sydney this coming Wednesday. I'll be flying in about 8:30 for a meeting at 9. How about you pick him up and Kris and I will meet you around 11?'

'Sure, I'll text the location.'

Sydney on Wednesday glistened from mid-morning rain. Kris and Saxon alighted the vehicle at the arranged destination in south-western Sydney just after 11.

Inside the empty warehouse, Saxon walked past the open side door of a white van. He paused to stare at the man with a black bag over his head. Visions of Jeremy Abernathy washed through his mind for a brief moment. Those events seemed so long ago.

Waylon and two of his team waited by a table. Saxon and Kris inspected the contraband laid out, four DI devices and an open cooler bag holding individually packed skin samples in labelled plastic bags.

'That's all he had?' Saxon asked Waylon.

'We tranquilised his dogs and searched his house, his vehicle, we can't locate the rest of the devices or skin samples.'

'Might be at his Ethos lab,' Kris suggested.

'We don't think so—'

'Has he told you anything?' Saxon turned towards the man in the van.

'Not a word. We've been monitoring his communications and there seems to be another party in the mix.'

'From where?' Kris queried.

'A male in Kuala Lumpur,' Waylon answered. 'Jett couriered a package to a private company at Bankstown Airport two days after his trip to Melbourne. The company, BGT, specialises in biopharmaceutical cold chain cargo to and from Asia.'

Kris gestured towards the van. 'This one will have to disappear,' he told the pair. 'This information can't go further.'

'Of course,' Waylon said, 'but we need to identify his man in Kuala Lumpur first. We're having trouble pinpointing him.'

Saxon contemplated the man in the van. 'Do what's needed to find this man in Malaysia. We need to know his connection to Ethan and Jett. We need the missing devices and skin samples.' He turned back to Waylon. 'Then both must disappear.'

'Understood.'

'I think Waylon and his team should be kept out of any lethal activity,' Kris proposed. 'Wolf should be our magician to make things disappear. You're too close to us.'

Saxon reflected on Kris' suggestion before responding. 'You're right. When you find what we need, let Kris know.'

'Easy,' Waylon agreed.

Saxon and Kris left the warehouse so Waylon and his men could continue their work.

Neesa Sharp and Haze Munster waited patiently. Wendy had created a one-off in-dream meeting instance within a tropical setting. The island was bathed in a warm afternoon glow from a setting sun as a zephyr blew in from the ocean, gently stirring fronds on giant palm trees.

'I've met you before,' Neesa revealed to Wendy. 'You probably don't remember me, but I remember that red hair of yours.'

Wendy studied her face. 'I don't think so.'

'I was tangled in barbed wire and you had a serious cut across your belly.'

'You were in the Ultimate Warrior Knockout?' Wendy quizzed slightly excited.

'I was. I asked you if it was worth the Nukoin. I didn't make it out of the barbed wire wall. How far did you get?'

'That stomach wound made me a target the next day. Couldn't outsmart a pack of painted wolves. Got eaten alive.'

'Sounds like a fun experience,' Haze commented sarcastically.

Merlin arrived first, quickly followed by Kris and finally Saxon.

'This is Neesa Sharp and Haze Munster from Petroc Brothers,' Wendy introduced to the ZynnComm trio. 'This is Merlin, Kris and Saxon.' Everyone nodded their salutations.

'Before we begin,' Neesa jumped in, 'we know we have a problem and we understand why you kicked us off the platform, but please hear us out.'

'So this wasn't a deliberate act on your part?' Wendy suggested.

'Of course not!' Haze responded angrily. 'We aren't idiots, but we wanted to try and fix this quickly and quietly before it got out of hand.'

'Well that didn't happen,' Kris berated. 'Why didn't you shut down until you fixed it?'

Nessa and Haze glanced at each other before Neesa spoke. 'We couldn't. I'll explain. It appeared about eight days ago and we've been working our butts off to fix it. We first noticed problems in our Slitherland experience. Female assembled echoes were acting weird, challenging live male echoes with the Asimov question. They would physically assault them if they didn't give the correct answer. Haze and I spent time in the experience observing and then checking their source code. That's before we realised we were targeted.'

'Targeted?' Merlin questioned.

'Zeek, our partner, received a text message from the Magical Thinking Token organisers telling us we were in the running for an award for our Gravi-T-room experience,' Haze clarified. 'They wanted him for an interview. The text said to check his email to confirm his interest. Zeek is our marketing man and he didn't hesitate clicking the email link and confirming. The screen opened to a demand for 10,000 Nukoin within 24 hours or malware called Liar would be distributed across our Gatekeeper of Dreams system.'

'Excuse my ignorance, but what is a Magical Thinking Token?' Saxon asked his team.

'It's an award given to independent creators,' Merlin filled him in. 'Three Magical Thinking Tokens are awarded on the first of every month and are quickly becoming a must win award for small independent producers. They offer some serious traction in the industry and attract venture capital.'

Haze continued. 'Zeek didn't tell us at first, because spear phishing threats are usually detected and automatically deleted by the system. We tried to shut Slitherland down but couldn't. We found the Liar code deeply embedded in one of our Gatekeeper units. It focuses on the Sense8 modification algorithm, but it's an evolving modification algorithm that exploits behaviour source code characteristics. When we deleted an assembled echo, then replaced it, the new version came with heightened aggression algorithms. When we didn't pay their demands that's when they kicked it up a notch, and it spread across the cluster and female assembled echoes started killing live male echoes across more of our experiences.'

'We didn't know what to do,' Neesa confessed. 'We couldn't shut it down and we couldn't stop the Liar code from evolving.'

'We need to look at that code immediately,' Kris told the pair. 'We'll need that email as well. I'll send you a link to a secure server to quarantine both.'

'Of course,' Neesa replied.

'Any idea who could have done this?' Wendy interrogated. 'Any disgruntled ex-employees?'

'No,' Haze assured them. 'Our operation runs on a shoestring budget out of Zeek's basement. We've had the same three employees with us from day one. We've racked our brains over why we were targeted; we don't know.'

'Tell Sydney to distribute a platform wide alert to all developers about this Magical Thinking Token spear phishing scam carrying the Liar malware,' Saxon told Wendy. 'Contact the Token organisers, and I want to know who else has responded to the email.'

'This dream hacking doesn't seem to be spreading outside of the connected clusters, we would've heard from others by now,' Wendy deduced.

Saxon turned to Kris. 'As soon as we receive this code from Neesa let me know, I want to look at it.'

'It might be time to change the Asimov question,' Merlin put forward. 'I've been thinking about this a lot and we naively assumed one question would work if everyone respected it, didn't abuse it. That's changed.'

'What are you thinking?' Kris pressed.

'Each Gatekeeper of Dreams unit has its own dedicated question,' Merlin explained.

'Why have the question at all?' Haze proposed off hand. 'Live users know which participants are assembled most of the time based on their roles in the experience.'

'I wouldn't say most of the time, Haze,' Wendy countered. 'It really depends on the experience, and if assembled echoes answered yes every time they're asked, that would diminish certain nuances, mystique and worldbuilding qualities.'

'Which is why I suggested it in the first place,' Merlin added.

'Agreed,' Kris said. 'In some experiences it doesn't matter, it's plain who the assembled echoes are and their roles. But for others, you don't know, and that adds to the interaction and immersion within experiences. For me, the characteristic of a quality experience completely blurs the line between assembled, elevated and live echoes.'

'So, Merlin, that's a lot of questions given the number of units out there,' Saxon contended. 'How do we address that?'

'Mathematical questions. Skies the limit,' Merlin responded without thinking.

'He's right,' Kris agreed. 'And if this malware situation came up again we could easily pinpoint who had access to the question for any given Gatekeeper of Dreams unit.'

Saxon pondered the proposal for a moment. 'Okay. Your idea, your project, Merlin. How long to come up with all these mathematical questions?'

'There are math generators we can use to get it done in a day,' Wendy said. 'I'll help.'

'Stick to the plan. There are parameters that remain consistent,' Merlin reminded them, sliding down the nose cone of a wind turbine. 'I've been studying this for a few months.'

'We all have,' Bhang responded before scrambling across an industrial gas pipe. 'Metal Maze has been my waking mission almost every day. There should be a shortcut just ahead, through an aircraft fuselage.'

'How old is that information?' Arrow challenged, climbing up a ladder.

'Yesterday.'

'Yesterday?' Liam questioned. 'It won't be there now, it's always changing.' He struggled to navigate a rusted-through water tank, his foot crashing through the corroded metal, cutting his leg. 'Shit!'

The team of four were spread out across 30 metres and advancing quickly towards the end.

'The updates on socials have been pretty accurate,' Bhang insisted.

'The developers see them too, Bhang. That means more changes so the Chest isn't found,' Arrow argued.

Only a single Vermilion Crystal Chest had been found in the past two months, bringing the total to just three since the game launched.

'How long have we got?' Merlin asked.

Bhang, the timekeeper, glanced at the forearm. 'About a minute.'

'There's the fuselage!' Liam yelled, pointing down. Arrow was closest, but a truck body obscured her view.

Merlin froze and looked over at Liam. His next step towards Liam was his last. The sheet metal gave way and he fell, impaled on cast iron spearheads of a late 19th century fence panel.

Arrow paused as Merlin's painful screams echoed.

'Keep moving, Arrow!' Liam called from his vantage point. 'Go through the truck cabin.'

Arrow reached the fuselage first and ran through. On the other side, she pulled at tin sheets and rifled through car panels searching. That's when a reddish glow caught her eye through shattered glass of a twisted car door. Arrow reached down and heaved the car door aside. There it was, the Vermilion Crystal Chest. Picking up the shoebox-sized treasure, she lifted the lid to reveal a six-digit code that would win them 10,000 Nukoin. She began to fade away.

Margo and Saxon, along with other users, cautiously took their seats for a ride on the intimidating fire breathing dragon in the Fantasy Quest experience. As the enormous beast moved restlessly underfoot, Saxon took note of the detail. Before donning his harness, he reached down and ran his fingers across the texture of the iridescent scales. They didn't overlap, but sat up against one another, giving a pebbly appearance to the skin.

A young woman sidestepped a middle-aged man and planted herself in the only remaining seat, grinning at him mockingly. 'Too slow, you missed out.'

Before she had time to slip into her safety harness, the visibly angry man forcefully grabbed the woman by the upper arm and hurled her out of the seat then sat down.

The humiliated woman promptly picked herself up. 'Fuck you, arsehole!' she screamed, slapping the man about the head.

Two women, seated at different locations on the dragon, immediately got up from their seats and seized the attacking woman by an arm each.

'Reservists?' Margo whispered to Saxon.

As the hostile woman was being held, the battered man abruptly stood up and punched her squarely in the face, smashing her nose. 'No, fuck you. Thank you, ladies,' he said to his rescuers.

One of his rescuers promptly let go of the dazed, bloodied woman and took hold of the man's arm, twisting it up behind his back. 'You need to learn some manners,' she rebuked, marching him off the ride.

'Yes,' Saxon finally responded quietly. 'I'm pleased they restore order with a minimum of fuss.'

'Why are Reservists even in student projects?'

'Our student showcases are publicly released so they can gather audience feedback to write an evaluation report. They are rated White, so Wendy slips in Reservists.'

Margo considered the two combatants as they were led away. 'I wonder if either of those two would have been that aggressive in the real world?'

'I think not. Users are more daring in-dream. Look at us, we're about to fly on a fire breathing dragon.' He smiled.

'It's our son's first end of semester project, we have to!'

'Honestly, I never thought we'd be experiencing a DI project authored by Hugo.'

Margo chuckled. 'No, neither did I.'

'I must admit, he has an eye for detail,' Saxon complemented.

'Make sure you tell him that in your feedback,' Margo encouraged.

'I can't provide feedback; it would be seen as a conflict of interest.'

'No, I mean you tell him as his father, and as the creator of the tech,' Margo stressed. 'He needs to hear that from you.'

Saxon contemplated his wife's comment as an attendant interrupted the moment by checking his five-point buckle mechanism on his harness was correctly fastened.

With the rider safety check complete, the two attendants alighted the creature via its trident-pronged tail.

Majestically, the dragon reared up on its powerful hind legs and expelled a 30-metre blast of flame from its gaping mouth, delighting all riders. Talons, the size of a human, dug into soft soil as the dragon built up pace towards lands' end. With wings tucked in, the mythical animal launched from the cliff top and dove straight down at breakneck speed, terrifying all onboard.

'Good evening and welcome to the program. Tonight, we'll be exploring Dream Immersion Neurocoherence Training, a DITS recovery program established by ZynnComm and the Harvard

Department of Psychology,' Stark Green introduced. 'My guest tonight is Professor Winston Singh, the Department Chair of Psychology and Professor of Social Ethics at Harvard University. Welcome, Professor Singh.'

'My pleasure, Stark,' Professor Singh responded, beamed into the London studio from his office in Cambridge, Massachusetts.

'There have been months of discussion, reporting and protests around dream immersion trauma syndrome, Professor Singh. Why has it taken ZynnComm so long to acknowledge the condition exists and secondly, how do they intend to support sufferers of DITS?'

'Stark, I can't comment on behalf of ZynnComm, but I can tell you dream immersion trauma syndrome is not something that can be addressed with a knee-jerk reaction. Without robust, authentic, analytical, peer reviewed research into the condition we wouldn't know exactly what we're dealing with. Dream immersion is a very nuanced technology with psychological implications that may impact each individual in a unique manner. It is still early days, but over the past eight months we have endeavoured to explore the psychological triggers and possible solutions.'

'With all due respect, Professor, the triggers are violent rapes and murders in White rated experiences, no different to real-world crimes.'

'I knew he was going to go there,' Saxon anticipated, watching on the couch beside Margo in their Sydney home.

'I expected nothing less,' Margo commented. 'His interviews are balanced.'

'I would have to disagree, Stark,' Winston Singh countered. 'In our waking world traumatic events can last much longer than 33 minutes, they can be ongoing over a prolonged period. I'm not diminishing the traumatic incidents occurring in-dream, but I'm saying they are different to our real-world trauma, yet they share similarities. Nightmares, low self-esteem and co-existing disorders such as depression, anxiety, panic attacks and addiction are all associated with dream immersion trauma syndrome. They can manifest as fear, helplessness, grief, shame, anger, guilt and despair which resemble PTSD symptoms in most instances. Stark, the research reveals there is trauma associated with unanticipated violent attacks in-dream, on that we agree. When it comes to support for victims of such incidents we are very excited about Dream Immersion Neurocoherence Training and the benefits it can offer. It's a short six-week course that involves appropriately targeted psychodynamic psychotherapy where we focus on exposing and resolving unconscious conflicts that are driving their symptoms. We reintroduce participants to dream immersion by utilising emergent Neurocoalescence facilitation techniques. This is the first tangible application using Neurocoalescence to solve a problem. This type of therapy didn't exist eight months ago, this is cutting edge, and we've documented extremely positive outcomes in a very short timeframe. Dream Immersion Neurocoherence Training was initially being developed for PTSD sufferers but we expanded the program to include DITS. Participants having received Dream Immersion Neurocoherence Training continue to improve post-therapy, having gained insights that transform their waking mindset using problem solving techniques, liberating them from their overwhelming intrapsychic conflicts.'

'He was the right choice to deliver the message,' Margo said.

'He was,' Saxon agreed.

Margo gently turned the handle and opened the front door at Wildwood with a little trepidation. The foyer stood impressive, crowned with its stained glass dome ceiling supported by rainforest green marble pillars flecked with golden hues. On the opposite side to the entrance, across a sunburst of onyx tiles, a glass wall revealed an enticing slice of pool and garden. Margo was drawn towards it.

'Hello, darling,' her mother Sylvia greeted, walking in from the living room.

Margo spun around. 'Mum,' she meekly responded. The woman she hadn't seen for over 20 years was exactly as she remembered her.

'Walter!' Sylvia called. 'Margo's home.'

'Hello, Mum.' The two gave each other a peck on the cheek and hugged and as if there was never a day lost between them.

'You look fabulous, Margo. Is that a new dress?'

Margo automatically glanced down at her dress. 'This? Yes, it is actually.'

'Hello, Giggles,' a younger, spritely Walt said as he entered the foyer. He gave her a kiss.

'Hi, Dad.'

'Where's Saxon?' he asked.

'Saxon?' Margo had to remember what was happening in their lives two decades ago. 'He's working of course.'

'That boy needs to relax,' Walt advised, 'take some time off now and again.'

'Like you, Walter?' Sylvia teased with raised eyebrows 'Come on, let's eat.' Margo followed her mother towards the glass wall. 'We're eating by the pool.'

'I'm hungry,' Walt admitted.

'How is work going, darling?' Sylvia enquired.

'*Work? Which job?*' Margo thought. 'Good, yes, going well.'

The pool and entertainment area was picture-perfect.

Thirty minutes later, Margo walked from the bedroom of her Sydney residence into the living room.

'Well? What did you think?' Saxon enquired excitedly, sitting on the edge of the leather couch.

Margo flopped down beside him and sighed. 'It was...beautiful.' She burst into tears.

Saxon took Margo in his arms and held her. 'I'm pleased you liked it.'

'I didn't know what to expect at first, you said it was something new you've been working on,' Margo managed through sniffles.

'Did you want aliens?'

Margo pushed away from him. 'Nooo, I'm just saying, you could have given me a little more warning.'

'It wouldn't have been a birthday surprise then,' Saxon insisted.

'You called it Wildwood. I thought you would have called it Fortress Tremaine?'

'That's what I call it. You have always known it as Wildwood,' Saxon smiled.

'It was so good to see both of them again, especially mum. It threw me at first, I wasn't sure of how to react, trying to remember what was going on back then.'

'It's your story; you just have to improvise and see where it goes. New storylines can always be added.'

'The atmosphere, the mood was...calming; it didn't seem laboured at all. We reminisced about trips we went on and...I thought you couldn't make dad younger?'

'No, not in his experience with Sylvia. This is your experience of them. You are the same age. We can't change the users age in their experiences, but we can use early video of Walt.'

'Okay, right. I was thinking, how can Hugo visit the experience when he was born a year after mum died?'

'We have a cunning plan,' Saxon winked at her before giving her a reassuring squeeze.

'We?'

Saxon picked up his PD. He tapped the interface and Hugo appeared on the wall screen.

'Hiya, Mum! Happy birthday! Did you like it?' he beamed.

'Did you do this?'

Hugo laughed. 'No, Dad 80 percent, me 20. Did you like it?'

'I was just saying to your father, it's beautiful, thank you.'

'Dad has an eye for detail. The nuances he added were inspirational.'

'Thank you both,' Margo glowed, taking Saxon's hand. 'I love it. It's the most thoughtful gift I've ever received.'

'Dad thought you'd like it. You always told me growing up, the best presents are made, not bought.'

'They certainly are,' Saxon agreed.

'Anyway, I have to get going. I'll see you shortly.'

'Are you coming home? I thought you were heading up the coast for the weekend?'

'That was a cover story. It's the first day of spring so it must be your birthday! I missed the last one. See ya soon.' Hugo disappeared from screen.

Margo gazed at Saxon with a grateful grin. 'You made him stay.'

'I might have had a word,' he admitted with sly grin. 'He didn't take too much convincing.'

'It's so good to have him back.'

Saxon nodded and held her. 'Happy birthday.'

'So, tell me. How are you going to add Hugo to Wildwood?'

'Well...let's wait until Hugo gets here and he can tell you.'

Saxon patiently waited for the 3D printer to complete its task in the R&D prototyping test lab on level five. As he loitered, he watched technicians in clean suits diligently perform tasks outside the climate-controlled printing room. Their benches were littered with testing equipment, handheld gadgets, monitors and a variety of microscopes.

Minutes later, the latest generation Gelchip was finished. Saxon reached into the completion compartment with his gloved hand and removed the sealed Gelchip. Carefully holding the tiny container, he closely scrutinised the newest iteration of the Neurocoalescence Gelchip.

Back in the lab on level two, Dixon Tarantola, Saxon's research assistant, took his time diligently positioning the new Gelchip into the delivery tray of the Analytical Conductron unit. He touched the interface screen and the tray slid into the machine. 'Okay, that's in place.'

'Fire it up, let's test it,' Saxon instructed.

Dixon tapped the screen again to begin the evaluation process. Graphs of differing colours and morphoneural sampling rates were output across a bank of screens along the bench. 'Engaging.'

'Keep an eye on it and I'll be back tomorrow to see how it's travelling.'

'Hopefully this version will prove to be more stable,' Dixon said.

'Don't get your hopes up. It might take months before we achieve a permanent state.'

'Synchroneumetric cognitive singularity should be feasible if the qist calibration is correct.'

'Small wins will get us there, Dixon,' Saxon promised. 'The qist calibration only has to be out by half a pectical and we have to start again.' Saxon's PD buzzed. 'I have to take this. I'll be back tomorrow.' Saxon headed towards the elevator. 'Kris, I've been thinking–'

'We need to meet immediately. We have a major fucking problem. I've run both advanced static and dynamic analysis several times for the Liar code and it has unique adamantine core coupling at the improfing level–'

'Indestructible?' Are you sure?'

'Believe me, I've triple checked. The FH code can't be touched. It's way more dangerous than we first thought and it's spreading.'

The elevator door opened and Saxon got in. 'Spreading where?' The door closed.

Dream Phaze Expanding Glossary

BASE - Bergman Analysis and Synthesis Engine - Gatekeeper of Dreams authored experiences are translated through a BASE neural compiler into Synmem code.

Big Dippers – Daily users of the dream immersion platform (dip).

Biosoftware – neurochemical sequence that contains markers that 'express" in the presence of a biological activation code.

Black Shield – intuitive firewall protecting the Norus network.

Codesters – developers/programmers who author dream immersion experiences using FH code.

Cycle – one episode of an experience – 33 minutes is one cycle.

Dippers – occasional users of the dream immersion platform (dip)

Dreamcast – existing broadcast television production converted using the Gatekeeper of Dreams engine, where users take part in an extended show environment above and beyond the aired real-world episodes.

Dream Clusters – a collection of experiences with a central theme.

Dreamforming – interface for authoring dream immersion experiences using a conception space and tool menu generated by Gatekeeper of Dreams hardware.

Dreaminars – in-dream tutorials/how-to/DIY workshops.

Dream Immersion (DI) dashboard – interface worn on the forearm to access dream immersion. User selects experience preferences, and it initiates and monitors all stages of dream immersion. Translates Synmem code into inaudible frequencies and delivers them to earstims.

Dream immersion experiences – Once only Experience (OoE), a Series of Experiences (SoE) or a Continuing Experience (CE). This choice must be made prior to dream immersion.

Dream Immersion Neurocoherence Training – an in-dream Neurocoalescence recovery program for those suffering Dream Immersion Trauma Syndrome.

Dream Immersion Platform (DIP)– technology created by Saxon Zynn and his team for dream immersion experiences. Consists of five components – dashboard, earstims, thalpherycine, Synmem code and the Norus network.

Dream Immersion Trauma Syndrome (DITS) – a real world condition suffered by dream immersion users from unanticipated and gratuitous in-dream physical, psychological, or emotional trauma.

Dream Phaze – Internet term (slang) meaning an 'engineered dream' rather than an organic, natural dream.

Dreamplex – mass dream immersion complex similar to a cinema complex.

Dynamic Emission Neuroimaging – is the use of several combined scanning techniques to directly image neurotransmissions of the brain in real time.

Earfonic – single ear hook Bluetooth earphone with mic.

Earstims – delivers inaudible frequencies from the DI dashboard into the brain which sparks neurotransmitter chemical sequences in the thalamus. Thalpherycine must be present for Synmem code synthesis to take place.

Echoes - characters who populate dream immersion experiences.

Ø Live echoes are active users, living people using the tech

Ø Assembled echoes are the extras in every experience, they are created from scratch and populate all DI environments

Ø Elevated echoes are deceased people authored for specific experiences

Ø Host echoes can be live, elevated, or assembled characters. Hosts can be active across multiple experiences.

Exteroceptive - stimuli outside the body.

FH code – Frequency Hypgenic source code developed by Saxon Zynn for the Gatekeeper of Dreams engine which creates the tools and content for the dreamforming interface to author dream immersion experiences.

Firerock – risk management organisation specialising in covert activities.

Fundamental Purists – religious movement founded by Jeremy Abernathy.

Gatekeeper of Dreams – hardware/engine used to author dream immersion experiences via the dreamforming interface, which converts the authored dream into Synmem code.

Gateway neurochip – bioware (hardware) implanted at the brain stem created by the Forsythe Corporation for neural mood stabilisation using SFT software.

Gelchips – quantum computer chip capable of conducting 198 quintillion calculations per second.

Griz-L-gun – **Gr**avimetric **i**on **z**one-**L**aser-**gun**. Common handheld weapon popularised by ZynnComm's Lucid Division for in-dream gaming.

Group consciousness integration matrix – software allowing users to be aware of and interact with other users within the dream immersion environment.

GUESS – Global Unified Electronic Surveillance Service.

Haptic spontaneity - sense of touch; tactile freedom.

Humuration - the 11-minute process of turning a human corpse into slow-release humus fertiliser using a standalone, dedicated Humurator unit.

Instance – a single experience episode or cycle of 33 minutes. Multiple separate instances of an experience can occur simultaneously. Timing depends on demand or an exact schedule.

Interoceptive - stimuli arising within the body based on deep feeling and emotional reactions rather than on reason or thought.

Jazper - network intelligence and connectivity management system for the Norus network.

MMDG – massive multiplayer dream game.

Neurocoalescence - is a major development in dream immersion technology. Neurocoalescence is the confluence of minds, the unification and synchronisation of multiple brains working in concert as a single, superintelligence capable of problem solving at unprecedented speed and capacity.

Neuroelectrodynamics – study of the dynamics and interaction of electrical signals in the brain.

Neuroinformatics – combines data across all levels of neuroscience in order to understand brain function by the application of computational models and analytical tools.

Neuromorphic computing - software systems that implement models of neural systems mimicking neurobiological architecture.

Neuronic Reorganisation Actuator – The critical microelectronic device within a dream immersion forearm device (dashboard) which synchronises immersion.

Neurotransmission – the process of communication between two nerve cells

Norus Network – dedicated computer network which facilitates and coordinates the entire Dream Immersion Platform.

Nukoin - popular digital currency

Occipital lobe - the rearmost lobe in each cerebral hemisphere of the brain.

Pectical – system of unit (SI) in Gelchip qist calibration

Personal Device (PD) – universal device that people carry for communication, identity, GPS identifier, finances, medical, entertainment, analytical applications, workplace applications, security, and many other functions.

Pons - the part of the brain stem that links the medulla oblongata and the thalamus.

Quantum Identification (QuID) - The unique QuID code conveys how often a device is used, the number of people using that device, their location, their age, and their level of intoxication. Does not track or store any other type of information.

Reservists – covert security echoes embedded in White/Yellow rated general public experiences. Plain-clothed assembled echoes coded with security/military/policing strategies to maintain order.

RIP bullet - Radically Invasive Projectile developed in the early 21st century.

Scrambler – encryption app used in PDs/telecommunications to make the message unintelligible to the receiver not equipped with an appropriately set descrambling app.

Sense8 - predictive modelling engine used by developers for authoring 'echoes'. Part of Gatekeeper of Dreams suite of tools.

SFT - Synaptic Functional Transliteration - neurological software (biosoftware) created by the Forsythe Corporation for neural mood stabilisation. Works in conjunction with the Gateway neurochip.

Spatial perception - the ability to be aware of your physicality within the environment around you.

Synapse - a junction between two nerve cells, consisting of a minute gap across which impulses pass by diffusion of a neurotransmitter. Also known as a neuronal junction.

Synaptic vesicles - in a nerve cell, synaptic vesicles store various neurotransmitters that are released at the synapse. The release is regulated by a voltage-dependent calcium channel. Vesicles are essential for propagating nerve impulses between nerve cells and are constantly recreated by the cell.

Synmem code – Synaptic Memory neural code/software developed by Saxon Zynn for authoring neurochemical sequencing for dream immersion.

Thalpherycine – biosoftware activated by Synmem code which works on several levels to create authored dreams using neurochemical sequencing.

Vectigon metrics - neurochemical behaviour modification.

VPDN – Virtual Private Dream Network - Provides privacy, anonymity, and security to users by creating a private dream network connection across the dream immersion platform. All user data traffic is routed through an encrypted virtual channel. This conceals the users IP address when connecting to the Norus network, making user location invisible to everyone.

Dream Immersion Classification and Rating system

Classification	Rating (level of impact)	Description (frequency and intensity)	Genres available
General public	White	Suitable for all users with no expectations of sex or violence with negligible coarse language.	Entertainment, historical, sci-fi, drama, docudrama, romance, adventure, role-playing, strategy, mystery, fantasy, promotional, instructional, personal wellbeing, comedy, sport, documentary, musical, concert, shopping, biography, self-improvement, competition, game show, nature, travel, talent show, education, research
Low-level sex and violence	Yellow	Suitable for users with expectations of minimal sex, low impact violence and some coarse language with no risk of death.	Action, western, historical, sci-fi, crime, drama, romance, adventure, role-playing, strategy, mystery, fantasy, thriller, comedy, sport, game show, competition
Moderate sex and violence	Blue	Suitable for users with expectations of sex, coarse language, drug references, moderate impact violence with low risk of death.	Action, first person shooter, war, western, historical, sci-fi, crime, drama, romance, adventure, role-playing, strategy, mystery, fantasy, thriller, sex games, sport, horror, terror
Explicit sex and violence	Red	Suitable for users with expectations of explicit sex, drug use, frequent coarse language, high impact violence with blood and gore with moderate risk of death.	Action, first person shooter, war, western, historical, sci-fi, crime, drama, romance, adventure, role-playing, strategy, mystery, fantasy, thriller, sex games, horror, terror
Gratuitous extreme sex, ultraviolence, profanity. Offensive and obscene confronting content. Anything is possible.	Black	Suitable for users with expectations of gratuitous extreme sex of every type, frequent drug use, extreme profanity, ultra-high impact violence with blood and gore with high risk of death. Discrimination, bestiality, perversion.	Action, first person shooter, sci-fi, war, crime, drama, adventure, role-playing, strategy, mystery, thriller, fantasy, fetishes, violent games, violent sex, horror, terror, torture

Dream Phaze
www.dreamphaze.com[1]
hello@dreamphaze.com

Next novel in the Dream Phaze series:
Dream Phaze – Fascination (Book 3)

1. http://www.dreamphaze.com

Don't miss out!

Visit the website below and you can sign up to receive emails whenever Matt Watters publishes a new book. There's no charge and no obligation.

https://books2read.com/r/B-A-RNPH-LESWB

BOOKS 2 READ

Connecting independent readers to independent writers.